CRUCIBLE OF SECRETS

Also by Shona MacLean

The Redemption of Alexander Seaton
A Game of Sorrows

CRUCIBLE OF SECRETS

Shona MacLean

Quercus

To Rachel

First published in Great Britain in 2011 by

Quercus
21 Bloomsbury Square
London
WC1A 2NS

A CIP catalogue reference for this book is available
from the British Library

ISBN 978 1 84916 314 9 (HB)
ISBN 978 1 84916 315 6 (TPB)

10 9 8 7 6 5 4 3 2 1

Typeset by Ellipsis Digital Limited, Glasgow
Printed and bound in Great Britain by Clays Ltd, St Ives plc.

Prologue

Aberdeen, Midsummer's eve, 1631

It could not be possible: but there it was, plain, clear, beyond dispute in front of him. Robert Sim, librarian of the Marischal College, lifted his eye glass and scanned the page again, but in truth, he knew that his eyes were as sharp as ever they had been, and he needed no glass to decipher the words. There could be no doubting it: the man with whom he had that very morning exchanged pleasantries, with whom he had been exchanging pleasantries for as long as he had lived in this town, was dead. What was more, he had been so for more than eight years.

ONE

The Library

Specks of dust danced in the beam of sunlight that fell across the smooth oak of the table in front of me. The smell of the wood took me back many summers, to the library of our rival college a mile away, and afternoons of accidental slumber of my own. At the other side of the room, I could see that only by dint of great effort could one of my scholars resist the urge to close his eyes and rest his head on the book whose swimming words had been eluding his grasp this last half-hour. In a few minutes more I would advise him to give up the fight and join his fellows in their games on the Links: few of them had been tempted to abandon the fresh air and sunshine for an afternoon in the musty silence of the college library. Certainly, the student who had scurried down the stairs as I had ascended them had been in some haste to escape its walls, not even taking the time to look at me as he'd thrown behind him some mumbled response to my greeting.

Robert Sim, the college librarian, was, as ever, bent over his work. He would have done well in the scriptorium of one of the old monasteries: a life of silence and scholarly labour would have suited him better than the engagement with society demanded in these changed days, but he had been born a century too late, and the library afforded him as safe a retreat as was to be had in our town. By his feet were two wooden chests, the keys of which he had attached to a loop in his belt. Since I had come in an hour ago, he had been carefully lifting items from the larger of the two and checking them against a list on his desk. Once or twice I had felt his eyes upon me, but the subsequent glances he directed towards my scholar made it evident that whatever he wished to discuss with me was for no one's ears but mine. Eventually, curiosity got the better of me, and I went over to the boy, whose head shot up in a sudden start of consciousness.

'Adam . . .'

'Mr Seaton! I was just resting a moment . . .'

I looked at the work he was labouring over. 'Ah, *The Politics*. I see you have not yet progressed to the eighth book. Perhaps you recall from your dictats of my lecture on the subject . . .?'

The colour rose in his cheeks and he shifted uneasily in his seat. 'I have not, I mean, I do not have . . .'

I decided to stop tormenting the boy. 'No doubt you will find the place when you return to your room later. While he censures the excessive physical training of such as the Spartans, Aristotle does allow that play is a necessary form of rest from the toils of the intellectual life.

4

Perhaps you would profit more from some exercise of the body – a game of football, or some golf, down on the Links – with your companions, than by continued slumbers over his words in here this afternoon.'

The colour blanched from his face a moment, to be replaced by a broad smile when he understood he was not being chastised. He was on his feet, his gown thrown over his arm all in one movement.

'Thank you, Mr Seaton,' he said, as he bolted for the door.

'Adam,' I called after him.

'Yes, sir?'

'The book,' I said, nodding towards the table where the great philosopher had been abandoned.

'Oh, yes, of course.' Affording me a sheepish grin, he was back at the table in two bounds, closing the book and returning it to Robert Sim, who did his best to hide his amusement under a furrowed brow of disapproval.

'You are kind to the boys, Alexander. They labour the more to please you because of it.'

'There is little to be gained from treating them harshly. Resentment will not breed good citizens.'

'You are at odds with Mr Jack on that point.'

'And on more besides. Should there come a day that you find me in agreement with Matthew Jack, on any matter, I insist you haul me before the principal and urge him to throw me from the college gates.'

Robert grinned. 'You may be assured that I would.'

I nodded towards his desk. 'Tell me, what are you busy at today – new acquisitions? Do not tell me the council has loosened its purse strings at last?'

He shook his head. 'A benefaction. Dr Gerald Duncan. He was an early graduate of our college and passed the last twenty years of his life in medical practice in the Low Countries – Friesland – at Groningen and, latterly, Franeker. He attained a considerable estate. His medical books he left to the University of Groningen, but the others he willed to us.'

'Is there anything of interest?' I said, beginning to scan the spines of the works on his desk.

'It is mainly political history, and works relating to the natural world. But yes,' he hesitated. 'There is something, however I . . .'

He glanced anxiously around him, ascertaining that we were, in fact, alone. 'I must talk to the principal first, but I would value your—'

At that moment we heard the sound of footsteps on the stairs. Sim looked towards the door, startled, and as William Cargill appeared in the doorway there was a drawing tight of the librarian's lips and the merest shake of his head.

'Tomorrow then,' I said, 'after the sermon.'

He nodded, composing his features in a greeting for my friend. 'William, it is not often we see you in here nowadays.'

'Not as often as I would like,' said William, striding in to the room with a degree of familiarity. 'My dull lawyer's

6

work leaves me little time for the perusal of literature.'

'It keeps the wolf from your door all the same.'

William grinned modestly. His calling had brought him far greater wealth than mine or Robert Sim's ever would us. 'I envy you these quiet hours, though. What have you been whiling away your time with today, Alexander?'

I indicated the work I had left open at my desk and he crossed the floor to look at it. 'Kepler. Mathematics was never my strong point. And besides, he is a little too fanciful for me.'

'You do not believe that God created a universe replete with secrets to be discovered, that the human mind might never be idle?'

'Hmmph. I think there are enough secrets in our corrupt world, here, below the heavenly sphere, to keep a man busy enough. What say you, Robert?'

The librarian weighed his words before replying slowly, 'I think you might be right.'

I looked at Sim for further explanation but he had turned away and begun to busy himself once more with the cataloguing of the books.

William closed the Kepler and brought the volume back to the librarian's table.

'I am not finished,' I protested.

'Oh, indeed you are. You must descend from your higher plane a while. Our wives and children have gone on ahead of me, and they will give short shrift to your philosophy. Baskets of food have been packed, rugs have been brought and commissions issued. I am not to emerge back out on to the street unless I have you with me.'

I sighed, knowing there was little point in further protest.

'Will you not come with us, Robert? You are under no obligation to open the library on a Saturday at all, you know.'

'I know, but I must finish this cataloguing, and then there are some accounts I must work on before I return to my lodgings tonight. Better to burn the college's candles than my own.' Although he affected lightness, I could see he was ill at ease, and I had no wish to prolong his discomfort by pressing him.

'We will not keep you from it any longer then, Robert. But we will talk tomorrow.'

'Yes,' he said. 'Tomorrow. After the sermon.'

TWO

Aftermath

Sarah's expression as William and I stumbled through the door of my house on Flourmill Lane a little before ten that night was a study in disbelief.

'What in the name of God . . . ?'

William held up a hand to stay her. 'Alexander will tell you. I'd better get down to Elizabeth before she hears all about it from someone else.' He nodded towards my left eye. 'I'll send up a steak for the bruise.'

He was gone, and my wife had still been unable to finish her sentence. I lurched towards the chair she hastily pulled out from the table for me, and sat down, grateful at last to be home. Sarah knelt before me and lifted my face the better to examine it. 'Are you going to tell me what happened?' she said at last, and then, 'Oh, no. Do not tell me you got into a fight with Andrew Carmichael?'

I shook my head and instantly regretted it, as a pain shot from my eye to the back of my skull. 'No, I did not fight with Andrew Carmichael.' Much though in my worse moments I might want to, but I could not tell her that.

'We sat a long time, William, Andrew Carmichael, John Innes and I, after you and Elizabeth left with the children. Somehow the wine William had packed took on something of the quality of that of the wedding of Cana and it seemed foolish to put it away before it was finished.'

She smiled a little indulgently. 'I guessed as much. And Matthew Jack?'

She had mentioned a colleague of mine, a fellow regent at the Marischal College, universally feared and universally despised, whose arrival amongst us on the dunes at the Links earlier in the day had brought an end to the charm of our picnic. It had been my fault: thinking to spare the scholars down on the strand, whom he was charged with overseeing, the burden of his company for half an hour, I had invited him to join us a while. His reply had been as graceless as I should have expected.

'I would not intrude on your time with your family.' There were still some in the burgh who took pains to remember that my wife had been carrying another man's child when first I had met her, and Matthew Jack was one of them. He had managed to invest the word *family* with such contempt that I had been sorely tempted to haul him down to the water's edge and hold his head under the incoming waves. I had settled instead for walking away, but it was too late. He had called after me. 'But as you already have company – I see John Innes there, and Andrew Carmichael, is it not? – I will allow myself a half-hour's respite to join them.'

The faces that had brightened in greeting when I appeared on the crest of the dune had fallen notably when they saw who I had brought with me, and within less than an hour Sarah and Elizabeth had gathered up the children – William's five-year-old son James, our Zander, the same age, and Deirdre, nineteen months, the blessing of my life – and taken them home. I would have left then too, had not Sarah stopped me.

'Stay. Spend a while longer here. You are too long indoors, out of the fresh air and sunlight, and you see too little of your friends. Elizabeth will not mind William staying, I am sure.'

'He would only be under my feet,' her friend had said, not looking up from her work of trying to dry her squirming son. 'See he does not darken my door until sunset.'

And so they had left us with the wine and what was left of the bread and cheese, by the still-smouldering fire. Andrew Carmichael and John Innes were regents at our rival university of the King's College in the Old Town, and talk between us soon turned to the poverty of our salaries and the scanty resources with which our scholars were forced to make do. 'At least we have acquired some new books for our library,' I said, and told them of the bene-faction Robert Sim had been cataloguing that afternoon, and what I knew of its provenance and contents. William remembered having met Dr Duncan once, many years before, when the physician had made a trip home to the town of his birth. John recalled having heard that he had been a good friend in his younger days abroad of our principal, Dr Dun. Matthew Jack, never to be outdone, claimed to have met him once, at a Scots service in the kirk in Rotterdam. No one had disputed this, for it was well-known that there was scarcely a college or a kirk in reformed Europe in which he had not set foot, however briefly. Both Andrew Carmichael and I were happy enough to confess that we had never heard of him before in our lives.

John, ever the diligent scholar, had pressed me for greater detail of what I could remember of the benefaction, and our discussion moved on to what might be the intellectual merits of its contents. Matthew Jack, as was his habit, had some sniping riposte to anything good anyone had to say about the authors under discussion, or of the late physician's choice of reading materials. It had been a great relief to the rest of us when he caught sight of two of the Marischal scholars breaking away from their classmates to try their luck with a group of young girls from the burgh. Within minutes Jack was back down on the sand and, having chased the girls away with threats of what he should tell their parents of their behaviour, was marching their two suitors back towards the town and the cold confines of the college walls.

I should then, perhaps, have offered to take Matthew Jack's place on the beach until his return, but I had a kind of fascination with Andrew Carmichael that would not allow me to leave the conversation of my friends while he was still part of it. Whether John Innes knew of this, I could not tell. William knew; he watched my every expression, measured my every word, because of it. And Andrew Carmichael himself knew, of that I was certain. I had not realised it until earlier that afternoon.

After we had left the library and the respectable confines of the town to join our wives and children in their picnic amongst the dunes of the King's Links, William had challenged me to a race. Our rivalry in this as in every sport was long-standing, and our progress from town gates to beach had been one of many misplaced elbows and attempted trips, shovings into bushes and much breathless laughter. By the time we had reached the brow of the dune where we were to meet our families, I was three strides in the lead and ready to crow at my triumph, but the sight I saw as I breasted that hill stopped me in my tracks, so that William all but careered in to the back of me. Elizabeth had taken my daughter and the boys to gather wild flowers amongst the rocks, and there, by the fire at which she had begun to grill some fish, sitting beside my wife, was Andrew Carmichael. The sight of him so close to Sarah hit me like a punch in the stomach.

He stood up, in some confusion, evidently as discomfited as I was.

'Alexander, I . . . William. Hello. Good day. You have come to enjoy this fine weather. I will not disturb you in your meal, I—'

'You will stay and share it with us,' said William, striding past me and avoiding my eye. 'And is that John Innes there with your students? Call him up to do likewise.' He then poured out and handed to me a beaker of wine from a flask he had had his steward pack. 'And take care the look on your face does not sour it,' he muttered to me, under his breath.

Yes, Andrew Carmichael knew. A man of learning, a decent man, a good man, they all said. The man, half the town knew, but none said to my face, who when I had been in Ireland, three years ago, had fallen in love with Sarah, my Sarah, and who was, as I could tell every time I forced myself to look at him, still in love with my wife.

My first reaction on seeing him there had been what it always was in that first raw moment – I had wanted to hit him. But I spoke the truth to Sarah when I told her that, no, it had not been in a fight with Andrew Carmichael that I had come upon my bloodied nose and swollen eye. For after Matthew Jack had left us, and we four remaining had been able to speak freely, I had realised there was indeed much more than our mutual love for one woman that Andrew Carmichael and I might have in common. And with William and John we had talked for hours as the sea below us advanced and then began to retreat again from the shore, turning from blue to green to gold, under a sky whose colours flamed and blazed in mockery of our Presbyterian world.

And so our evening might have ended, had it not been for the commotion that reached us from the beach just as the embers of our fire were grown cold and the wine finished. The students of the King's College and the Marischal College, forgotten all by their masters, had taken up a game of football, and as was inevitable, had come to blows. As was the tradition between them, old enmities between colleges, family feuds of many generations' standing, found expression on the sands. The student who had been left in charge of the Marischal scholars came racing up the dune. 'Mr Seaton, come quick! Alexander Irvine and William Forbes are in the middle of it. If someone does not stop them, there will be murder down there.'

And well might there have been, had we not between the four of us managed to separate twenty young men revelling in the fights and grievances of their fathers and grandfathers, but not before I had taken an elbow in the eye and an upper cut to the chin from a boy who did not see at whom he had lashed out until the deed was done. Matthew Jack had arrived back from his locking-in and haranguing of the two young gallants from earlier when the fight was at its height and our efforts looking in danger of being overwhelmed. Little affection though I had for him, I could not help but admire the bellow that issued from his throat, and the instant effect it had on those who were subject to his discipline. For a man so mean of frame, his very presence could inspire a great deal of terror. Poor John Innes, on the other hand, could inspire none, and had it not been for the assistance of Andrew Carmichael, their charges from the King's College might have rampaged long into the night. Eventually the two groups were separated with an effusion of blood and swollen eyes, but fewer broken bones than might otherwise have been the case.

As the scholars of King's were led away back towards the Old Town, Matthew Jack had refused my help with our own, and driven them down towards the new burgh, declaring as he went, 'These wretches will be lucky to set foot outside the college walls again between now and Christmas.'

I refrained from pointing out that the term would be over in little more than two weeks. I also knew that I, with the rest of the college, would be forced to spend an hour of my time on Monday morning in the college courtyard, watching Matthew Jack administer to these boys the beating of their lives.

Sarah listened to all this as she tended my eye and chin. The promised steak had been brought by a servant from William's house and I had been instructed to apply it to draw out the bruising. 'William was a little dishevelled looking, but he did not look to have been injured,' she said.

'No. His time in the law courts has kept him a more wary antagonist than I am.'

'And the other two?' she asked lightly.

I searched her face for some change in expression, but saw none. 'Andrew took some blows to the shins, and John was winded, but that was all.'

She smiled. 'I cannot imagine poor John in a fight.'

My saintly friend had been of little use in the fracas. Had

it not been for the assistance of Andrew Carmichael his scholars would have trampled him underfoot. I was not disposed to tell this much to my wife.

'And Mr Jack has the boys back in the college?'

'Aye, pity help them, for they will need it.'

'Will they be all right? Tonight? None of them was injured?'

'Some,' I said, 'although not greatly I think. I doubt whether Jack will rouse himself to check.' I got carefully out of my chair. 'I should go and see to it, and make sure that Dr Dun has my report of what happened down there today. Matthew Jack's idea of the truth isn't as other men's.'

Sarah put a hand on my shoulder. 'Not yet, Alexander. You are in no fit state to go anywhere. You need to sit at rest a while and take a little food, to restore some of your strength. Besides,' she added with a frown, 'you cannot go to Dr Dun with ripped hose and a head full of sand, to say nothing of the blood on your shirt.'

'I must see to the boys, Sarah.'

'They are near enough grown men, and will come to no harm for your taking half-an-hour's rest. You staggered in that door; do not tell me it was just the effects of William's wine that made you do so, although I doubt Dr Dun would think so well of that either. And you do not need Matthew Jack noising it about the town that you are a drunkard.'

And so, given no option, I did as she bid me. I let her finish bathing me and and took some broth and dozed an hour in my chair. I went nowhere near the college, nor indeed out of my door for an hour or more after I had first intended to. I wish to God that I had done.

THREE

The Scents of the Night

When I did venture out, it was not quite dark yet in the streets of the burgh, the late June light refusing until the last necessary moment to yield to the Sabbath. Nevertheless, lamps and candles were being lit inside homes where the evening light could not reach, up closes and beyond courtyards, through thick stone walls and shuttered windows.

There were one or two other solitary figures still out – I could not tell in the grimy grey who they were, and we none of us glanced more than a moment in each other's direction – whatever business a man had out in the town at this hour of the night was his and not that of some passing stranger. It was a time when men took refuge in the shadows. Shadows, the word William had used when, on our way home from the fracas on the Links, he had finally broached the subject I had known would come.

'You have no cause, Alexander, to suspect or mistrust him. He never set out to wrong you. Indeed, he did not wrong you, and you know that.'

'I know it,' I said, 'but do not expect me to be at ease in his company: I do not like to see him close to her. Can you not understand? She is my wife!'

'Now, yes, she is your wife. But she was not then, three years ago, when you disappeared into the night, taking ship for Ireland and a family you had scarcely spoken of. She was not your wife, nor your anything, and you had had two years by then – two years, when you might have secured her and did not.'

'You know why – I did not think, I—'

'You. Always you. But what of Sarah? Mother to a bastard child, servant in another man's house, holding her head high in the face of all she knew was thought and said about her, and about Zander. You left her without having spoken a word to her. You left a scribbled note and went, and we thought you dead. Andrew Carmichael did not swoop down on her like some bird of prey, or fox in the night. He came to my house seeking my counsel on a matter regarding the law. He came a second time, and then a third, at my invitation, and it came as no great surprise when Elizabeth pointed out to me that he was falling in love with Sarah. Sarah did not return his feeling – she was in such a shock at your sudden leaving, such a certainty that you were dead or had gone to another, that she could not, whoever might have spoken to her. But he did speak, and he spoke kindly, and he listened to her and was a friend to her when you had abandoned her. And yes it was because he loved her and it was not done with disinterest, but who amongst us has ever loved with disinterest?' William's anger was risen now, and I knew it because he kept his voice so low. 'And I'll tell you this, Alexander. Had the day come when she had lifted her eyes to him, reached out a hand to him, been ready to go with him, I am not the one who would have stopped her, nor Elizabeth either.'

This stopped me in my tracks, for he, my best friend, had never told me this before. 'But she never did, and he did not press the matter. He let her understand that when she was ready, he would be there, waiting. And that is all he did, and all she did, which was nothing. And from the day you returned, he stepped back into his shadows, and I do not think he ever spoke to her of it again.'

Yes, Andrew Carmichael was in the shadows, but those shadows were hanging over my life and try as I might I could not shake them off.

I sought to drive these thoughts from my mind as I crossed from the Guest Row over the Broadgate to the college. The buildings that rose above me, behind the houses and booths that fronted the street, were almost entirely in darkness; one or two lights flickered behind narrow windows on the turnpike stairs, but none from the students' chambers. Even the gatehouse was in darkness and the porter away from his post. This was unusual, and increased my concern for the boys who had been left in Matthew Jack's care. I made my way down a side alley that would bring me out by the wall of the college garden. I knew that the gate leading from the garden to the library courtyard was not beyond the ingenuity of a man of my height and years to scale.

I was surprised to find the gate to the library close ajar and creaking lightly on its hinges. I could not think who amongst the students could have been so careless on this of all nights, when Matthew Jack, and evidently the porter also, would be on the prowl along the corridors and stairways. A light from above caught my eye, a tiny flicker through a gap in the library shutters; I remembered having noticed it as I'd passed earlier with William. I had been all for going up to tell Robert to go home for the night, but William had persuaded me that I was in greater need of getting home myself, and so we had left him. I was surprised, all the same, to see that he was still there – he must have fallen asleep. It would not have been the first time, and yet I knew he had to read in the kirk early the next morning, and that it would not do for him to appear before the congregation unwashed and in his workday clothes. I decided to go and rouse him before I went to look for Dr Dun or to check what Matthew Jack had done to the boys.

The night-time scents of the garden still hung in the air, the honeysuckle and the climbing roses that tumbled over the walls and trellises contending with one another for mastery of the falling dusk, but as I rounded the corner in to the library courtyard another smell, sickly, warm and cloying, rose above all the other usual odours of the place: the smell not of the college close but of the flesher's yard.

I almost stumbled on it in the half-light: the shape

sprawled across the cobbles a few feet from the library steps, its dead eyes looking up at me in mute appeal, was Robert Sim. Flies were already busy about the blood congealed at his throat.

FOUR

The Library

Dr Dun knelt on the ground, carefully making such examination as he could beneath the lanterns held by the college porter and one of the baillie's men. The principal lifted Robert's head gently and I saw that the right side of the librarian's face, where it had lain on the ground, was caked in dirt and blood. Dr Dun had seen such sights often enough before, but it was a minute before he found his voice.

'There can be no doubt, Alexander. He has been murdered. You see the wound at his throat?'

I nodded, not wanting to look again at the bloodied mess that had once been my friend. Behind me, I could hear the porter retch.

'And here,' continued the principal, pointing to the dead man's palms, 'you can see the gashes where he sought to defend himself. It looks to have been a small, but very sharp knife.'

The baillie spoke to me. 'Have you found any such knife?'

I shook my head. 'I have not looked . . . I ran to get the

porter – to fetch Dr Dun and yourselves, then I came back to stay with – Robert.'

'You did right,' said Dr Dun, brushing dirt from his clothes as he stood up, not noticing, it seemed, the brown smears of blood on his cuffs and the hem of his cloak. 'This is a bad affair and, and, I fear it will reflect badly on us.'

The baillie was a man of business, with little time to spend on civilities. 'It is indeed a bad pass.' He tilted his head. 'And it is Robert Sim?' The principal nodded. 'How long do you think he has lain dead like this?'

Dr Dun shook his head. 'I cannot be certain. Not long. The body is not yet stiff and the blood not fully congealed.'

'And do you think he was slain here?'

The principal indicated the state of Robert Sim's face, and his fingernails. 'I think you can see here and here that he made some effort to drag himself along the ground, towards the courtyard. Robert Sim was meticulous in the cleanliness of his hands. He would allow no one with dirty hands to touch the books in his care. He kept a basin of water and a drying rag up by the door there for that express reason. Even I was directed that way more than once. But look at his own fingers – they are caked in dirt and blood. He must have clawed his way along the ground. He did not get very far. Also, the blood has not spread greatly. I would think he died very close to where the assault took place.'

The baillie nodded. 'At the bottom of the stairs here.' Then he turned to the gatekeeper. 'Mr Sim lived in the town, not in the college, is that not so?'

The man nodded.

'At what time did he usually leave the library on a Saturday?'

The man looked troubled. 'The library is only supposed to be open until noon on a Saturday, but sometimes Mr Sim had work of his own to do and he . . .'

'So he had no usual time of leaving?'

'It would change from week to week, but he never stayed later than eight in the summer, five in the winter.'

'But he did not leave tonight?'

The gatekeeper looked from the corpse to the baillie and back to the corpse, as if the town magistrate lacked in something.

'I think what the baillie is asking,' I said, 'is did Robert Sim leave earlier in the evening, and then return?'

'I could not say.'

Dr Dun now interjected. 'Do you mean you were not at the gate?'

The man was firm in his own defence. 'I would have been, but Mr Jack arrived back from the Links with the scholars and he was in very high dudgeon. There had been some fighting and trouble, and he called upon me to see to it that every one of them was locked in their chamber for the night, but only after the rooms of the likeliest had been searched for weapons. He has had me patrolling the corridors and landings half the night.'

The principal ran a hand over his brow and muttered, 'He goes too far, always too far.' And then, barely able to mask his anger, he said to the gatekeeper, 'So what you are saying is that anyone other than the scholars under guard could have left or entered this college tonight.'

The man was surly. 'The gates were locked.'

But we all knew there were places, not just the gate I had come in by, but breaches in our crumbling walls, sorely in need of repair, where a careful and agile man might pass unseen.

'Would that he had come with us,' I murmured.

'What?'

I told the baillie of our invitation to Robert to join us on the Links.

'When was this?' asked the principal.

'In the afternoon, at around three. I had been working in the library for an hour or so.'

'Who else was there?'

'No one. When I left with William Cargill, Robert was alone.'

'Then I think we had better see what the library has to tell us, do not you, Baillie?' said the principal. Taking the lantern from the porter he set his foot on the bottom step and led us up the outer stairs.

The door was unlocked, and there was no sign of the key.

'That is not right,' said the gatekeeper. 'He never went out and left the place unlocked, never once. He kept the key on its ring at his belt.'

'Perhaps he had not yet intended to leave for the night,'

said the baillie. 'Perhaps he had merely gone out for a moment for air, or to meet with someone else in the college.'

'He would still have locked up,' I said. 'He would allow no one to remain unsupervised in the library – master or student.'

The principal concurred. 'And besides,' he added, indicating the corpse on the ground, 'he has with him the satchel that he used to carry work back and forth from here to his lodgings. He was going home.'

Below us, the constable knelt and undid the buckle on the worn leather satchel. He rooted around in it a moment, and brought out a large, hide-bound ledger, with the symbol of the incorporated trades embossed on the front. 'There is only this, nothing else.'

The book was passed up to the principal, who took it in his hand and nodded. 'The Trades' Benefaction Book.'

I had seen it often before – folio, bound in pigskin. 'It was on his desk in the library this afternoon,' I said. 'It was this that he planned to work on tonight.'

'Well, his assailant had no interest in that, it would seem.'

The constable laid aside the satchel before carefully unclasping and sliding the belt from Robert Sim's body. There was no ring of keys around it, but the thong from which the ring had hung had been cut.

'Someone has evidently forced the keys from him, dead or alive,' said the baillie.

Dr Dun pushed open the door and led us into the library. I don't know what I had thought we would find in there –

blood, broken glass, splintered wood, torn and flung-about books, signs of a struggle – but as one candle after another was lit in the sconces along the walls, there was very little evidence of any of that. In fact, at first sight, the place did not seem greatly altered from how it had been in the afternoon. Desks and chairs were where they had been, books were on their shelves, not strewn on the floor. Not even the inkpot on the librarian's desk had been overturned, and yet I had a strong sense that the place had been searched. The door of a press was not quite properly closed; a candle had burned right down to the wick, as if it had never been put out; one or two books had not been pushed right in on their shelves, as Robert Sim would have taken care to do. And on his desk, as it always was, bound in leather and kept in the librarian's own neat hand was the register of readers. Its companion, the library catalogue, bound in identical style and kept in the same hand, was gone.

The principal, his hand resting on a lectern Robert had often used, was also looking around him, noticing, I was certain, the same things I myself had noticed. The baillie and his constable found less to interest them, the former soon making his own assessment, and implying in his tone that he looked for no other.

'Well, there is little amiss here. Evidently Robert Sim had left for the night and was assaulted and robbed outside. His assailant, finding nothing of value here, made off into the town unobserved, it would seem.'

He had begun to walk back towards the door when a

shout from the constable below took our attention. He shouted again for the baillie. I was first to the stairhead and saw, in the intermittent light from his swaying lantern, a set of keys and something else that briefly glinted as the light swept over it; it was a knife, small and lethally sharp, picked up a moment earlier from a dank corner beneath the stairs. It was evident to us all that this must be the instrument that killed Robert Sim, but only once I had suggested it and the principal confirmed it did the burgh's officers realise what it also was: a doctor's scalpel.

The baillie directed the constable to try the keys in the library door, and carefully took the scalpel from him. The blood was brown and dry on the blade, and smeared on the handle. He held it out towards us. 'You are certain that that is what it is, Dr Dun?'

'There can be no doubt. Every doctor and surgeon in the town will have one.'

The baillie shook his head. 'Well, I'll hazard that there is one doctor or surgeon in this burgh who has one less tonight than he had this morning. The first thing to be done is to draw up a list of all the physicians in this and the Old Town.'

'And the first name on that list will be my own,' said the principal.

The baillie made to protest, but Dr Dun held up a hand to stop him. 'There can be no partiality, no respecting of persons in the search for the perpetrator of this brutal deed. You will find such a list in the third drawer of the tall

Dutch chest in the room next to my chamber. I will have one of the students copy it for you.' He turned then to the gatekeeper. 'And you will grant the town's officers access wherever they might wish. If the truth be hidden somewhere in this college, it will be found out. And now, Baillie, you will excuse me, for the hour is late and I must speak with Mr Seaton about how this business is to be managed here, within these walls.'

The baillie's mind was on the matter of doctors and their knives now. 'We will begin our investigations in the town tomorrow. I know the final examinations are almost upon you – we will strive to avoid disruption of the college business. I am greatly obliged for your assistance, Dr Dun.'

Finally, the principal and I were alone, and I was not greatly surprised to see Dr Dun turn once more towards the library. 'Now, Alexander, before we find the answers, I think we must first know the questions, don't you?'

Again, I was struck by the strange but oddly imperfect tidiness of the library. In a place that was usually silent, the heavy silence of the night, punctuated only by the sounds made by Dr Dun and myself, was like a third presence. The principal placed the Trades' Benefaction Book on the librarian's desk. 'The catalogue is missing,' he said, as much to himself as to me.

'I had noticed that.'

'What else?'

'Very little. That is what seems so strange. One or two

books do not look quite right on their shelves – I suspect, should we look, we would find that some of them are not in their proper place.' I cast my eye about me again. 'That box of mathematical instruments, beneath his desk there, is somewhat askew. One of the press doors has not been shut properly. I think the place has been searched, very carefully, by someone who knew exactly what they were looking for.'

Dr Dun nodded. 'I believe you are right. But what was it, and did they find it?' He sighed deeply and sat down in Robert's chair. 'Let us be systematic.' He pulled towards him the ledger in which Sim recorded the names of those using the library along with a note of what they had consulted. The ribbon marker was still at Saturday's page, and my own name the last one on it. 'It was a quiet day,' said the principal. 'Three readers in the morning, and only one other than yourself in the afternoon.' He turned the book towards me and I scanned the short list of names. There was my own, with the Kepler registered beside it, and the scholar who had been slumbering over his Aristotle until I had sent him out into the sunshine. Two other scholars, of the senior class, had been in in the morning, but it was the third name that caught my attention: John Innes, my friend and regent in the King's College.

Principal Dun must have caught the look on my face. 'Is there something the matter, Alexander?'

'No, I , I . . . it is just, I didn't expect to find John Innes's name here.'

He smiled. 'Come now, you know we have an arrangement with the King's College whereby their masters might
consult our library and ours theirs. And you know, while
he lacks your own depth of insight and sharpness of mind,
poor John is the most diligent of all the regents. Although
. . . I suspect Principal Rait will have some harsh words
for him over today's fracas at the Links.'

'I must bear much of the responsibility for that – I should
have gone down onto the beach when Matthew Jack left
to take the others back to the college earlier on.'

He looked up at me from under his eyebrows. 'He had
no business leaving them, and you were not the duty regent
today. But that is not our concern at the moment. Does
this register bear out what you know of yesterday, that
there was no one else at work in the library when you were
here in the afternoon?'

'No – but wait, yes. Malcolm Urquhart, of the fourth
class. He was leaving as I arrived.'

'Hmm. Perhaps he had consulted nothing.' He closed the
book. 'Well, I would like you to seek out each of the people
named here, find out from them exactly when they were
here, what and whom they saw. And heard.'

I nodded, glad that it was I and not one of the baillies
who would be interviewing my friend John Innes, but troubled still, not by the fact that he had been in our library,
but that in all of our conversation of the librarian and the
new benefaction, he had not mentioned his visit once.

The principal ran his hand along the arm of the librarian's

chair and closed his fingers over the curved end of it, the oak rubbed smooth over the years by the man who had so long sat in it. 'Robert, Robert.' It was the first time I had seen Patrick Dun appear dejected, as if the burden of his office had become too great. 'How was he, when you saw him?'

I took myself back to earlier in the day. 'I did not think he was . . . altogether himself, not quite. He seemed agitated, a little distracted. In fact, there was something he wished to discuss with me. Something he was going to tell me, but William came in and he changed his mind.' And then I remembered. 'He said he needed to talk to you first.'

Dr Dun raised an eyebrow in interest. 'To me? Did he give you any idea of what it was about?'

I shook my head. 'I took it to be something to do with the benefaction. There was something in it, I think, that troubled him. He did not come to see you?'

'I had been out at Belhelvie, and was not back in the town until after eight. I am sorry to say I had very little thought of the college or the library, and went directly to Benholm's Lodging.' I knew the thought that was in his mind: the journey from Belhelvie to his town residence at the top of the Netherkirkgate would have taken him within a hundred yards of the college and the library close, where Robert might already have been lying dead. He rubbed his left hand across a weary face. 'Tell me what you know about this benefaction.'

'It was an acquisition, lately come to the college from the Low Countries – Groningen, in fact. A doctor—'

Dun interrupted me. 'Duncan, Gerald Duncan. Of course. I had a letter from Franeker that it was on its way. Gerald was a good friend to me, many years ago, when I first went to study under Dr Liddel at Helmstedt. We corresponded for a good while after I left, but, sad to say, I never saw him again. He made for himself a very creditable career in Germany and then Friesland, but I do not know that he ever returned home.'

'He did once, at least. William Cargill recalls being a boy and meeting him at his uncle's house.'

The principal looked surprised, but this was not the time or place for reminiscence on old acquaintance, and he returned to the substance of the matter. 'So, Sim was cataloguing Gerald Duncan's benefaction.'

'And the catalogue is gone,' I said, 'so we now have no way of knowing what was in it.' Familiar as I was with this place, without the catalogue I could not have told which of the hundreds of books on open shelves or shut behind the high glass doors of presses might be from Duncan's collection.

'You despair too quickly, Alexander.' To my astonishment, he moved a stool to the shelves behind Sim's desk and, climbing on to it, reached up with his hand to what appeared to be an empty space on the second highest shelf. 'We are fortunate that Robert Sim was a little shorter than I am myself,' he said, as he drew from the back of the shelf a length of string with, on the end of it, a small key. I helped him down and he strode across the room to a chest in a dingy far corner of the library, where only old maps and scientific instruments awaiting repair were kept. He turned the key in the lock of the chest and opened the lid, a broad smile spreading over his face as he did so. 'I often used to berate Robert, gently, for his excessive caution in his dedication, but I do not do so now.'

From the chest he lifted out two pieces of paper, which he handed to me. Along the top, in a hand I did not know, was written, *List of the Books Mortified to the Marischal College in Aberdeen by Dr Gerald Duncan, Franeker.* And beneath the lists were the books.

'I don't understand,' I said.

Dun smiled. 'There is no great mystery. It has been a rule of this college for as long as I can remember that any books coming into its library had to be signed for not just by its librarian, but also by its principal. Robert would have resigned his post rather than stray from such a regulation. He may well have finished cataloguing Duncan's benefaction, but he would not have put a single volume on the shelves until I had countersigned his receipt, which – as you see,' he said, indicating the space beside Sim's signature at the bottom of the second page, 'I have not yet done. If the book – or books – his assailant was looking for was amongst Duncan's benefaction, he will not have found it. Only Robert and I knew that this old chest was the library's strong box, or where the key was to be found.' He handed me Robert's library key, and that to the strong box. 'You must examine these lists, Alexander. Look for what it was that Robert saw. If I had the time to do it myself, I would, but I must keep a firm grip on the rudder of this college if I am to steer her through the troubled waters of the next few weeks. For now though, it grows late, and I must give thought to tomorrow.'

At the top of the stairs, Principal Dun paused, and turned back to me. He spoke quietly. 'There is one more thing I must ask you to do, for I can think of no other who could do it discreetly and in whom I have greater trust.' I waited; it was evident the principal took no pleasure in what he now had to say. 'The baillie and his constables will investigate this matter as the town deems fit, but Robert Sim was one of our number, and deserved well of us. I want you to look into his private life, his life outside these college walls. It may be that it is there, and not here, that the answer to this horror is to be found.'

FIVE

The Books

I watched my wife through the thick glass pane of the window. The glow of one small candle set on the windowsill was all the light to be seen now in the courtyard off Flour-mill Lane where our small house jostled for space with five others. Clay pots of thyme and rosemary were bracketed to the wall, and tubs of chives and lavender flowered by the doorstep. Their scents contended in the fallen darkness with the peaty smell of smoke rising from the chimney, drifting out on the night air, away from the animal odours of the backlands, where dogs, pigs and fowl were at rest for the night. She was sitting by the fire, untwisting her hair from under the cap where she had kept it all day. I liked to watch her sometimes still, unobserved, to have again that feeling that had gripped me, attended my every step, my every thought for two years; that I had come upon the one that would make me whole, and that if she was almost, almost, beyond my reach, she was utterly beyond that of others. And then to walk in and to touch her, brush her cheek, her fingertips with mine, was to live again, for a moment, the first time.

Sarah looked up as I opened the door, only a flicker of a second between seeing me and the smile coming to her face.

'You are so late, Alexander. I had begun to worry that you had fallen amongst more mischief.'

'I had not expected to find you still up. You should not have waited for me.' I knelt down before her, taking her hands in mine, and told her as gently as I could what had happened.

She could say nothing coherent for a few moments, half-formed questions dying in disbelief on her lips. Tears filled her eyes and spilled out over the lashes. I wiped them away with my hand.

'Hush, hush.'

'But he was so good – what harm was there ever in Robert? What would he have ever done to anyone, that he should die like that? He did not deserve that.'

I could summon no words, no platitude, no portion of the scripture to answer her. 'It is not ours to know.' I could not say that to my wife, the well-worn admonition to those seeking to understand the mind of God. For I knew that what I had seen in the library close that night had been no work of God.

'Robert shall have some justice in this world, we are determined on that.'

She looked up at me, instantly suspicious. 'We?'

'The burgh authorities have begun their investigations, and, God willing, they may find the perpetrator, but the principal has asked that I should assist him in looking into matters in so far as they affect the college.'

'But why you?'

I shrugged as I stood up. 'Because I am the oldest of the regents, I suppose. I do not think he altogether trusts Matthew Jack, and the other two have – well, they have not lived in the world as I have.' And because I knew Death in ways they did not. I had seen Death and tracked its malign pathways in ways they had not.

I could see my answer had done little to ease the concerns creeping into her mind. 'What are these matters?'

I poured myself a beaker of ale from the jug on the sideboard. It was warm and tasted stale. 'They concern the library, for the main part. I am to interview the students and masters who were in there yesterday – their names are in the register – and I have been examining the books Robert was cataloguing when he died. It seems obvious to Dr Dun and to myself, that whoever killed him took his keys from him and made a careful search of the library. If we can find what he was looking for, it may help us to discover who he is.'

Sarah's face paled. 'Do not tell me you have been in the library until now?'

I nodded. 'Well, yes, where else?'

'Are you gone mad, Alexander? You were there, until now, alone?'

40

'Yes, I . . .'

'What if he had come back? What if this murderer had come back there and found you? What would have happened . . .?'

I went to her and took her by the shoulders. 'He no longer has the key. The constable found it, dropped beneath the library stairs. And you forget: I am no gentle Robert Sim: I can defend myself.'

'Can you, Alexander?' She reached up and touched my still-tender eye, and then her eyes went to the silver scar at my throat, made by the knife that had come close to killing me in Ireland, less than three years ago. I could not have hidden it, but I had often cursed the night I had told her of how in Ireland I had come to believe I would not live to see her face again.

I stroked her hair and kissed it. 'If God had not meant us to be together, he would have found a thousand ways by now to part us. Do not fear for me.'

She sniffed then straightened herself. 'If I do not, who will? You take no care for yourself. Look at that shirt!'

I looked down at myself and smiled. It had been warm, still, in the library that night, and the books of Duncan's benefaction very dusty. The sleeves of my best college shirt, assiduously scrubbed by Sarah on a weekly basis and put over my head by her little over three hours ago, had not fared well in my labours, and were now a mottled grey. I pulled the shirt over my head and dropped it in her laundry basket. 'What would I do without you?' I said, pulling her to me.

'I do not know. You will just have to see to it that you do not find yourself without me.'

Later, as she slept, I lay with my hands behind my head, listening to the sounds of the sleeping town. The moon cast its pale blue light through our unshuttered window, illuminating the bare wooden floorboards and the open hatch down to the kitchen below, from where I could hear the even sounds of our children's breathing in their box bed. I imagined Robert Sim's silent room, the bed in his lodgings not slept in. The image of his body sprawled on the cobbles of the library close came to my mind and I sought to chase it away. I took myself back over my last two hours in the library, with the list written in Robert's own hand, and the chest of Gerald Duncan's books.

Robert had been meticulous, and he had already assigned to each book a shelf-mark, lettered for the benefactor and numbered according to subject matter and date of publication. The most recent of the works had taken little of my time – a printed and bound set of graduation theses from the University of Franeker for the year 1622. 1622: I had been immersed in my divinity studies and in the throes of my first experience of love. I wondered how the young graduands of Franeker had fared in those years since their laureation, which paths in life they had taken. The first few paragraphs of their dedication contained the usual fulsome panegyric to the college's benefactors before descending to reminiscences of friendships formed.

I remembered my own inaugural disputation, prior to my promotion and graduation as Master of Arts in philosophy. My own parents had not been there, my mother dead and my father not at ease in such gatherings, but my friend Archie's parents had been there, Lord and Lady Hay, come down from Delgatie with their Katharine. My Katharine. And Jaffray had been there, Dr Jaffray, almost a father to me, come down from Banff to join in the festivities for the boys he had always loved so well. I had made my defence and been greatly lauded as had my fellows, and we had had our laureation and feasted in to the night. A golden day. It was as well we had not known what was to come.

And what had happened to these boys, with their great hopes, passing out of Franeker into the world? It was not good to dwell on such thoughts; I passed quickly over their dedications to the meat of the matter: the theses proposed by their professor and defended by the graduands themselves.

There was little in the set of propositions that was greatly contentious, or would have given too much difficulty to a competent and diligent student. Nothing that would have been of too great concern to the civic or religious authorities of our town. I could see nothing in any of them that could be construed as a danger to our society or to anyone in it. Certainly nothing that might have caused Robert Sim's unexpressed concerns of yesterday or have precipitated his death.

I moved on.

The most interesting to me amongst the books in Duncan's gift, perhaps because of my growing curiosity about the lands across the North Sea, was a finely bound 1616 edition of *The History of the Frisians*, by Ubbo Emmius, late Principal of the University of Franeker. Aside from my sojourn in Ireland, I had never journeyed beyond these shores, and the histories of the places and peoples across the seas held an increasing fascination for me. I resolved to come back and read Emmius' work when this business was done with. Of less interest to me was his *Opus Chronologicum*, published in Groningen in 1619. The warm personal dedication inside, written to Duncan in Emmius' own hand, reminded me that the Scottish doctor had practised for many years in that region, and the two had evidently been friends.

There were more histories – of the Franks, the Romans, the Germans, of Poland and of Spain; re-tellings of battles at sea between Christians and Turks, the siege of Rhodes and the capture of Famagusta. There was even an account of the activities of the Jesuits in Japan. Duncan had travelled in his mind to places and amongst people I had not even begun to imagine.

Most of all though, Duncan seemed to have interested himself in the minerals of the earth and the possibilities they offered to the man who might fully understand and master them. These were the most numerous and evidently well-thumbed of all the books Sim had catalogued on the day of his death. Clearly, my countryman had grown increasingly interested in alchemy as he had entered upon old age. As I worked my way down the list, I began to suspect that the conventional works on minerals and fossils were a mere supplement, or even a screen to the more occult works gifted by him to our college. As well as some works of Paracelsus and the *Magiae Naturalis* of Gianbattista della Porta, there were numerous alchemical books and pamphlets by authors I had never heard of. I had never felt any great attraction for the Hermetic quest, the searching after a secret, unifying knowledge, known to the ancients but lost to us. My earliest teachers had been of the view that the mind of God is not for man to know, and that those who sought that knowledge through the symbols and artefacts of His creation were at best deluded and at worst blasphemous. It was not a matter I often reflected upon, natural science not being in my field of interest, and I had no time for those who peddled little more than fantasy and magic.

What I had not told Sarah was that by the time I had replaced the final book from Duncan's collection in its box, my eyes stinging and my head sore, I had begun to fear, a little, the unknown evil that had walked amongst these shelves only a few hours before, searching for what I myself sought. As a cloud passed over the face of the moon, and the darkness of the library's many recesses deepened, I had become more and more aware of the silence of the place, the emptiness of all human presence. The lighting of another candle to better illuminate the tiny print of the volumes in front of me served only to cast shadows where before there had been none, to suggest movement where there was only stillness. The usual silence of the streets at night heightened my sense of isolation, and my fear, and I checked more than once that I had bolted the library door from the inside.

After I had locked the books and catalogue safely away once more, I had to force myself to return to Robert Sim's desk and to think, to consider whether anything in my examination of the books of the benefaction had brought me any nearer to understanding the murder of the librarian. But there was nothing, nothing there that could, as far as I had seen, have occasioned his need to speak to Principal Dun, or his hesitation to talk to me.

I forced myself again to picture Robert Sim as I had last seen him before his death; to picture the desk at which I now sat. What had been there? The catalogue, yes. But what else? The register – what I had found in the register was of greater concern to me than anything I had seen in the catalogue, but that was the work of tomorrow. And then there had been the Trades' Benefaction Book – found in that bag, lying, bloodstained, on the cobbles when the man's body had been found. I knew that Dr Dun had taken it from the hand of the constable, and had some idea he might have taken it for safe-keeping before the baillie's men came to remove the body of the librarian. There was nothing I could do about that tonight: I would speak to Dr Dun in the morning.

★

He felt sick to his stomach, but his stomach was empty from retching. It was too late now. The blood from Robert Sim's neck had curdled on his shoe and he had not noticed it until he had reached home the night before, under cover at last of the blessed darkness. He had washed his hands and face and stared at his own image in the glass and asked himself whether it could really have been him who had done such a thing. He could almost have persuaded himself that it had been another. He prayed God that it had been another, and then he had bent to remove his shoe, and felt the sticky dampness on his fingers. He had lifted his fingers before his face and seen the brown smear on them, smelt it, and the sweet, molten odour of it had made him vomit.

He had slept, eventually, and the tensions and exhaustions of the day had left him too tired, he thanked God, for dreams, but it had been on waking that the nightmare had returned, for only for the briefest, most blissful of moments, had he forgotten what he had done. He had expressed his shock when he learned of Sim's death, found the right words, if such there could be; fulfilled the duties of the Sabbath, somehow. In all, he had acted as would have been expected of him, but now, wakeful and alone as others slept, he could scarcely stop himself from shaking, and no matter how tight he held himself, he could not blot out the hollow of dread that filled his stomach. But he must think, think. A day had passed and no one had accused him. He had searched every shelf of the library and had not found what he sought, but no one else had done so either, or he would by now be tethered in the tolbooth, a doubly condemned man. It might be long enough, if ever, before anyone came upon that which he feared was still there, somewhere. For who would

*look as Robert Sim had looked? A man might have it before his
eyes and not see what it was that Robert Sim had seen. And yet,
perhaps Sim had passed what he had found to another. He would
know soon enough, no doubt. All he could do now was to continue
to play his part, and in the passage of time, perhaps, the horror of
yesterday would be forgotten and the cause of it never known. He
looked once more in the mirror, and he could begin to believe it had
been another man, and not him who had committed that terrible
act at all.*

SIX

In Search of Robert Sim

There was little that could be done in my researches in to Robert Sim's life on the Sabbath, and so Zander was delighted to see me still at home when he tumbled from his bed, rubbing the sleep from his eyes on Monday morning.

'Is the college closed today?' A better idea. 'Is it a holiday?'

'Not a holiday. A few more weeks yet till that. But I have some work to do in the town for Dr Dun, and so he has had someone else take my classes today.'

His face became serious. 'I hope it is not Mr Jack; I do not like Mr Jack.'

'Mr Jack strives as he does that the boys might make the best of themselves, but he is maybe a bit harsh on them.'

'He has a bad face,' persisted Zander, 'and I do not like him.'

'Zander!' said his mother. 'A man cannot help his face.'

'No, but the fellow might smile occasionally,' I muttered to her, under my breath, to be rewarded with a warning look and a wet rag with which I was instructed to wipe my daughter's face.

'Are you going back to the library this morning?'

'No,' I said. 'There are some matters Dr Dun wishes me to look in to in town.'

'What matters?'

I shook my head, indicating Zander, and she did not pursue the matter.

'Have you time to walk with us then, to the Cargills' house?'

'I do, but I had not thought you went so early. Does Zander not go by himself these light mornings?'

'He does, and Deirdre and I stay here and see to our work, do we not, my pet?'

Deirdre laughed, and threw the rag I had left sitting by her to the floor.

'But today we go early to Elizabeth's. She is to order new linen. There is a weaver in town newly returned from the Netherlands with a wondrous skill, they say, and all the latest in Dutch fashions. Elizabeth wants my help in going through her linen chest, to see what she will need.'

'If she does not already know what she needs, she cannot truly be in need of it at all.'

'Alexander! I sometimes think you would be happier living like a monk in that college of yours. It is no sin to have nice things that you have worked to earn.'

I stroked her face. 'I know it is not. And if I could provide for you as William does for Elizabeth, I would. And I would never be happier anywhere without you. I fear I would make a very poor monk.'

She flushed, and carried on with the business of clearing the table, her back to me. 'You provide for me everything I could want. Everything.' Then she looked at me, her expression changed, humorous. 'And do not for a moment think to talk William out of allowing Elizabeth her new linen; she has promised me their old.'

'Well then, I will tell him they are in need of some new Italian crystal also, for I have had my eye on those goblets of his for years.'

I walked with the boys the extra two hundred yards or so from the Cargills' house to the English school, set behind the wall of the kirkyard. There they would learn their letters and their morals until the time came for them to go up to the grammar school. And then, just as it had been for William and myself, it would be off to the college and the world beyond. I watched them run through the gate, Zander never looking back, and wished I could hold back time.

It was good to be out in the town, in the early morning sunshine, away from the library and the confines of the college walls. I was stopped two or three times by towns-folk wanting to know about the murder of Robert Sim. I gave the same answer to all of them: it is out of the college's hands; it is in the hands of the baillies. The answer seemed to satisfy them well enough. But I had not spoken the truth: the baillies may well have been about their business over the murder, but so was I. I turned down the Netherkirk-gate and skirting St Katharine's Hill by Putachieside, I headed for the Green. Far now from my lecture room, I was nonetheless on the college's work, and I had hopes that I might find amongst the dyers and the weavers at the Green answers that had evaded me amongst the dusty books and faded pamphlets of the library.

The house of Janet Simpson, brewster, widow to a long-dead dyer, was at the east side of the Green, near to the old Carmelite yards. Janet had the ground floor in a tenement of three storeys, and to supplement the meagre income of her trade, she had taken as lodger Robert Sim. I found her in the backland, already at her work at the mashing vat, while her daughter prepared the fire under the cauldron.

The daughter looked up briefly. 'Our ale is not ready. Anna Wilson down by the burn has ale for sale today.'

The widow straightened herself when she saw who it was that her daughter was talking to. 'I do not think Mr Seaton is here to buy ale.'

'No,' I said, 'I am not.'

She wiped her hands on her apron. 'Come inside. Jessie, see to the masher.'

It was a moment before my eyes accustomed themselves to the dim light of the room in which the women cooked, ate and slept. Little enough light found its way into the backland of the tenement, bounded as it was by others of two and three storeys, and almost none came through the one small window to this room. A smell of bannocks from the oven filled the place, and I noticed a tray of them already cooling on the table. I suspected Janet supplemented her income with some extra trade which the bakers and the town's authorities would not like. It was no concern of mine.

She placed a bannock and a beaker of ale in front of me. 'I had been expecting you – you or some other from the college.'

'Have you had the baillies here yet?'

A twinkle came into her eyes and she nodded towards the cooling bannocks. 'You do not think I would have those sitting out for all to see if the baillies had not already been and gone?'

I smiled. 'No. Were you ... of any help to them?'

'What is it that you do not want them to know?'

The shrewdness of her question took me by surprise. 'I don't know. But most men have something. I will not cast any blame on his memory if there is nothing good to be gained by it.'

'Then I will tell you what I told them: Robert Sim was a good tenant; he gave me no trouble. He paid his rent on time, never came drunk to this house or took trouble to our door. He brought no visitors here and no one ever came here looking for him. He went early in the morning to the college, where he took most of his meals. He returned late. He kept his chamber tidy and never had a day's sickness that I know of.'

'And that is what you told them?'

She got up and went to the oven. 'That is what I told them because that is what they asked me.'

'But there is something more.' Some indecision in her eyes told me that she had not told me everything. 'Had Robert said anything to you ... had he been acting in any way differently of late?'

I saw her hesitate.

'Please, Mistress, you must believe me. I am here on the college business, on behalf of Principal Dun, but Robert was also my friend. I do not seek to blacken his name or look for scandal for the sake of scandal. If there is anything you know that might be of help in finding out his killer, I urge you to tell it to me.'

Carefully, she lifted another tray from the oven and then turned to face me. 'It is little enough. In another man, it would scarcely have taken my notice.'

'Go on.'

'In the last few months, since the turn of the year, Mr Sim had taken to going somewhere on a Friday or some-times a Saturday night, every two or three weeks, perhaps, and not returning until late.'

'It was not simply that he was working longer in the library?'

She shook her head. 'I do not think it. On those nights, he would return earlier than usual from his work and take his supper here, rather than in the college, and then go out again. Sometimes he would have his satchel with him, with a book or books in it.' She paused a moment. 'And that is another thing. Until this change in his habits came about, he never took books from the library home with him, never. Only some accounts he worked on for the guilds.'

I did not doubt this. Robert had always been vigilant in upholding the regulations that forbade the borrowing of books from our library. Unlike the scholars and masters of the King's College, we at the Marischal were restricted to consulting them in the library itself. Not even the principal was permitted to take a volume beyond its walls.

'Did you ever see what these books were?'

She shrugged. 'I saw them on his desk when I went in to clean his chamber, but I cannot tell you what they were. I cannot read. My daughter knows a few letters, but she was never in that room – it was for her own sake as well as his.' She fixed me with a warning look. 'I will not have burgh gossip about my daughter.'

'Do not fear for that; there will be none from me.'

Satisfied, she continued. 'They were not always the same books. They changed from time to time – I could tell by the size, and colour and age of them – but they were of no interest to me, and I doubt if I would know them again.'

I doubted it also, and it would serve little purpose to have the old brewster woman look over the hundreds of books on the shelves and in the presses of the library in the hope that she would recognise those she had once seen in Robert Sim's chamber.

'When was the last time Mr Sim went out in this way?'

She needed no pause to think. 'It was the Friday before last.'

'Eight days before he died?'

She nodded curtly, and I thought my questions were finished, and was about to ask to see Sim's chamber when she spoke again.

'He didn't come back.'

'What?'

'That last Friday. He didn't come back. Not until the Saturday night. I am a light sleeper: I would have heard him come in. And besides, his bed was never slept in.'

'Did you question him about it? Did he tell you where he had been?'

She gave a humourless laugh. 'I am a widow woman, Mr Seaton; I earn a crust brewing ale and by having a lodger sleep in the only decent room in my house. It is not for me to question where the librarian of the town's college has spent the night.'

She was right, although many a landlady would not have been so reticent. I recalled some of the misdeeds of my own past and darker days, and the righteous fury and many last warnings issued to me by my landlady in the school-house of Banff. I recalled also the nature of some of those nights when I had stumbled late to my own bed, or not at all. 'Had he been drunk, do you think? Or with a woman?'

She raised an amused eyebrow at me. 'That I cannot tell. But I think you are more of an age than I to tell how a young man spends his nights away from his own chamber.'

I had no answer for her and she gave me the key to Sim's room. 'The baillies have already searched it, but they found nothing. I took the trouble to go round it with them. Lock the door when you are finished, and put the key back up on the shelf there. I must get on with my work.'

I watched her go back out to her yard and then turned the key in the lock. Sim's room, with the shutters pulled open on a window looking out on to the thoroughfare, had better light than had the kitchen, and I did not need the tallow candle the widow had given me. I stood in the doorway a moment, looking round at the small chamber. It could have been any man's room; any unmarried man. There was a bed with a small chest under it, a small fir table and stool, and a simple sideboard below the window. Robert's winter cloak and the gown he kept for the Sabbath and for college ceremonies, hung from a hook on the back of the door. A pair of riding boots lay under the bed.

I checked the chest first. It contained only two winter blankets and some clean linen.

Above the table, fixed to the wall, was one flimsy shelf. On it were a Bible, a book of psalms, an old childhood catechism, and something I would not have expected to find there: the first of what I knew to be three parts of Luther's translation into German of the Bible. I opened the volume: it had been printed in Frankfurt in 1595 and gifted to the college by Dr Liddel, Dr Dun's old teacher from Helmstedt and a generous benefactor of education in our town. The work should have been locked safely behind the glass door of a press in the library along with the rest of Dr Liddel's benefaction, not sitting openly on a shelf in a poor room rented from one of the town's brewsters. I turned the volume over in my hand, prior to setting it down on the bed, that I might not forget to take it with me when I left. I had not known Robert even understood the German tongue.

I went next to the sideboard. Placed on top were a pitcher and bowl, rough local work, nothing to the pieces of Delft-ware in my own chamber, so treasured by Sarah, gifted to us on our marriage by that same old, loving landlady of mine. Beside them a cloth and a hairbrush. The drawer beneath contained nothing I would not have expected to find there: two clean shirts, a winter jerkin, spare hose and stockings, good winter gloves of sheepskin and a hat, evidently of the same manufacture. In the cupboard below were two plates, a knife and a cup that must have been Sim's own, an empty leather flask of the sort a man might use when travelling, and a walnut box, bound with leather straps. It was not locked, and the straps were not properly tied: the baillie's men, I supposed, for Robert would never have been so careless. Inside was a small amount of money, Scots and English, with a few Dutch and French coins of little value. Robert's contract with the town as the college librarian was there too, along with testimonials from his university teachers and the minister of the parish a few miles away where he had grown up. I took a few minutes to read them, but they were of the sort I had seen many times before, and told me nothing new.

I was about to leave the room when I noticed I had

knocked Robert's boots askew when moving the chest from under the bed. It could not matter to him now, but the sight of the boots looked wrong in the well-ordered room. I lifted the left one to straighten it, and was surprised by the weight of it. I balanced it against the right and found that it was indeed heavier. I slid my hand down inside the leg of the boot and my hand closed around something hard and smooth which turned out, when I extracted it, to be a small replica of the walnut box whose contents I had already examined. This one, evidently missed by the baillie's men, was locked. Nowhere in the room, or about the pockets of Robert Sim's clothing, could I find a key. And then I remembered: I searched in the pocket of my breeches and drew out the library keys found near to Robert Sim's body. Nestling amongst the larger college instruments was one very small key of finely worked brass. I slipped it in to the lock and it turned without complaint. I had not stopped to think what I might find in that box, but when I opened the lid, I felt only a surge of disappointment, for all that was there was a scrap of paper, folded. When I opened it I saw that there were only two words on it, written in Robert Sim's own, precise hand. The words were known to me from some-where, the knowledge of them tantalisingly close and yet I could not place them: Jachin and Boaz. I folded the slip of paper and put it in my own pocket. Then locking the box, I slipped it back into the boot and under the bed once more, not forgetting, as Robert's landlady had instructed me, to lock the door of the dead man's chamber as I left it.

'All will be as it should be, Mr Seaton?' was all she said to me as I passed back out into her yard.

'Yes, Mistress,' I said. 'All is at it should be.' I held up the bible to show her. 'I am returning this book to the library – it is college property.'

I was about to turn up the close leading from her small courtyard to the street when the silhouette of a man appeared at the end of it. I squinted against the sunlight to make him out. As he emerged in to the light I saw that it was Richard Middleton, a physician not many years older than myself who had settled in the burgh while I had still been in Banff. He stopped short a moment when he saw me.

'Mr Seaton, I . . . it is . . . I had not thought to find you here.' His accent still held traces of his Lanarkshire childhood, and had not been hardened by our harsher northern tongue.

Nor I you, were the words that came to my mind, but I managed to stop myself from uttering them. Richard Middleton, tall, fair, graceful and elegantly dressed, was known to be a favourite amongst the rising families of Aberdeen; I doubted that he had many patients down here amongst the widows and lower craftsmen. 'I am here on college business. You will have heard what happened to Robert Sim?'

He nodded. 'At the sermon, yesterday – the people could

talk of little else. What a horror to happen, within the college walls.'

'Yes,' I said, 'it was.'

We appeared to have reached the limit of our conversation, and Middleton did not look anxious to prolong it.

'Well,' I said, putting on my hat, 'I will leave you to your business. Good day, Mistress. Doctor.'

'Good day, Mr Seaton,' said the widow, never for a moment taking her eyes from the physician.

SEVEN

The Register

I was shown in to the principal's private chamber a little before mid-day. He looked weary, and I guessed he had not slept well.

'The sight of Robert Sim as we found him is before my eyes every time I close them. It would have been a thing bad enough, had it happened in a back street of the town, some silent and dark alleyway where men forbear to wander after dark, but somebody came deliberately within our college walls to murder him. It is an evil I do not understand.' He looked at me and his eyes were red-rimmed. 'But we must seek to understand it, Alexander. What have you found?'

And so I told him of my visit to Robert's lodgings, and what I had learned from his landlady. He looked a little surprised to hear of Sim's recent night-time wanderings, but he had been long enough in the world not to be shocked by them.

'It was a lonely life he led. It may be that he had found some comfort or companionship at the end of it. You will be discreet in your enquiries? It cannot harm him now, but

he was a good man, and I would not see his name maligned.'
I assured him I would, although with regard to the change
in Robert's nocturnal habits, I did not see how I was to
proceed further, discreetly or otherwise.

'As to the matter of the books he was taking out of the
library, only Robert himself would have been able to tell
us what they were. I wonder at him having Dr Liddel's
Bible in German, though, for he did not have the language,
you know.'

'Perhaps he was learning it.'

'Perhaps so. It is a pity he had not come to me. I lived
so long in Germany that I still wake up some mornings
thinking in that tongue.' He sighed. 'That is the register
you have with you?'

'That is my task for this afternoon – questioning those
who were in the library yesterday.'

'Good,' he said, and looked as though he would move
on, but he evidently sensed my hesitation. 'There is something else, Alexander?'

'The Trades' Benefaction Book: I cannot find it.'

He opened a drawer in his desk. 'I judged it best to keep
it safe, here. The trade guilds do not like their business to
be known, and there is much of their business in these
pages.' He opened the ledger at the Coopers' page and
showed me. 'Each of the larger guilds has its own account,
detailing its payment for the support of scholars here or in
the grammar school, who have a call through kinship on
the charity of their craft.'

I knew that already. It was the only way that many an orphaned son of a craftsman had any hope of an education.

'But here,' continued the principal, drawing my attention to the fine detail of the accounts, 'you see the contributions of individual members – the amount and frequency of their payments, whether and for how long they have fallen into arrears, the extent of any procedures begun against them. There are names on this list that might surprise you, and not all of these people would be happy for their laxity in payment – their fall in standing within their craft – to be noised abroad.'

'But it is hardly cause for murder,' I said. 'And anyway, surely there are other ways that a craftsman's financial affairs can be brought to public scrutiny.'

'Several,' agreed Dun. 'All the same, take care where you keep this book.' He closed the volume and handed it to me. 'But now,' he said getting up heavily from behind his desk, 'while you look into the business of the dead, there are matters of the living I must attend to: Matthew Jack beat the boys too hard this morning, far too hard.'

It had not taken me long to track down the three students whose names were written in the library register for Saturday, and I had them brought to me at the library from their classes, one at a time, in the afternoon.

The first two boys had very little of interest to tell me. They had been in the library from nine in the morning until eleven. The only other reader to come in during that time had been a regent from the King's College. He had still been there when they left. They were not sure of his name. But I was; it was there in front of me in Robert's hand in the register. That would be a more awkward matter, and one I had put off until the evening. Robert Sim, they told me, had been no different from any other time they had been in the library: courteous, but not given to personal exchanges or pleasantries. Each one looked mightily relieved as I thanked him for his help and dismissed him back to his class.

The final name in the register, other than my own, was that of Adam Ingram, the sleepy scholar whom I had finally released from his labours over Aristotle to go and join the others on the Links. I had expected him to enter the library immediately after the latter of the others had left it, but it was almost five minutes later that I finally heard a step on the bottom of the stairs. I did not think it was him at first, so slow was the trudge that brought him to the library door. I turned to face it as it opened and could not stop the sound of shock that escaped my throat: he was hunched slightly, holding himself awkwardly to one side, and taking slow and painful steps. He was not looking at me, but down and away to the floor like a frightened dog, and the hand that held his cloak across him had two long and angry gashes across the top and knuckles. I recovered myself quickly and hurried over to take him to the nearest seat.

'Adam, for the love of God . . .!' And then I realised:

Matthew Jack. My voice fell flat. 'Mr Jack did this to you.'

He swallowed with difficulty and nodded.

'I cannot believe Dr Dun allowed it.'

'He . . . he did not,' said Adam, his voice hoarse, as if he did not trust himself. 'He was not there for the start.' I could believe it: the principal did not like to see the boys punished, and often found a reason to absent himself from their public whippings. He swallowed again. 'I was the fourth. By that time Mr Williamson had gone to fetch Dr Dun; he put a stop to it as soon as he saw. Too late for me and the other three, but the rest were spared it, thank God.'

I put my hand over his but removed it instantly as he flinched under the pain of the open wounds. 'Adam, I promise you this: if my word bears any weight with the principal, Matthew Jack will never again lift his hand to a boy in this college.'

He nodded again, looking at me at last, with bloodshot eyes rimmed with red. He took in the room, as if adjusting to where he was, and why we were here. 'It seems different now,' he said at last. 'Everything looks the same, but it is different.'

He was right. There was the same curved wooden ceiling, the same fir beams supporting it above the rows of shelves and high glass-fronted presses that lined the walls. Windows, tall, narrow and arched as in a church, let in just what light they had always done at this time of the day, at this point in the year, but the absence of the constant presence of the librarian, the knowledge of what had happened to him, rendered the place crypt-like.

I poured him a beaker of water and waited as, with trembling hand, he took some. 'Now tell me about Saturday,' I said. 'Tell me about the time between your arrival and my own. Who else came to the library during that time? Did anything occur that struck you as strange? Did any change in manner overtake Mr Sim whilst you were here?'

He thought back. 'I came in shortly after midday. I had taken my dinner in the hall with the others but wanted an hour or two of quiet study before going down to the Links. I met the porter and two of the college servants coming down the stairs; they had just delivered some books that had been waiting a few days down at the docks, while the town and the college wrangled over who should pay for their transport up to the library. The servants were grumbling greatly about the weight of one of the boxes. When I got up to the library Mr Sim was bent over a large wooden chest and was lifting a letter from it. And he was smiling, at the books themselves almost. He put the letter – or list, I think it was by the look of it – down on top of an open ledger on his desk, and fetched my book for me. I thanked him, and he bent again to the box, and started to lift the books from it, one at a time. I think he had soon forgotten I was there.'

I had seen Robert in this state many times myself, when he was at his most content. 'And that was it? No one else came into the library between then and when I came up myself, at around one?'

He was, like me, looking at the names on the register. 'No,' he began, and then, 'but wait, yes. Malcolm Urquhart. You would have passed him on the stairs.'

'I did. And a foul enough mood he seemed to be in. But Mr Sim did not write his name in the register.'

'He did not stay. He had not come in to consult a book – he did not even sit down. He only wanted to speak with Mr Sim.'

'And did he?'

Adam nodded. 'He kept his voice low – I don't think he wanted me to hear, but I had a good idea what it was about, anyway.' He looked a little uncomfortable.

'Adam, sometime between when I last saw him alive and when I found him dead, Mr Sim was murdered down in that courtyard, a few yards away from where we now sit; he was left to crawl on the ground in his own blood. His killer then came up the steps and walked up and down this room, opened these presses, scanned these shelves. If anything you saw or heard in here might lead us to the identity of that person, you must tell me.'

The boy looked frightened, for which I was a little sorry, but I had the feeling that soft words might not unlock his tongue. 'It was not Malcolm Urquhart, Mr Seaton, I am sure of that. He can have a fiery temper, but he would never have done such a thing. '

'What did he want with Mr Sim?'

'He wanted him to allow him off with the final library payment. He has not the money to pay it, nor any of the other expenses of his graduation. Malcolm has only what his brother can afford to give him, which is very little – he is schoolmaster at Banchory – and some help from the laird of Crathes, who is his brother's patron. It would have been enough to see him through his studies had Malcolm lived as other poor scholars must.'

'But he has not, has he?' I knew Malcolm Urquhart, with all his wit and dangerous charm, had run with the high-born. I had assumed that, just as I had been myself, he had been supported by the family of one of them.

'He is heavily in debt. He will not graduate if he cannot pay his fees, or persuade the college to wait for them.'

'Has he gone to the principal yet? Or his regent, even? Dr Dun and Mr Williamson are good men. Malcolm Urquhart would not be the first scholar to find himself unable to pay his fees.'

Adam shook his head. 'He could not. He was cautioned twice last year, threatened with removal, after being found in a tavern in the Old Town, both times with a woman. He was not . . . wise . . . with what money he had, and now he will pay the price. He thought that Mr Sim might have been more lenient with him over the library dues than those who better know his past transgressions and the cause of his misfortunes.'

I remembered the ill-humour in the boy's mumbled response to my greeting as he had gone past me. 'I take it Mr Sim did not turn a kindly ear to his plea?'

'I do not think so, for Malcolm seemed very angry; he –

he knocked something from Mr Sim's hand before making off down the stairs.'

'Then I hope he has cooled his heels by now, for I intend to talk to him next. Do you know where I might find him at the minute?'

The apprehension in Adam's eyes turned to genuine surprise.

'Do you not know, Mr Seaton?'

'Know what?'

'Malcolm Urquhart is missing; nobody has seen him since Saturday afternoon.'

EIGHT

The Round Tower

I was glad to get out of the college, away from its damp corners and crumbling walls into the bright sunshine of the June afternoon. The cawing of the gulls, white pennants gliding and curling against the endless blue of the sky, mocked the men moving silently beneath them along the gloomy passageways of our citadel of learning.

'Will you be back today, Mr Seaton?' called the porter, as I went past his lodge and out onto the Broadgate.

'No, Stephen, I do not think so. Why?'

'Because Dr Dun has told me I am to lock the gates when the bell at the Grayfriar's Kirk tolls six tonight, and not to open them again before six tomorrow, should even the bishop himself come banging on the doors.' Such hours were common in the winter, but in the summer months the gates were not usually locked until ten at night. The principal was clearly in fear that the murderer of Robert Sim had not yet finished his business with the Marischal College.

On another day I might have gone by the King's Meadows and out past the Links to Old Aberdeen, but it was no pleasant errand I was on, and I had not the leisure to enjoy the afternoon sun as its rays sparkled like crystal on the waves chasing each other to the shore. Instead, I would take the more direct route between the two burghs, out along the Gallowgate and past Mounthooly, to ascend the Spittal hill and come down the other side on to College Bounds and the Old Town.

It was not yet three when I crossed the Powis Brig on to the High Street of Old Aberdeen. It was quiet here, so much quieter than the New Town that I had come from. It was not a market day, so what trade there was took place in booths at the fronts of people's houses, their gables jostling for space around the market cross. I turned off the High Street and through the archway into the King's College. The gatekeeper hardly lifted an eyebrow to see me pass; he had held his post over twenty years, and remembered me still as a young scholar there myself, struggling to keep the misdemeanours of Archie Hay from the sight and ears of the college authorities.

'A fine day, Mr Seaton.'

'Aye, Geordie, a fine day.'

I crossed the quad and sat on a bench outside the door to the common school of the college, from where I could see all comings and goings in the students' and masters' lodgings. Many of the students had abandoned their chambers to study and dispute with one another on the grass, while others sat talking quietly on benches. It was with some reluctance that I passed through the doorway to the round tower of Dunbar's building and began to ascend the steps to John Innes's chamber.

None amongst the students I passed questioned me; from my frequent visits here, my figure was almost as well known to the scholars of King's as it was to those of Marischal. I came to the top floor, and knocked lightly on John's door at the far end of it. There was no reply, and I tried once more, louder this time. I heard a shuffling noise on the flagstones, and the sound of an iron bolt being drawn back. The door opened as far as the chain linking it to the jamb would allow and a voice, John's, but low and cracked, called, 'Who is there?'

'It is me, John – Alexander. Will you let me in?'

The chain was dropped, and the door drawn back further. I stepped carefully over the threshold and into a place more gloomy than the corridor I had just left. John's chamber faced south, but today its one small window was shuttered fast against the bright mid-afternoon sun, and little light found its way into the room. The air inside was fusty and stale. It was a moment before I could see my friend: he was standing, hiding almost, behind the door. When he saw that it was indeed me, he pulled me further in and shut the door quickly behind me.

'John,' I said, 'are you all right? What is the matter, man?'

'Who saw you come here?'

'Who? I don't know . . . nobody. Everybody.'

He sat down on his narrow bed in the far corner of the

chamber and ran his hands through his thinning hair. 'It cannot be long,' he said. 'It cannot be long.'

I drew up a stool in front of him and forced him to look at me. 'What cannot be long? John, what is this about?'

He shook his head and continued to mutter.

'John, tell me, what is it? Is it something to do with the rumpus down at the Links between the students on Saturday? Are you being blamed for it?'

'The students? Hah!' he laughed a moment, as if I were stupid, and continued to shake his head. Something in his look recalled me to the reason I had come here today in the first place. I let go the hands I had taken hold of, and sat back a little. 'John, has this something to do with Robert Sim?'

The name seemed to pull him back, instantly, to where we were. He lifted his head and looked directly at me now, his pale blue eyes unflinching. 'Yes,' he said slowly, 'I fear it has everything to do with Robert Sim.'

This at least cut through the awkward preliminaries. 'Tell me what you know about Robert's death.'

He looked away and drew a hand across his forehead. 'I know nothing of Robert's death, save what I have been told: that you found him in the library close on Saturday night, with his throat cut.'

'It was less a cut than a stab in the neck,' I said, 'but . . . the effect was much the same, although Principal Dun thinks he perhaps lived longer after the attack than he might otherwise have done.'

74

John was hunched, and seemed to cower a little further in on himself. 'How long . . .?' he began. 'How long do they think he might have lived?'

'Twenty minutes, perhaps, little more.'

'And no one heard him call out?'

'No one. I doubt it would have made any difference had anyone done so in any case. So great was the loss of blood, Dr Dun thinks nothing could have been done for him.'

'No,' answered John, not seeming convinced. 'Has his killer been found?'

I shook my head. 'We are scrambling in the dark. Talking of which, can I open these shutters? I can hardly see you.' It was then, when I pulled back the shutters and let the light flood in from the window, that I saw what a truly dreadful condition John Innes was in. His hair was dishevelled, and his normally clean-shaven chin covered with what looked like two days' stubble. His eyes, pale and watery under their sandy lashes at the best of times, were pink, from sleeplessness or weeping. The air around us, such as it was, was foul.

'When did you last leave this room?' I asked eventually.

'Last night, for the Sunday service. Andrew Carmichael took my classes for me today. He told the principal I was ill.'

'And does he – Carmichael – know what it is that is the matter with you?'

'I told him it was grief over Robert Sim, and God knows, he was a friend and I do grieve over him.'

'But there is something else, is there not? Something you are afraid of?'

He stood up and went to the washbowl on the deal table beneath the window and splashed some water on to his face. 'It is nothing I can tell you about, Alexander.'

I almost laughed. 'John? What has there ever been that you could not tell me? Am I not your friend? Have I not been your friend these seventeen years? What have you ever done in all that time that you could not tell me?'

He said nothing for a moment, did not turn his gaze from the window.

'My life has not been as yours, Alexander.'

'I know that. Which one of us can say our life is as that of another? We are bound together by something more than what we have become. Surely ours is a brotherhood?'

He turned at last, and smiled a little. 'Yes, Alexander.' He pressed a hand to his heart. 'Ours is a brotherhood I will value until the last breath leaves my body. You must promise me you will not forget that.'

'Of course, but . . .'

'No, you must promise me.'

'You have my promise.'

'Good. That is a comfort.' He lowered his voice. 'But there are other brotherhoods, and . . .'

He hesitated.

'You and Robert Sim were in some form of brotherhood together?' I had heard of fraternities of men, scholars, divines, in the Netherlands and in Bohemia, Germany, but never in Scotland. 'Is there some fraternity here? In Aberdeen?'

He turned away again, shaking his head once more, wringing his hands. 'Forget that I spoke, Alexander. I should not have spoken.' He looked at me again, desperation in his eyes. 'For your own sake, forget that I spoke.'

I started towards him. 'No, John. I am . . .' But before I understood what he was doing, he had crossed the floor and wrenched open the door.

'Go!' he shouted. 'Go!' He pushed me out in to the corridor and slammed the door shut once again behind me. Before I could gain my senses I heard the key turn in the lock and the bolt shot to.

I had never seen John, meek and mild John, act in this way, never heard him talk so wildly. I stood there a few minutes, knocking, calling his name, but to no purpose – I did not hear another word or sound from the room, and in time I had to leave off and turn back towards the stairs, having learned much to alarm me, but nothing of John's Saturday morning visit to the library and still less to help me understand the killing of Robert Sim.

Had it been possible, I would have gone then to seek out Dr John Forbes, professor of divinity in the King's College, and for many years mentor and friend to John and me both, but I knew he was away in Edinburgh, on business for his father, the bishop, and so there was no one here to whom I could take my concerns. I went slowly back through the quad, paying little attention to the scholars around me; so absorbed in my thoughts that I was not looking where I was going, and on turning under the archway that would take me back out to the High Street, walked right into Andrew Carmichael, sending flying the lecture notes he was carrying.

'Alexander . . .'

'Andrew . . . here, let me help you with these.' We bent together to pick up the papers. 'Geometry,' I said. 'Perhaps you would like to come down and give my third-year class a lesson. The finer points of Euclid seem somewhat to have eluded them.'

He laughed. 'And me. Were it not for these dictates of my old professors at Herborn and Franeker I fear I would be lost myself.'

The papers, as I handed them back to him, were now somewhat dusty and in a disorder that would take him some time to sort out.

'Andrew, I am truly sorry. I was not paying proper attention to where I was going.'

'You do seem somewhat distracted.' He waited, and I almost let the moment pass, so that he began to turn away. I made the decision. 'Andrew, is there somewhere private that we might talk?'

'There is my chamber, up there.' He indicated a window in the Dunbar building.

'Near to John Innes?'

'Directly below him.'

'Perhaps that would not be the best place today.'

I looked back towards the quad and then out to the High Street; where there were not students there were townspeople, going about their business from booth to booth, talking with their neighbours in doorways or across dikes, hanging out linens or watching children play on the greens. There seemed nowhere where two men might talk and their conversation not be remarked and overheard. After a minute or so of us both casting around, Carmichael indicated the garden of the Mediciner's manse. 'I am sure Dr Dun would have no objection to our talking there.'

Patrick Dun, my own college principal was also, through lack of personnel and as a testament to his own great experience and abilities, Mediciner of the King's College here in Old Aberdeen, and in virtue of his position had a house and garden from the university. I agreed with Carmichael, and we had soon crossed the street and passed through the ornate iron gates in to the gardens of the Mediciner's manse. It was a place where I had spent many happy visits since my return to Aberdeen from Banff five years ago. Dr Dun had been the very first, after my marriage to Sarah, to invite me to bring my wife and child to dine at his home, and he had made sure too that everyone knew he had done so. He might as well have stood at the market cross and proclaimed that my wife would be accepted by all in the two colleges or they would answer to him.

Carmichael and I chose a stone bench at the end of the path between orchard and herb garden, far from the street yet far enough from the house that we would not be overheard by any in it. I knew it to be one of the principal's favourite places, in his rare moments of rest. Roses clambered over trellises and up the wall behind us, to spill out over the bounds of the manse as if seeking their freedom, and the rays of the sun fell upon a granite dial, the craftsmanship and precision of which Dr Dun took great pride in. Carmichael stopped to admire the piece. He ran his hand over its contours, its edges and grooves. He walked around it, admiring and inspecting its various faces, examining it so closely he might have been trying to measure its angles by his eye alone. 'The complexity is astonishing,' he said at last, 'the execution perfect.'

'I have often admired it,' I said, 'but in truth, I am a poor judge of its function; I know only that it is a thing of great beauty.'

'Beauty, yes,' he murmured, 'but beauty without function is an empty thing. The man who conceived and executed this was a master of his craft.'

'Are you a student of sundials?' I asked.

He shook his head. 'No, but my father was a stonemason. His was workmanship of good quality, but he never produced anything like this. This is the work of a mathematician, a true architect.'

His words recalled me to the reason I had brought him here in the first place.

'An architect,' I echoed. 'Like Vitruvius.'

He took his eyes from the dial and looked at me, a little puzzled. 'Vitruvius? Yes, perhaps so.'

'Tell me, Andrew, do you teach the works of Vitruvius here?'

He breathed out heavily and came to sit beside me. 'A little; I teach his theories: his concept of the architect, of his place at the apogee of all the crafts, of the skills required of him, but as to the architecture itself . . .'

'And John Innes? Does he also teach Vitruvius to his students?'

Carmichael frowned. 'I do not think so. John has the second class. He is too busy trying to impress upon them some semblance of knowledge of Latin and Greek. Why? What is your interest?'

I had come this far, it would have done more to prick Andrew Carmichael's interest should I retreat from the matter now than if I told him all that I knew.

'My interest is in why John should have taken the time, on Saturday morning, to go down to the New Town and consult the works of a long-dead Roman architect in the library of the Marischal College, and never to mention to me having done so. He had been in our library on Saturday morning, but did not say a word about it down at the Links in the afternoon, when we were talking about Robert and the new books that had arrived.'

Carmichael frowned. 'You are right, he did not. It is strange – I have never known John Innes to dissemble, nor come anything close to it. But, you know, he is not well just now, Alexander. He has not been right since we heard of the death of Robert Sim.'

'Robert's death. That is what I need to talk to you about, for it seems to have sent John into a terror, to have driven him half-mad almost. I knew they were friendly enough together, and God knows, Robert's death is a hellish thing, but I did not know them to be close, or to have particular connections to one another.' I did not know how to say it. 'Had Robert – had Robert been visiting John here of late?'

I saw a wave of stunned comprehension pass over Carmichael's face, followed by disgust. 'You are asking me if there was some unnatural relation between them? My God, Alexander, I thought you were John's friend.'

I lowered my voice. 'I am, and that is why I can ask you such a question, for I believe you are too. I must know why John has got himself in such a state.'

'It is not over the murder of a lover, I can assure you of that. The only times I ever saw Robert Sim here it was in our own library, or at graduation feasts and the like when the student was known to him. I do not know that I ever even saw him in private conversation with John.'

'And what of John? Has he behaved differently at all of late, in the last six months perhaps?'

Carmichael plucked at some lavender from a nearby border and crushed it between his fingers.

I offered more. 'Has he spoken to you at all of brother-hoods, fraternities?'

At this he gave off his crushing of the herb. 'Yes,' he said, animated now, 'yes, he has. Perhaps four months ago.'

He looked again at the sundial. 'And that would explain the Vitruvius, too.'

I moved closer to him. 'Slow down, you begin to lose me.' He lifted a hand to stay me while he let the thoughts follow their paths and connect.

'About four months ago, on a Friday evening, after all our duties were done and the students safely accounted for, Dr Forbes invited John and myself along with one or two others to take supper and have a hand of cards with him. I was glad to go, for the nights were still long and dark and there is little enough entertainment to be had in the evenings, but John declined, citing prior arrangements. Now, as you know, John is not a man to have "prior arrangements". I noticed that he did, occasionally, leave the college on a Friday evening and return late, but it was not my place to question him on it. Then, after several weeks, perhaps two months of this, he approached me and asked if we might speak confidentially. We went to his room and he began to talk to me about the Hermetic quest: he had become fixated on the idea that there is some secret knowledge of the ancients that will unlock for us God's great plan of the universe, that will help us find the essence of that universe deep within ourselves, and that the discovery of this essence, this element, will lead to universal harmony, the key to solving all the problems and contentions of the world.'

'The great quest of the alchemists,' I said.

'Yes. And he had been studying the works of Paracelsus.'

'Which ones?' I knew of the Swiss physician,

Theophrastus Bombastus von Hohenheim, or Paracelsus as he had called himself, from long discussions by the fire of my good friend Dr Jaffray in Banff. Jaffray was a great admirer and follower of Paracelsus' method in the diagnosis and treatment of the sick, the physical examination of the patient and the application of alchemical knowledge to the diseased element, and he enjoyed recounting tales of the contempt for authority that had seen the Swiss hounded from one university town in Europe to another, but he deplored what he and many others saw as the descent into magic of Paracelsus in his later years.

Carmichael spread out his hands. 'I don't know. I believe he had begun with the medical works, but moved on.'

'And this was the practice of their fraternity?'

'I believe so. And I expect,' he continued, 'that this new-found fascination with what is fundamental to us and to the universe would explain also his interest in Vitruvius.'

'I see that.' I knew that the Hermetics venerated Vitruvius and his views on architecture as the greatest of sciences, necessarily encompassing all forms of human knowledge and endeavour. And the greatest architect of all was God, the universe His divine and perfect creation of which each one of us was an interlocking part. We would all come together to realise the perfect vision of His creation, if only the secret behind it could be understood. No more war, no more illness, no more hunger, no more hatred, drought or famine. 'But what has all this to do with Robert Sim? With brotherhoods?'

Carmichael chewed at his bottom lip a moment. 'I cannot say for certain that it has anything at all to do with Robert Sim, but as to fraternities – well, at the end of his discourse on the promises of Hermetic knowledge, John asked me tentatively if, in the course of my studies abroad, I had ever come across any who might have been of a secret society of Hermetists, in pursuit of this knowledge. I told him I never had, and that should I have done, I would have counselled them to look to the world they can see, and not try to conjure the secrets of a world beyond their senses.'

'What was his response?'

He shrugged. 'He was disappointed, I think. He told me that should I ever reconsider my views, he would be there to listen. At the time I thought he meant nothing more than companionship, friendship; the idea that he meant some sort of actual brotherhood never entered my head.' He put the lavender down on the bench. 'Is there such a fraternity here?'

Mindful of John's evident terror, his pleading that I should forget he had ever spoken of it, I answered Andrew Carmichael as honestly as I could. 'He has not told me that there is.' In my mind, however, I was now certain that there was, and that John Innes and Robert Sim had been amongst its number. What I had to do, and what Andrew Carmichael could not help me with, was discover who else had been in their brotherhood, and what danger they might thereby have placed themselves in.

I thanked Carmichael for his time and asked that he keep

a close eye on John's health and state of mind, and let me know if he worsened. He promised that he would, and we parted at the gate to the Mediciner's manse, two men now uneasily aware that they might be friends, if the one could forgive the other for having married the woman he loved, and the other in turn forgive him for having loved that woman in the first place.

NINE

Women's Tales

Once back in the New Town I made directly for William Cargill's chambers in Huxter Row, behind the Town House and the sheriff court. The last stalls of the Monday market were being packed up now and the traders returning to their homes and yards, leaving the dogs, gulls and indigent to scavenge what they could from what was left. I passed the tolbooth, the burgh prison, ignoring the cries of those inside who extended their purses through their barred windows in the hope of passing charity, and then turned down the vennel to the small, turreted building where William and his fellow advocates rented rooms. The vennel was busy and the entrance hall to the advocates' chambers busier: the sheriff and his deputes would sit in court the next day to hear the grudges and grievances of inhabitants of the shire, one against the other, to listen to the arguments of procurators for one party and against another, and to direct juries of the defendants' peers and neighbours.

As I was about to enter William's rooms, I found myself flattened to the wall by the sweep of four retainers of the laird of Tolquhoun, followed by the laird himself, dragging his young son, briefly a student of mine, almost by the scruff of the neck. The laird took notice of me at the last minute.

'Ah, Mr Seaton is it? I would that I had never put this scoundrel to that damned college of yours. I should have sent him for a soldier instead, if the soft heart of his mother had not intervened. My purse would be all the fuller and that of your friend William Cargill a deal lighter. Good day to you, sir.' And he pushed the sullen boy ahead of him, and out into his last evening of freedom in the town of Aberdeen.

William was rubbing the backs of his hands over his eyes when I went without knocking into his rooms. He looked up with a start as I closed the door behind me, and sank back in relief when he saw that it was me.

'It has been a long day then, my friend,' I said as he reached for a bottle of Madeira wine and two glasses.

'You can have little idea. I swear to you, Sodom and Gomorrah would have been spared, had the good Lord but waited for a look at Aberdeen.'

I sat back and sipped at my Madeira. 'I thought you lawyers spent your days on dry and dusty disputes over boundary walls, the incursions of beasts onto the corns of neighbours, the testaments of the dead.'

'*Some* lawyers do, Alexander, *some* do. But it has fallen to my lot, it would seem, to be beset with the miscreant offspring of every landed family in the north.'

I laughed. 'And who would pay for Elizabeth's fine new linen if they went elsewhere?'

He held up a hand. 'Please, Alexander, do not start me on that. I have had Duncan rumbling in my ear for nigh on a fortnight about the wanton profligacy of it, the claims of the kirk and the poor upon my every last shilling. Anyhow, enough of my petty troubles. Do you make any progress in your investigations?'

And so I told him what I knew, of Robert Sim's change in habits over the last six months, his taking of books from the library, his night-time ventures, and that I thought John Innes was in some way involved. Strangely, he did not seem altogether surprised to learn of Robert's clandestine wanderings, but the mention of John Innes's name gave him greater pause for thought.

'John? Are you certain?'

'I am certain of very little, but he is far from himself, and what Andrew Carmichael told me suggests that John also has taken to night-time wanderings over the last few months. As to this talk of fraternities, I do not know what to make of it. It is not something I am in a hurry to pass on to the burgh authorities. Talk of secret societies is apt to make the wrong people jump to the wrong conclusions.'

'You are right there.' William went to his door and called through to his clerk that he was not to be disturbed for the next ten minutes.

'What have you heard? Is there something you give credence to?'

'I am a lawyer. I give credence to nothing other than that my name is William Cargill and that I live in the burgh of Aberdeen. But as to what I have heard regarding Robert's murder that might have some possible connection to the truth – well, of course, there might have been the motive of robbery, but what would a common thief know of the value of one book as against another? And there is no coin or plate or plenishing of any worth to be found in the Marischal College library. The actions of an angry father or jealous lover I would also have discounted, were it not for what you have just told me about Robert's movements, alongside another rumour I heard today.'

'What rumour?'

'That the kirk session will soon hear an accusation of adultery made against Rachel Middleton.'

'The physician's wife? William, you are in jest.' Rachel Middleton was the wife of the young doctor I had seen the previous morning just as I was leaving Robert Sim's lodgings. She was not native to Aberdeen, but had lived here several years, in a house left to her by her brother, a master stonemason. She and her husband did not move in the circles familiar to me, and I could not have said I knew either of them well, but in all the time I had lived in the town I had never heard a whisper of scandal against her.

'The reputation of a young woman is not something I care to jest about, Alexander, even with you.'

'But on what grounds? That she is – well – womanly of

SHONA MACLEAN

figure and does not mix much in the town, from what I know? That her brother Hugh left her wealthy?'

'That may well be what fires the malice, but it seems there may be grounds to suspect her virtue. It is rumoured that Robert Sim was a frequenter of her house on more than one evening when her husband was not there, after the drummer had gone through the town and the clocks struck nine, and that he was not the only one.'

'Surely you cannot think John . . .?'

'I do not know what to think, but John is a man, like the rest of us.' He looked at me sharply. 'I have heard no other names, mind, only rumours of other men besides Robert, and you tell me his throat was cut with a scalpel?'

'It is what we found, and Principal Dun thinks it is very likely the murder weapon.'

'Well, Rachel Middleton's husband is a physician, is he not?'

I remembered again the startled look on Richard Middleton's face as he had met me in the pend to the old brewster woman's yard. 'And he might have . . . because of his wife. But surely . . .'

'In truth, Alexander, I do not know what to think. What I know of the man says it is hardly likely.' He got up and stretched his arms. 'Anyway, I have had enough of this place and its troubles for today. Come home with me and make an early supper with us. Sarah and the children will still be there, I am sure – Elizabeth was determined that the sorting

91

of old linen and the choosing of new would make a day's work at least.'

The bells of the Grayfriar's Kirk had just tolled five as we turned on to the Broadgate, the college buildings rising up to our right behind the houses fronting the street. We were about to cross over to Guest Row when a commotion from the gates of the Marischal College took our attention. I recognised the voices, but could scarcely believe my ears, or indeed the evidence of my own eyes, when I saw the cause of the disturbance: Matthew Jack, his face scarlet and contorted with fury, was being bodily removed from the college grounds, the porter and one of the burlier college servants having each an arm as they hauled him through the gates. Beyond, in silence, Principal Dun watched, his face as cold and unmoving as stone. A scuffed wooden chest and a leather satchel I knew to be Jack's were, I saw, already on the street. One of my fellow regents stood by the principal and spoke for him.

'Your business here is finished, Matthew Jack. It will be made known that you are no longer to consider yourself a regent of this college, and henceforth you are not permitted entry within its gates. You will be handed over to the magistrates of this town should you ever seek to enter here again.' And then the gate was shut, and principal, regent, porter and servant gone from view, leaving only Matthew Jack on the street with his miserable belongings, ranting at the gate that had just been barred to him.

'You think to silence me, Patrick Dun, but I will not be

silenced. I know what I know, and that will I make known, and then we will see who is brought before the magistrates and, aye, higher authorities, and how many remain in your college!' And then, the spittle still on his chin, he slung his satchel over his shoulder and began to drag his chest down towards town, and I knew not what shelter.

William stood, silent and astonished before turning to me. 'Good God, Alexander, the expulsion of Matthew Jack from the college, and, God-willing, the town, is a thing much to be desired, but over the heads of what has this happened today? What is the man raving about?'

I shook my head. 'Nothing that I know of, but as to his expulsion, I can guess.'

'What?'

'He near enough maimed some of the boys today for the fight down on the Links on Saturday. As hebdomodar it was his right to punish them, but what he did in the college courtyard this morning was beyond all natural justice. I am not greatly surprised that Principal Dun has taken this course. Well, this will cut short my investigations, such as they are. The college cannot sustain the lack of two regents as well as the librarian, with the examinations so close.'

William turned away from the college. 'No doubt you're right, and you'll be much wanted within those walls over the next few days. But come back with me tonight; give some of your time to the children — and to Sarah.'

'Has Elizabeth said something?'

All William's ease of manner was gone from him now,

and he struggled under my question. 'She thinks . . . that things between you are not as they once were.'

His awkwardness was matched by my own, and at first I did not know how to answer him. 'It may be that I have been staying too long at the college, that I have left her alone too often. But the summer vacation is almost upon us, and then I will make things right.'

He put an arm on my shoulder. 'I'm sure that you will. Now let us leave the town to its own business a while, and see what dramas the world behind my door has waiting for us.'

Little more than five minutes later, I was through William's door and being threatened with a description of the new linens to be ordered. The weaver, a pleasant-looking fellow a few years younger than myself, with something of a twinkle in his eye, was introduced to me as Bernard Cummins. His name was something familiar to me, but I did not know why. He was making ready to leave, and I didn't trouble myself much over where I might know him from. Taking me for William, who had been caught up by a fellow advocate a hundred yards from his door, Cummins assured me that his prices would be fair, and that should any of his work not meet with the lady's expectations, she would be under no obligation to take it, and I under none to pay for it. I expressed great relief at this, explaining that I was but a college regent, and not the wealthy master of the house.

'Ah, but you have been blessed greatly by Fortune in

other ways,' he said, smiling over at Sarah before taking his leave of Elizabeth and setting out into the street, his very profitable order tucked in his pocket.

'Well,' I said, 'he will set the ladies' hearts a-flutter, I am sure. I see he will beguile his way into all the wealthy houses of Aberdeen, and empty the coffers of many an unwary husband by his charms.'

'Nonsense,' said Elizabeth, flushing. 'It is just that his years away from Scotland have taught him proper manners as well as better weaving. Sarah and I are in two minds as to whether to send you and William to Holland, to acquire there by example what nature has left wanting.'

'Indeed, I would not waste your time on that, for William has been often to Holland, without any improvement that I can see, and I am sure that what has done him so little good would do me none whatsoever.'

I spent a few minutes more in the kitchen, as Sarah told me all the news of the day, before taking a copy of the weaver's order through to William's study, as Elizabeth had asked me to. As I approached the door, snatches of an unusual sound reached my ear – a man's voice, singing, in a tongue I could only guess to be the French. I pushed open the door carefully and walked quietly into the room, only to come on William's aged manservant, Duncan, bent over a case of instruments which he was lovingly cleaning. The old Presbyterian looked up with a start, caught in mid-verse.

'Well, Mr Seaton. I – I did not hear you come down the corridor. I had not expected anyone. Mr Cargill . . .'

'William will be a few minutes yet. He has been caught up with some business on the street.' Some devilment in me would not let this chance for mischief pass. I set the papers carefully down on William's desk. 'Do you know, as I came close to the door I thought to find some troubadour in the room, or my friend the music master of Banff at the very least, so sweet were the sounds coming from here.'

Duncan's face and neck became suffused with scarlet. I pressed on.

'French, was it not?'

He took a deep breath, through gritted teeth, and then his shoulders sagged and I instantly regretted making fun of the old man.

'Aye, French it was. It is many years since I have heard or spoken the tongue, but today, as I was cleaning Dr Cargill's instruments, it took me back. The sunlight coming through the window and the summer sounds of the birds, they all took me back. All foolishness, an old man's foolishness.' He picked up the small, silver medicine goblet he had been cleaning and returned it to its place in the box.

I tried to picture him, over thirty years ago, not a young man even then, but a few years older than I was now, servant to a wealthy Aberdeen merchant, in France to see to the buying of wine. In an inn in Besançon one evening, they had come across a group of young medics, freshly graduated from Basel. Amongst them had been James Cargill, William's uncle, a young man from Aberdeen who had left the burgh a poor scholar, and would return a fully qualified physician. The merchant had greatly taken to the young doctor, and while he himself had further south still to go, he had sent his servant, Duncan, back north with the young man, fearful of the troubles that might befall him alone on the journey. And from that day Duncan had been a servant to the Cargills, and would be now until the day he died. He shut the case and locked it away in its usual cupboard, along with the notebooks and letters that had lain there fifteen years, since William's uncle's death.

William's arrival brought us both a welcome release from the awkwardness.

'So, is the fellow gone?' he asked, as he breezed in, setting his hat on its nail by the door.

'Who?' I asked.

'The weaver fellow. Am I safe from having to pretend I care about linens?'

'To me, at least. He went about two minutes after I arrived. He left that for you.'

William picked up the copy of the order and blanched a little. I leant towards him and whispered in his ear, 'The touch of lace on the pillows will help you sleep especially well, apparently.'

He glared at me, and filed the paper away with other household expenses.

Later, in our own home, once the children were sleeping, as Sarah and I lay together I told her of my day.

'I thought it was only the matters of the library that you had to see to,' she said.

'I did not know how to tell you that I was to probe into Robert Sim's secrets, his private life. I do not like to look into another man's life.'

She was lying with her back to me and I had my arm around her waist. I could not see her face. 'Better, perhaps,' she said at last, 'than to look into your own.'

'Sarah.' I put my hand up to her face and felt the moisture on her cheek. 'Sarah, look at me.' She turned towards me but still she would not look in my face. 'Sarah, I have wronged you; I have listened to the poison of rumour in the town and I have wronged you. I have wronged Andrew Carmichael also, I know that.' She was watching me now, as the last pink light of the day spread over our bed and onto the bare floorboards of our room. I swallowed. 'I spoke with him this afternoon. I had to go up to the King's College, to see John, and I met with Andrew afterwards. What William and others have often sought to tell me is true: he is a good and decent man. I cannot condemn him because he has loved where I love, because he wanted what I have, before that thing was mine.'

'I was always yours, Alexander.'

I pulled her closer to me and kissed her, and held her there a long time, and then, 'Sarah,' I said, holding her back a little from me, 'what do you know of Rachel Middleton?'

She frowned. 'Rachel? The doctor's wife?'

'Yes.'

She sat up, hugging her knees to her. 'Not a great deal. She is a little older than me, I would say. Perhaps twenty-eight or twenty-nine years old. She arrived a few years ago with her brother who had come up from Glasgow, I think, to do the finishing work on Craigston Castle. Her husband had been completing his medical studies abroad and soon joined them. When the work at Craigston was complete, they moved into the town. Her brother was killed in a fall two years ago and left her wealthy – she and her husband live in his house. She does not mix greatly, does not encourage company, I don't think, and they have no children. Why?'

'And what do they say about her, the gossips in the streets and in the market place?'

She turned on me. 'You know I do not listen to these women, that I have good cause, that–'

'I know that. But you must have heard something?'

'Truly, I have not. Although . . . she is a woman who attracts notice, and that is rarely a good thing for one who came a stranger to the burgh. There are those who do not like her for that she holds herself aloof – but why should she not? Why should she wish to be forever mixing with those of no interest to her? But I haven't heard any tales against her – yet. Do you tell me that you have?'

'Not I, but William: the session will soon hear accusations of adultery against her. It has been brought to their ears that Robert Sim, and other men too, were night-time visitors to her house, at times her husband was not always present.'

'To consult her husband perhaps?'

'Sarah, how often did you hear of Robert being ill? Never once.'

She went to pour herself a beaker of water from the pitcher on the sideboard. As she was padding back to the bed, she stooped to pick up something that had fallen from a pocket of my breeches to the floor. A small, folded piece of paper. She opened it and froze.

'Sarah? What's wrong?'

She said nothing for a moment, continuing to stare at the paper.

'What is it?'

She looked up at me, her face pale in the first shafts of moonlight. 'Alexander, where did you get this?'

I recognised now the thing in her hand. It was the note I had found in the small walnut casket hidden away in Robert Sim's boot under his bed. 'In Robert Sim's room. I could not think what it meant at first, but it has come back to me now, although why Robert took such pains to hide it, I do not know. Jachin and Boaz – the names of the great pillars at the entrance to Solomon's temple.'

She shook her head slowly. 'No,' she said at last. 'Gilbert Burnett.' Her mouth was scarcely able to form the name that had never before been acknowledged in our home. The name of the master stonemason in Banff, in whose house she had been an abused servant, until his rape of her had been discovered in her pregnancy with Zander, the boy who was now my son. 'Gilbert Burnett, in his drunkenness and swagger told me once: it is the Mason Word.'

TEN

The Lodging House

I had returned to my duties in the college because I had thought I was needed, but I had been as well, I think, to leave my scholars to the ministrations of John Strachan, the divinity scholar and mathematics regent who had had charge of my classes in my stead. My mind was whirling with words spoken the previous night, and a fleeting image at the edge of my vision early this morning. I hardly knew what lectures I gave, or how my scholars answered my questions. It was a relief to all, I think, when the bell sounded for the mid-day meal.

The dining-hall, usually a cramped and lively place in spite of frequent exhortations to silence and decorum amongst students and masters, was still and sombre as I took my seat at the top table beside the principal and the remaining teachers, the silence issuing from the two empty seats at the end of our table overwhelming everything save the all-pervading odour of mutton fat.

The principal seemed to have less stomach for his food than I did myself. Plucking at a piece of oat bread and hardly touching his ale, he exchanged only the occasional remark with the professors on either side of him. I suspected what had to be said between them over the expulsion of Matthew Jack had been said already, in their private rooms and away from ears that did not need to hear.

'Have the boys heard?' I asked my fellow regent, Peter Williamson, in as low a voice as he could hear.

'I would think the whole town heard, the racket Jack was making when he was put out at the gates.'

'I saw him myself. Where has he gone?'

'No one knows. Some say he has left the town to try his luck elsewhere, others that he has left Scotland altogether.'

'Would that we were that fortunate,' muttered the regent to my left. 'I was with the porter to oversee the packing of his bags. Jack ranted that we would hear more of him, and that it would be changed days for this college when we did.'

Peter Williamson poured himself another beaker of ale. 'Empty threats,' he said. But I remembered what Jack had shouted as he'd been left outside on the street, that he was being forced from the place because of what he knew. And I also realised that if no one had seen him about the town since then, no one had seen him leave it either.

I rose with everyone else when the principal got up to leave soon afterwards. As he passed behind me he touched me lightly on the shoulder. 'You may go now, Alexander.'

That morning I had told Dr Dun of my fears for my friend John Innes in the King's College, and of what William had heard concerning Rachel Middleton. He had agreed that I should talk privately with the doctor's wife, and had also urged me to try again with John. So, for a third day, I left my scholars in the hands of John Strachan, and went out into the town.

The young physician and his wife lived in her brother's old house at the top of Back Wynd, on the corner where Upperkirkgate meets the Schoolhill. Behind it lay the churchyard. There was no reply to my rap on the front door, so I went down the pend at the side and in through the builders' yard there to the backland of the Middletons' house. The gate was bolted from the inside and as I knocked I caught sight of a small movement behind the half-opened shutter of a window above me. I knocked again, never taking my eye from the window, and after what seemed to me a long time, I heard footsteps and the opening of the back door of the house. The bolt was drawn back and the gate opened to me.

I had never before spoken to her, nor indeed seen her at close quarters, but I saw she was as different from her husband as flame to water. Where he was slim, pale, angular, she was curved where a woman should be curved, her move-ment was flowing warmth, her eyes hazel and her hair a chestnut that sparkled almost auburn in the sun. Hints of lemon and thyme drifted to me on the air.

I had thought what I would say to her, the questions I would ask – I had discussed them with the principal even – but as I sat down opposite her at the bench by her back door, those scents took me back to a fleeting moment earlier in the day, when I thought a figure pulled back into the shadows of the college gateway as I'd passed, and instead I heard myself asking, 'You have been looking for me, Mistress, have you not?'

She poured something from a pitcher into glass beakers and offered one to me.

'A mint cordial,' she said. 'It is cooling.' She took a sip and put her glass down slowly. 'I have been looking for you, yes.' She looked directly at me. 'I need your help because I do not know where else to turn, or even what I should ask for, but I know that I need help.'

'Take your time.'

'You were Robert's friend.'

'Yes.' I waited while she searched for the right words.

'He told me that, that you were his friend. That you were a good man.'

'I am no better than any other, but I was his friend, and would be so to those he cared for.' She looked down at her hands. 'I know he visited you here, at night.'

She seemed a little startled that I had come so quickly to that point, but she recovered herself.

'Who told you that he came here?'

'I know that a report has been made to the session that Robert came here, and others too.'

'I knew there would be, eventually. And the nature of this report?' Her face was defiant but I could see a tear in her eye.

'Do you really need me to . . .?'

'Yes, I do.'

'It questions your virtue.' There was no gentle way of saying it. 'I think you should prepare yourself for an accusation of harlotry in connection with Robert's visits.'

She took a deep breath, almost relieved, it seemed, to have heard the worst. 'They will not prove it.'

'That is not my concern. You must understand I do not come here to judge, still less to speak for the session. My only end in this is to find justice for Robert, but I think it is true that he came here, is it not?'

'Yes,' she said at last, 'it is true.'

'When did it begin? When did he start to visit here?'

'Six months ago perhaps, but as to the beginning, it was longer ago than that.' She looked up brightly. 'You did not know my brother?'

I shook my head.

'Hugh was a stonemason, a master of his craft. He was a good deal older than me – he had been my mother's first child, I her last. When Richard, my husband, was in Germany pursuing his medical studies, Hugh took me in. I managed his house and he took care of me. He found work aplenty here, and brought other masons to work with him. When Richard at last returned from the continent, Hugh allowed us to live here together. When he died, he left me this house. The men he worked with went their own way, and I lease the yard out to one of his old apprentices, a master now himself, for a reasonable rent.'

I could not see how any of this touched on the fate of Robert Sim, and my impatience must have shown on my face.

'I am coming to the matter now,' she said. 'We lease out the yard, but the lodging house the workers stayed in when they were not engaged on projects out in the country is there.' She pointed to a squat stone building at the far end of her own garden, near the kirkyard wall. 'My husband is often called out at night, or away for a few days, to see to patients. I did not wish to have a group of men living so close. A little over six months ago, I decided we should clear out the lodging house and lease it to some family, or a young married couple. Richard saw to the clearing, with the help of a friend . . .' Here she hesitated.

'A friend? Who? Robert?'

She looked away from me. 'Not Robert. I cannot tell you his name. But he came, and he helped. Some of what they cleared from the place – a few tools, some materials – was sold to other craftsmen in the town. But they found something in there – I don't know what – that made them stop in their work. I wanted to go in and sweep the place out, for it had not been swept or cleaned since my brother died, but my husband would not let me – he said he would do it. And indeed, for the next few evenings, he and his friend worked at the place with brooms and buckets, and had candles burning and a fire in the hearth at night. It was shortly after that that Robert first came. I was out, fetching coals, when he came through the gate. Richard was not here and had not warned me to expect anyone, and I was so frightened to see a man just come through the gate like that, I dropped the coals. Robert insisted on gathering them all up and taking them into the house for me.'

'And that was the beginning.'

'If you like,' she said.

How far could I probe into those moments, those small incidents that can take two people from acquaintance, to the first awareness of desire, to love? Robert had not chosen to confide in me about Rachel Middleton, and those remembered moments were all that she had left. I would leave them to her. But then, a possibility entered my mind.

'You were going to come to me for help. Is it that . . . are you with child, Robert's child?'

'What? No, no.' She shook her head, emphatic. 'It is not that at all. It is just that – we have few friends in the burgh; our own doing, our own choice.'

It was a strange admission, but I had not the inclination to pursue her on it. 'But your husband's practice does well, does it not? He attends to several patrons of wealth and growing influence in the town.'

'Oh, yes. But none of them would endanger their own position to help us, should danger come.'

'What danger are you talking about? Do you believe your husband found out about your adultery with Robert? That he murdered Robert Sim?'

'No,' she said, angry, determined. 'No!' Her eyes had

filled with tears. 'Before now, I feared only malice, and that I have faced before and faced down before. But now, after Robert, I do not know. I fear for my husband; we have no one to turn to and no one who will speak for us. Robert always said you were a good man. And that you had courage.'

I could not understand her, and she did not seem to understand why it was that I could not. 'I fear Robert spoke too well of me, but I will be a friend to you. I can only do that if you are honest with me. You must tell me the truth about your husband and his friends.'

She looked to the ground, biting her lip, the tears spilling over now.

'The meetings. I know – or I greatly suspect – Robert was involved in some secret society. From what you have told me, I believe it met here, at your house.'

She shook her head.

'Rachel, you must tell me what you know, or I cannot help you.'

'I know that, but they did not meet here in the house, it was down there.' She pointed to the lodge. 'They would spend three hours there, sometimes longer.'

'How many of them were there?'

She thought for a moment. 'Four; never more than four, I think.'

'Your brother, Robert Sim, John Innes and who else?'

'John?' she faltered. 'How? No, I . . .'

'I am near to certain that John was one of their number.

And he is in a state of terror. For his sake, you must tell me the truth. I will tell no one that I had it from you.'

At last she nodded.

'Was it John who came here to help your husband in the first place, when he was clearing the lodge?'

'No, it wasn't.'

'Then who?'

'That I cannot tell you.'

'Cannot, or will not? Mistress Middleton, this man's life may depend on it.'

'I know that, but my husband has sworn me to secrecy on the matter, and I cannot go against him. He too is fearful, but I do not know what he is fearful of. And I fear for him, that whatever evil was behind Robert's death might seek him out too.'

I stretched my hand across the table briefly to touch her fingers. 'You must trust me. If I am to help your husband, and John Innes, I must know as much as you can tell me. Who is the fourth man? It is not Matthew Jack?'

'Matthew Jack?' Her face paled. 'Not him, no not him. He did come here once, one evening, but he had not been invited and was not wanted. It was the evening of one of Richard's meetings, and Matthew Jack came not long after Robert had arrived. He knocked only once on the door and then walked right in – and found the three of us seated around the table, having our supper before the others arrived. Matthew Jack demanded to know what Robert was doing here, and what he had in his bag.'

'His bag? The satchel that he always carried with him?'
She nodded.

'What did they do?'

'Richard lost little time in putting him from the house,
and telling him that should he ever come back he would
have the baillies on him. He has never been back here, but
I have seen him around the town, and the way he looks at
me sickens me to my stomach.'

'The way he looks at you?' She flushed and I realised
what she meant. 'I think you need to be careful,' I said. 'If
your husband must go to his patients in the night, tell him
he is to take you first to my house.'

'Your house?'

'My wife Sarah will be there; there will be no scandal.
I think you should not be alone at night.'

'Since the night of Robert's death, Richard has not gone
out to patients.'

'Have you been in the lodging since your husband and
his friends began to hold their meetings there?'

'Never. He asked me not to go in there, and he took all
the keys.'

'And you have no notion of what it was they found, or
of the nature of their meetings?'

She shook her head. 'They met for study and conversation, fellowship, that is all.'

'But why then the need for secrecy?'

She looked out over her garden, where bees were busy
amongst the marigolds and daisies. 'I am sorry, Mr Seaton,

I was not privy to their secrets and did not seek to be so.'

I could believe her, but there must have been something. 'His bag, that Matthew Jack demanded to see. Do you know what was in it?'

She smiled. 'Now that I can tell you. Books. With Robert, what else but books?'

Books. The books his landlady had seen.

'Did he ever show you these books?'

'No, although we spoke of books often. I assumed he and my husband and the others studied these together. Robert had no knowledge of German, and Richard has made it his own.'

'They were written in German?'

'Some of them, I think. Others in Latin. There were notes, too, in Robert's own hand.'

'Could you tell what these notes were about?'

She shook her head. 'One of the books, I presumed. I could make out nothing more than the title he had written at the top of one of the pages: *Fama*. That was all I saw.'

Fama. Now I knew now why John had spoken of fraternity. I swallowed the last of the mint cordial Rachel Middleton had poured for me and rose from the bench, putting on my hat as I did so.

After a brief farewell with a promise that I would come back the next day, I was gone, leaving the strange young woman to grieve for the man who had never been her husband, and fear for the one who was.

ELEVEN

Brothers of the Rosy Cross

I cursed inwardly as I found the library to be locked and was halfway back down the outer stair before I remembered that I myself had the key. It was the third I tried that finally opened the door for me.

It had been only three days since Robert Sim's murder, but already the place had taken on the musty smell of disuse. I left the door open in the hope that some of what little air there was in the day might find its way in to the room. The register was still in the locked drawer in which I had left it at the end of my last morning's work in here, beside it the catalogue. I understood Robert's classification of works on the shelves, but was not yet fully conversant with the system set out in the catalogue itself, and it took me some time to find the entry that I was looking for. I had begun to think Rachel must be mistaken, or that what she had seen was not to be found in the library at all, but at last I came upon it, in Robert's own hand: *at Cassell, Wessell Presses, 1615, Allgemeine und General Reformation der gantzen Weiten Welt. Beneben der Fama Fraternitatis, des Löblichen Ordens des Rosenkreutzes.* I noted the shelf mark and was across the library floor in a moment, scanning the spines of the books in front of me, and then I had it in my hand: the *Fama*, bound with its sister work the *Confessio*, the proclamations that had set the thinkers of continental Europe alight with excitement and expectation, the great manifestos of the Brothers of the Rosy Cross.

I did not sit at Robert's desk, as I had done on my last two visits, but in my own accustomed place, beneath the high west window, where the light was better. My German was not of the best, being so out of use since the days when I had still lived in Banff, and Dr Jaffray had taught it to me for, he said, my own edification, but what I suspected was his own entertainment.

It should not have taken me more than an hour to read through what were, in essence, little more than pamphlets — a fable and a call to arms — and yet the memories and images brought to my mind by what was in them kept me there at my desk much later in the afternoon than I had planned. I read the tale, a myth, of a German monk, Christian Rosenkreutz, said to have been dead over a hundred years. Rosenkreutz, it was claimed, had travelled to the East, to Arabia to learn the knowledge of the ancients, the knowledge handed down to man by God in the earliest times, but corrupted through the ages. This knowledge, this key to understanding the book of the universe, had been lost to us in the West, buried under the inventions and encumbrances of the scholastics and the Papacy. Rosenkreutz had studied with the most learned Arabian scholars of the day, before continuing on to Africa, where knowledge was exchanged and ideas perfected. He had travelled at last to Spain, ready to share these marvellous gifts, the fruits of the great Hermetic quest, with Christendom, to offer the secrets that would unlock the mysteries of Creation and bring to an end illness, famine, war. He should have been feted, welcomed with open arms, but instead he had been mocked and scorned by those who had a greater interest in keeping the world in darkness.

This had not been the end of Rosenkreutz's tale. According to legend, he had returned to his native Germany, and there gathered to him three others of like mind. This new fraternity, the brotherhood of the Rosy Cross, took it upon themselves to part and travel through Europe, in secret, dressing in the clothing of those whose country they were in, adding to their knowledge and understanding of all disciplines and ministering to the sick. They agreed to meet once a year, in a spirit of brotherhood, to exchange and further perfect their knowledge, and that they should each choose a successor to carry on their work on their death. And so it had gone, but as the first and then second generation of brothers had died out, their successors lost touch with one another, even to the extent of not knowing where the original brothers were buried. And so it might have ended, but now came tidings of great joy, for the tomb of Christian Rosenkreutz had been found, and in it all the treasures, the secrets, the knowledge he had garnered. And at last the brotherhood, the secret successors and custodians of that great treasure, were ready to make themselves known, and to accept into their fraternity others who would truly know God and understand His universe.

I had been a young scholar at the King's College when first these pamphlets had become known. They had caused little excitement amongst us or our teachers, other than to afford some amusement at a pleasant story, or words of caution against secret societies promising hidden knowledge: such were the haunts of alchemists, cabbalists, magicians — all suspect. We knew what lay down that path, in our Presbyterian Scotland, with our king safe on England's throne.

But elsewhere, in the German lands, in Poland, in Bohemia, in England even, the effect of these pamphlets had been quite otherwise. A flurry of writings appeared all over Europe, announcing their authors' urgent desire to be accepted into the fraternity. Some attacked the brotherhood, accusing them of being Jesuits. Others argued that God had already given us signs of revelations to come: new lands across the oceans had been discovered with peoples previously unheard of, writings long lost had been found again, new stars discovered in the heavens. The time of Revelation was at hand.

There might have been little enough harm in all of this, had not the myth of the brotherhood become enmeshed with the great disturbances brewing all across Europe, where the Catholic Habsburgs and the Papacy sought to maintain control over the Holy Roman Empire, the German lands, in the face of rising Protestant peoples and princes. The Rosicrucian promise became entangled with the belief that Christendom was in the last days of a dark age and approaching the dawn of a new, that the days of the Papacy, and of the Habsburg Empire, would soon be over, swept away at last. It was proclaimed that the eagle of the Habsburgs would finally be vanquished by the rise of a lion, the Lion of Heidelberg, Frederick, Elector Palatinate, husband to the daughter of our own King James, and briefly the great hope of Protestant Europe.

There had been such hope in those days amongst those who sought the Philosopher's Stone, that essential element we shared with every other thing in the universe. But those hopes had died at the hands of the Habsburg armies at the battle of the White Mountain, outside Prague, where the Bohemian forces of Frederick of the Palatinate and Elizabeth Stuart, his queen, were utterly crushed, and the Holy Roman Empire, the length and breadth of the German lands, plunged into war, starvation, disease, despair. Such had been the gifts of the Philosopher's Stone.

And I had lost my friend there, too. My dearest friend Archie Hay, gone to fight for Elizabeth of Bohemia, and dead, with so many others, in her cause. I closed the book and almost laughed, so ludicrous was it that anyone ever had, yet more so that they still should, take seriously this tale of the Rosy Cross, this fable of a dead monk and his buried treasures. But there were those who had, it seemed: the physician Richard Middleton, the librarian Robert Sim, my friend John Innes and some unnamed other had created such a fraternity of their own. And of those four, one was now dead and another driven almost mad with terror. Returning the book to its shelf in disgust, I took up my hat and left the library.

It was now long past noon, and the sunshine of earlier in the day had gone, leaving behind it an oppressive grey heat. It was as if the absent wind had taken the air with it, too, for I had to labour to draw breaths from the meagre store around me. Faces that earlier had been cheery in the blue-skied morning now looked bothered and disgruntled. I was not at the King's Port before I felt the first stirrings of a throbbing behind my temples, and I knew without even looking at the sky what weather we were to have.

I had it in mind to stop before I got to the King's College, at the Snow Kirk, and order my thoughts, set out to myself exactly what I must say to John and what I must ask of him about his brotherhood. I suspected he would be no better in mind and body than he had been when last I had seen him, and feared indeed that he might be worse; whatever words I used must not be wasted. As I was about to turn from the road on to the path that would take me to the kirkyard, a movement at the edge of the kirk itself took my eye. It was Andrew Carmichael. I was about to raise an arm in greeting to him when I stopped, frozen by what I saw. For there was a woman with him. He had one hand on her shoulder, and with the other was tenderly brushing the hair back from her face. My stomach lurched and it seemed that every voice I had ever heard screamed through my head, for I did not need to see her face to know that it was Sarah.

★

The heat was building and there was no trace of wind. He had often cursed the wind, the wind that went through you in this corner of Scotland as it did in no other. It would find its way through every layer of clothing, every wrapping a man might have, to travel through him and on to its next victim, but today, how glad he would have been to feel a current of air, fresh, cold, cleansing, on his face. Today, though, there was none of it.

He looked out to the sea, hazy under the heavy heat of the sky, to what he had known once but could no longer see. How had it come to this? When had the turning been taken that had left him with blood on his hands, the turning that had led to the murder of Robert Sim? Had it been here, a matter of a few days ago, as he had looked in the librarian's face, in his eyes, and seen the answer to his question before it had been asked? No, for Robert Sim had not been the author of his own Fate.

When then? Where? Far from here, far to the south, standing in the cold stone hallway of a tower house, a letter in the bag at his feet, hearing of the death of a father and a grandfather?

No, not then. He must go further back. Back across that sea and years ago, long before he had known the name of Robert Sim, to two young men at a crossroads, far from home. Two young men, companions together through years of study in Germany, in France, in the Low Countries, returning at last to the place of their birth, to settle to the lives and affairs of men.

'One last adventure, one last place to see; so few of our countrymen have been there – and none that I know of,' his companion had said, as he looked at the road leading further to the flat lands and marshes of the north.

His eyes had been on the other road, the road for Rotterdam, and the ship that would take them home at last. But as ever, his companion had won the day, and they had turned for the north-west, and the road the signpost told them would take them to the town of Franeker.

Then, perhaps, yes it had been then. But if not then, before that and before that and before that, to the beginning of time, when God had decreed that he was to be of the damned. For that one thing he knew above all else: he was damned for all eternity.

TWELVE

The Storm Breaks

My scholars had never been so silent. They sat, dumbstruck, some of them not even lifting their pens and others letting them drop after the first few words, as I tore through the texts before me and gave the commentary of my life: nothing I had ever thought or felt about the authors whose work I had in my hands went unsaid, and where I thought them in error, blind or foolish I vented bile. When the bell sounded that would release my students to their breakfast, not a one amongst them moved.

I looked at them and had had enough. 'Go!' I shouted, and then more quietly, as I tied the strings on my notes, 'just go.'

I myself could not face the other regents, the professors or even the principal. I had no stomach for food or drink anyway, and so did not leave the lecture hall. I lay my head on the desk and wished for peace. After a little time, John Strachan, who had been taking the class in my absence, appeared in the doorway.

'Are you alright, Alexander?'

'What? Yes, yes, I am fine,' I said, raising my head and running a hand through hair that had not been combed since the previous morning.

He looked unsure, but proceeded cautiously into the room. Evidently, some of the students had been talking to him, and warning him what he would find.

'Are you not going to breakfast?'

'No, I am not hungry.'

Still he lingered, and I managed to muster some semblance of decency under his concerned gaze.

'Is there something you need of me, John?' I asked.

'It is only that the porter is looking for you. William Cargill's servant is at the gate and wishes to speak to you.'

'Duncan? What could Duncan want with me?' And then I knew it. Sarah. He had been her quiet champion since the day he'd met her. He had come to talk for Sarah, who would not come to the college herself.

My voice, when it came, was hoarse. 'I cannot see him.'

Strachan looked at me. 'Alexander, he is an old man. It is no small thing for him to come here . . .'

I pressed the backs of my hands to my eyes then lifted my head once more. 'I know that. I know it. And it is no small thing for me to say I cannot see him. Now please John, just leave me, and go.'

With no option, John Strachan went, and my thoughts for the next ten minutes until the return of my scholars were even more miserable than they had been before.

It was my misfortune and that of my class that the rest

of the morning was to be given over to Ethics. The anger was out of me, and I could only mumble desultorily on the subject until I could decently set the students to debate amongst themselves upon it. How they conducted themselves for the next hour-and-a-half, I could not tell, noticing only when the last of them to leave the room told me that the bell had gone for the mid-day meal.

By now I had begun to feel sick, my stomach empty and my throat parched. I pulled myself up and, remembering to take my notes and books with me, headed down towards the college buttery, where I begged a loaf of bread and some cheese from the cook's boy, and took a jug of wine from the cellar before retreating with my meal to what was now my sanctuary: the library.

I passed by my accustomed seat, and Robert Sim's desk. I had tried, last night, in an effort to shut out the images that were crowding my mind, to search the register for the names of those other than Robert himself who might have taken an interest in the *Fama* of the Rosicrucians. I had burned the candle to its base but had found no one. And now, in the light of the day that showed up every speck of dust, every scuff on the floorboards, every knot in the wood of the place surrounding me, I could pretend no longer. Everywhere, I saw Sarah with Andrew Carmichael. I took myself to a darkened corner, where the shelves of the north wall met those of the east, and slumped down with my gown pulled around me, brought the jug to my lips and began to drink. The wine was sour in my gullet and burned my stomach, but I thought if I took enough of it I would not notice. I tore a hunk of the bread but could not swallow it. I curled up on the floor and prayed for sleep.

And I did sleep. A deep sleep, a sleep that filled the cavern of my exhaustion. Once or twice, a noise of knocking, a voice, my name, penetrated somewhere through that wall of sleep, but not far enough to wake me. But then, it must have been hours later, a hammering, louder and louder, and a shouting of my name I could not ignore. It was William Cargill's voice. At length, I came to and stumbled towards the door, fumbled with the lock until I had it turned and opened the door to him. With him was Dr Dun, the principal.

What they saw when they looked at me told in their faces.

I saw the relief flood William's face. 'Alexander,' was all he said.

The principal shut his eyes a moment. 'Thanks be to God. We had feared you dead.' Then he turned to William. 'I will leave you now. See that you take him home, and that he rests.'

We waited until Dr Dun had made his way back down the outer stairs. William looked at me and shook his head. 'Am I to be let in, or shall we have it out here, on the stair head? For I swear to you, man, I am not leaving this place until I know what madness has taken hold of you.'

I dropped my hand from the door and walked back into

the library, leaving him to follow me, which he did. He sat against the edge of Robert's desk and I went over to my sleeping place and picked up the jug of wine. I offered it to him and he gave a curt 'no'.

'Are you going to tell me what this is about, Alexander?'

'You had better ask my wife.'

'Your wife? You can speak to me of your wife? Sarah was at our door, with your two children under her arms before five this morning. She had not slept the whole night, and was scarcely fit to speak by the time we got her inside. It took long enough to convince her — although I was hardly sure myself — that you had not been murdered. I went to the college myself, but the porter was under orders from the principal to let no one in before breakfast. All the fellow was able to tell me was that he had seen you come into the college last night, like a man that had seen the dead, that you had spoken to no one and that he had not seen you leave. How do you think Sarah took that news, after what happened to Robert Sim? And I had to leave them, because I had business with Thomas Burnett of Leys out at Crathes — I am just this minute back. And what do I hear the moment I enter my chambers? That Duncan — Duncan who is hard put to walk the length of the backland of my house these days — came up to the college asking to see you and was turned away.' His face, sweating though he was in the heat, was now white with rage. He breathed heavily, twice, and spoke very slowly. 'What is this about, Alexander?'

I was not sure that I could form the words. 'It is about . . . Sarah. And Andrew Carmichael.'

'Ach!' He turned away in impatience. 'Not this again. How many ways do you need to be told? There is nothing . . .'

'I saw them, William.'

'What?'

'I saw them together. Yesterday. At the Snow Kirk.'

'The Snow Kirk? But why . . .'

'I had just come up the Spital Hill and was about to go down to the Old Town when I saw them come round from the back of the kirkyard. You will say I was mistaken, but I know I was not. Oh, God, William, his hands were on my wife.'

And then I couldn't get the words from my throat, I couldn't see him any more; everything was blurred and hazy before my eyes, and William was across the room and had me by the shoulders.

'Alexander, this cannot be what you think it is. There must be some good reason for it.'

'What? I watched them there, I saw how he looked at her as she walked away, and I swear to you, William, I wanted to kill him. If I could have moved, made one foot go in front of the other I believe I would have killed him.'

'But you did not. Did he see you? Did either of them see you?'

'No. I went down behind a wall until they went their ways. Then I stayed there, for hours, just sat. Eventually,

I came back down here. I didn't know where else to go.'

I ran a hand through my hair, only too conscious now of the sight I was presenting to my friend. 'And the children, they have not been alarmed?'

'You are in the college so much, I don't think they would have noticed anything amiss, had it not been for Sarah's distraction. Zander knows there is something wrong, and Deirdre has been asking for you.'

'I should have thought of the children.'

'Come back, come back with me, and see them now. The rest can be dealt with later.'

So I left the library and the college with him, but I did not go down to William's house. Instead I went to my own, to wash myself and change my shirt and shave my face. I had not quite finished that last when I heard the sound of Zander's feet in the close and soon he was bursting through the door, filled with questions. I told him I had been engaged on secret work of great importance for Dr Dun, and that I was sworn to reveal the details to no one. He was delighted and impressed. And after him came Sarah, with Deirdre in her arms. I took my daughter and held her to me, but I could look only at my wife. And I truly looked at her. The sun had bronzed her arms and neck and scattered tiny freckles across her skin. I wanted to undo Carmichael's touch, to erase from my mind the memory of his fingers on her face. But I found I could not speak, still less make a move towards her.

'Alexander,' she said. 'Where have you been?'

I put Deirdre down and told her to go and look for her brother.

'Have you not spoken to William?'

'He told me he found you in the library, that you had been in the college all night. What were you doing? Why did you not come home? Or send me a message?'

'A message?' A voice in my head, a warning voice, was telling me to go no further. 'How could I send you a message when I did not know where I should find you?'

On her face was a look of utter incomprehension, and the beginnings of some anger.

'Where *you* should find *me*? Where you, who can slip from our bed yesterday morning without a word, and not return, until forced to, by William Cargill, tonight, again without a word, without a thought for us, should find *me*? Where else would you find me but here, looking after your children, or with Elizabeth? Where else?'

'At the Snow Kirk, Sarah; I would find you at the Snow Kirk.'

Everything stopped. I could see, all movement in her seemed to cease, aside from a panic that darted through her eyes.

She put out a hand to me. 'Alexander . . .'

I shook it off.

'Alexander, please, listen to me.'

I stopped at the door, taking down my light hide jacket from the nail where it hung there. 'Listen to you? Dear

God, Sarah, I cannot look at you.' I let the door swing shut behind me as I left.

My footsteps took me to Maisie Johnston's house, to the parlour where I had so often sat and drank with my friend Archie Hay in our long-gone student days. I had rarely gone there since then, and since my marriage, not at all. It was not a place a respectable man should be seen, and for a college regent to be found there would bode very ill indeed. I ordered English beer, and then asked for *uisge bheatha*, the whisky distilled in Speyside and the mountain glens to the west. Maisie denied that she had it.

'Come, Maisie, you had it ten years ago, why not now? If Archie Hay was sitting here before you, would you tell him you did not have it?'

'If Archie Hay was sitting here, I would commend my soul to God and leave Archie to the Devil, for he has been dead nigh on eight years, and can have no honest business with me. But Archie Hay was not a college regent.'

'My silver is as good as his.'

She smiled at last. 'Alexander Seaton, you never had any silver.' She opened a small cupboard and drew something from the barrel in there. She brought the glass of golden liquid over to the far corner in which I sat. 'Have that for free and go home to your wife.'

I set my pouch on the bench before me and said, 'Take my money, Maisie; I will be here some hours yet.'

It was indeed a good deal later that I at last decided to go home. I had not the stomach for the beer, and the whisky, fine though it was, only served to invigorate the pounding in my head. The cold mutton Maisie had brought me lay uneaten on its platter. I dropped more money than was needed on the table and left.

It was a short distance from Maisie's place to my own house. There were few, very few out on the streets at this time of the night, even on a summer's evening, and I was glad of it. I passed by the gable end of Rachel Middleton's house and remembered the promise I had made to her yesterday afternoon that I would return today. I considered for a moment, but her husband would no doubt be at home, and I had little inclination to meet the physician under the gaze of the woman I knew had betrayed him with my friend. And if he were not there, it was too late to call upon a woman on her own. I looked to the sky: it was turning from sulphurous yellow to a deep and threatening grey. At last the weather was going to break.

All was quiet in the house when I arrived home. A few coals still burned on the fire but there was no other sound or movement downstairs. The children slept soundly in their bed in the wall, Deirdre's fingers as ever rubbing a lock of Zander's hair. I could hear nothing from upstairs, save the occasional creak of wood in the light wind that was getting up. I took the little pillow from the chair, carved by Duncan, on which Deirdre liked to sit, and set it on the floor in front of the dying embers in the hearth, lay down and closed my eyes. Tomorrow. Time enough to begin to put right the wreckage of this family. I would listen to Sarah tomorrow.

I think the storm must have been raging a good while before I knew it, for before I was truly awake I had become gradually aware of the flashing of light in the darkness. It would have been well after midnight when I heard the first of the children's cries, Deirdre first and then Zander. By the time I had roused myself and crossed the room to them, Sarah was at the top of the wooden steps from our room: she was down them in a moment and had Deirdre in her arms while I tried to persuade Zander that the world was not about to end. A sudden flash of light, followed very quickly by a clap of thunder, split the sky and illuminated her face as she turned it towards me. There were no lies in that face and I wanted to go to my wife and hold her, and forget that there had ever been such a man as Andrew Carmichael.

Just then, above the sound of the storm, I heard a shout from the courtyard. I wrenched open the shutter at the window, and at first I could see little, but then another flash of lightning showed a woman's form, drenched, her face desperate. It was Rachel Middleton and she was banging on the door, shouting my name.

THIRTEEN

The House of Jewels

I could hardly persuade her to come into the house, still less to sit down. She was talking before she was through the door, but making little sense.

'Is it the session?' asked Sarah from behind me.

'I do not think it, at this time of night. Rachel, is it the session?'

'No, no, you must come, please. It's Matthew Jack; he has my husband.'

'Jack? Where?'

I managed to unfurl her fingers from their grip on my shirt front and get her over to a stool by the hearth where Sarah had begun to rekindle the fire. Only then did I realise that Rachel Middleton had only a nightshift under the dripping shawl that was falling from her shoulders and not a pair of shoes to her feet. 'Calm yourself and tell me.'

She took a breath and began to speak more slowly. 'They are in the lodging. Matthew Jack came to the house, in the night. Richard had been sleeping by the fire and Jack must have got past him – I woke to find him standing by the bed. He has always looked at me, he . . .' Her face twisted in disgust, and I knew what Matthew Jack had intended. 'I shouted out for Richard and he came running from downstairs. When Jack saw him, he brought out a knife. He warned me he would kill him if I made a move, and was forcing him down the stairs before I understood what was happening. By the time I dared to get out of my bed and go to the window, I saw that Jack had the knife at Richard's back and was pushing him down through the backland towards the lodging. I got down and outside as fast as I could but I could not see them – they were gone.' She clutched at my shirt once more. 'Please come; I think he will kill him.'

I was glad that I had not undressed for the night, and grabbed my cloak and sword from their place by the door. 'Sarah, I am going for William. Bolt the door and keep the children upstairs.' I told Rachel to stay with my wife and ran to get my friend.

I could not help but wake the whole household in waking William, but once he realised I was not at the end of some drunken episode, it did not take him long to understand what was wrong. He dressed quickly and also fixed on his sword.

'You'd better take Dileas too,' I said, indicating the large shaggy hound who was docile as a lamb with the household, but who would not, I was certain, scruple to rip out the throat of any who meant his master harm.

And so we were running in the night, through the storm,

the dog bounding ahead of us, seeming to know where we were going, and in only a few minutes we had reached the physician's house at the top of Back Wynd. The gate at the bottom of the pend was unlocked, and soon we were down the close and in the backland of the house. The builders' yard to our left was shut up and in silence, with no sign of movement in it, but the hackles were now up on the back of Dileas's neck, and he had started up a low growling. The kitchen door to the house was swinging open, banging against the wall in the wind, but we ignored it and went after the dog, more carefully now, down through the backland to the lodging at the end, where a dim yellow glow showed in one of the windows.

He had the knife to Richard Middleton's throat.

'Call off your dog.'

'Matthew . . .'

'Call off your dog, Seaton.'

I looked at William.

'Leave, Dileas.'

The hound, still growling and never taking its eyes from Matthew Jack's right hand, retreated a few steps towards its master. Matthew Jack and his prisoner were in the far corner of the lodge's one room, their faces flashing white as the lightning sent out its bolts over the burgh. Jack, shorter but burlier than the physician, had his victim on all fours in front of him.

'He is somewhat like a dog himself, is he not?'

'Matthew, let him up. This can serve no purpose.'

'No purpose? I want him to know what it is to be treated like a dog, to grovel. What are you doing here anyway, Seaton. I suppose the whore called you?'

Middleton risked Jack's wrath by lifting his head. 'Rachel — is she safe?'

'She is with my wife.'

At this Jack let out an unholy laugh. 'What a cesspit you crawl in, you so well-*respected* men. I suppose you have been attending to the doctor's wife while your own takes her pleasures in the Old Town, Seaton.' He snorted phlegm. 'And you too, William Cargill, who have such fears of getting another child on your own wife, you have no doubt taken your turn with Seaton's trollop.'

This was too much for William and he let go the dog with a yell of 'throat'. As Matthew Jack saw the animal lunge at him he lashed out frantically. In a moment the dog was on him and had him pinned to the ground, the knife had clattered to the floor, and I was rushing towards Richard Middleton. I took hold of his arm to pull him clear of Jack and the dog, but he cried out in pain and I let his arm drop again. I felt a sickly dampness on my palm. Where it had touched him, my hand was thick with blood, as was the blade of Matthew Jack's knife.

Dileas had a huge paw on each of Jack's shoulders, and was snarling in his face in a manner that left me in no doubt that the beast with whom I let my son roll on the ground and who carried my daughter on his back was perfectly capable of killing a man, and ready to do so. Jack screamed and writhed under him, but Dileas would only listen to one human voice amongst all the sounds of the storm, and that voice did not call him off a second time.

'Take the knife, Alexander,' said William, kicking it across the floor to me. 'I am going for Vedast Lawson.'

In the ten minutes or so it took William to return with the baillie and two of the town's officers, Jack began to understand that the dog would not be letting up his guard duty, and gave up his screeching for help. The dog relented in so far as to moderate his snarling to a low, warning growl, which bespoke his menace with equal eloquence.

'Call the brute off, Seaton,' Jack managed to croak at last.

I shook my head. 'He would not listen to me even if I had a mind to, and I do not have a mind to.'

'I should have known . . .'

'Hold your peace, Matthew, or he'll have your throat.'

Holding the knife rigidly in Jack's direction, I risked a glance at Richard Middleton, who had been dragging himself along the ground to find support against the wall. He winced with every movement.

'Where are you cut?' I asked him.

'Just the arm,' he managed to say.

'It should have been your heart.'

I rounded on Jack. 'Hold your peace, I said, for may God forgive me, it would give me little grief to see you carried from here a corpse.'

'I think it likely that God will have other work with you than forgiveness, Seaton, and with our friend the physician and all his unnatural practices.'

A swift snarl from the dog silenced Jack again and I was able to bend once more towards the young doctor, who had propped himself now against a long-cold chimney breast. His skin had taken on a greenish hue, whether through loss of blood or the effects of the lightning that intermittently illuminated us all for one another, I could not tell, and beads of cold sweat had begun to form on his forehead. 'Help will be here soon.'

And it was. The dog heard the voices first, his master's voice and others, running down through the backland to the lodge, shouting. William was first through the door, followed by Vedast Lawson, the baillie, and two of the town's stoutest men. William called off the dog and the men had Jack's hands shackled behind his back in minutes. 'I'll have that knife off you as well, Mr Seaton,' said Lawson, indicating the gory weapon I had almost forgotten I was still holding, which was more akin to a butcher's knife than a doctor's scalpel.

'Gladly,' I said, handing it over to him.

After the baillie and town's officers had gone, hauling Matthew Jack, still spewing out his venom, to the tolbooth, I assured William that I would be fine on my own with Richard Middleton. He was reluctant to leave me, and would only do so on condition I kept Dileas with me. The hound's agitation had scarcely abated, despite the removal of Jack, and I was not quite sure he was what was called for to put the physician at his ease, but William was insistent. When I agreed to the dog's staying, he left, content, first to go to my house to let Rachel Middleton know that all was well with her husband, and then to go home to reassure his own family.

I bent down and looked at the blood seeping through the sleeve of Richard Middleton's shirt, from the knife-wound on his arm.

'That looks to be deep. I should have asked William to go first to the college and fetch Dr Dun. I will take you to the house and then get him myself.'

'No.' He was trying to get to his feet but could not and sat down again. 'No,' he said again, more forcefully this time. 'I will see to it myself; I am a physician, remember.' He looked at me with a degree of hostility in his eye, but it did not last, and was replaced by something resembling defeat which pervaded his long, angular frame. 'I am a physician.'

A physician, yes. 'Tell me what you need.'

'My instruments are in a case in the kitchen. I will also need a basin of water and some clean linen, torn into strips.'

Leaving the agitated dog guarding the door, I quickly fetched what he had asked for and was soon, under his instruction, helping him to clean and dress the wound. I helped him on with a clean shirt, and persuaded him to drink some water I had brought fresh from the well outside.

William had left an extra lantern with us, and as Middleton drank I was able to look properly around the lodge for the first time. It was then that Jack's words, scarcely registered at the time he had uttered them, came to the forefront of my mind and I saw what it was that had made him speak of Middleton's 'unnatural practices'. What I had taken for the chimney breast of a fireplace such as would be found in any habitation was, I now saw, something quite other — it was the breast of a furnace, and not a furnace such as my father had used at the smiddy. Two sets of bellows lay on the floor, and ranged against a wall was a collection of large vessels only some of which I recognised: vessels for descension, sublimation, calcination. By the other wall, a water-cooling still. Set along a wooden bench were glass and copper vessels of almost every description: alembics, phials, flasks and basins. Below it mortars and pestles, tongs, a steel chisel, a basket of coals. Shelves above held jars and bottles of substances I could not begin to guess at, and near the door was a cabinet of drawers such as would be found in a spice-merchant's booth or an apothecary's shop. I did not need to ask him, for I knew: I was in an alchemist's laboratory.

From his place slumped against the cold furnace, Middleton had followed the direction of my gaze. 'It is not as you think.'

'You do not know what I think,' I said, when I could find my voice.

'Alchemy is what others call science, what I practise here

is but another form of what metal-workers, glass-blowers, apothecaries and others do openly, for the common good.'

'Then why do you conduct in secret what they do openly?'

'Because the art which I practise is misunderstood, as you have misunderstood it. What I carry out here is not some form of dark magic, but investigations into the possibilities of natural science. I am a healer, and I seek to understand how better to heal.'

I drew closer to the bench and bent to examine a book lying open there. 'You follow the teachings of Paracelsus.'

'To a point. I have limited interest in his more . . . esoteric speculations.'

'But as you say, it is a distinction that can be difficult for the casual observer to make. One such as Matthew Jack, for instance.' Then one of Jack's threats, thrown out as he was being dragged away, came back to me. 'This is what he spoke of when he said justice may have eluded you in Paris, but that it would not do so here, that he would make you known. You knew him in France?'

Middleton laughed weakly. 'Knew him? I knew him as a dog knows a flea or a sheep a tick. You could not be a Scotsman abroad in the same town as Jack and not know him, though, dear God, I tried hard enough. He was of the view that our common nationhood created a bond between us that would see him welcomed into my circle of friends – small as it was.' He winced and shifted slightly against the furnace. 'A half-hour in the man's company would make

SHONA MACLEAN

anyone wish to avoid him, and Heaven knows, we put up with him for longer than that. My friends and I made it clear to him eventually that he was not welcome amongst us: he saw to it that we were hounded from the city.'

'How?'

'Accusations, playing on people's fears. And now he will do it again.'

'What fears exactly are you talking of? Is this something to do with Robert and your fraternity? The Brotherhood of the Rosy Cross?'

I had surprised him.

'Robert told you?'

'Robert told me nothing. That part I have worked out. So there is such a fraternity, here in the burgh?'

'Not now, I do not think there can be now. We hoped . . . but things were taken too far, and now we have called down evil and retribution on ourselves.'

His voice was becoming hoarse and he was having difficulty speaking. I brought a beaker of water to his lips.

'I will take you into the house.'

He shook his head. 'No. Not yet.' He had begun to shiver, and his breathing was coming heavily, but he seemed determined to talk. I sat down beside him on the beaten earth floor of the lodge. 'Take your time, then, and tell me from the beginning.'

'The beginning was – when was it? Ten years ago? No, thirteen perhaps, at Heidelberg.' He smiled to himself. 'I cannot believe I was ever so young.'

'You are hardly old now.'

'I am thirty-five, but of late I feel I have lived more years than I have numbered.' A pause, then, 'Were you ever at Heidelberg?'

'I have never been to Germany at all.'

He looked a little surprised, just for a moment. 'Then I do not know how to begin to describe to you what you will never see. The Elector Palatinate was in his castle, with his princess, our princess, Elizabeth Stuart at his side. Their court was magnificent. Philosophers came, great thinkers from all over Europe, there were plays, pageants, encouragement of all the arts and sciences. The gardens were beyond what you could ever imagine. They were the work of a supreme architect. Every mathematical principle was explored, experimented with, enacted.'

I began to think his wound and the fever he was evidently at risk of were affecting his mind, and it must have shown in my face, for he grabbed my arm and spoke to me urgently. 'No, you must see, you must understand. These gardens were the fruit of the application of perspective, proportion, geometry, to the living earth. The principles of mechanics were brought to bear on water, on wood and stone. A man could walk in these gardens and hear music issue from fountains, enter grottoes in which statues moved and sang. It was at the University of Heidelberg, in the shadow of that Eden, that the manifestos of the Rosicrucian brotherhood first came into my hand. It seemed in those days that everything was possible, that scholars and thinkers, artisans and masters of all crafts, might share their skills and knowledge and strive together to better understand and realise God's plan for His greatest creation.'

I recalled the sentiments from the pamphlets I had read only a few hours previously in the library. 'I am familiar with the hopes stirred up by the *Fama* and the *Confessio*. You were caught up in the furore?'

'Oh, yes. I and my friends. We longed to join that fabled brotherhood of the Rosy Cross.' His eyes were bright, living the memory. 'We searched, we asked all the learned men we knew, but they could not help us. We did as others did – so young we were, so presumptuous – we published pamphlets, proclaiming our support, our urgent desire to join with the brotherhood, to obtain the keys to the lost knowledge of the past, that we might join in the building of a new Eden, an ideal state. And then . . .' His voice trailed off.

'And then?'

'And then, nothing.'

'Nothing?'

'There was no further manifesto; there came no response, to us, or to any other who sought the brethren. They remained hidden from the world, cut off, their secrets with them. And then came the horror.'

I did not need to ask what the horror was: the defeat of Frederick and Elizabeth of Bohemia at the battle of the White Mountain and the vengeance meted out on their Palatinate by the Habsburgs. Imperial forces under Spinola raped, looted and pillaged down the Neckar to Heidelberg itself.

'I was still in Heidelberg when the Spaniards came. I saw then what the alchemists, the Hermeticists, the Paracelsians are all searching for. I saw the Pan within, that essential element that makes us all a part of one another and of everything around us: our utter brutality. And the alchemy required to reveal this was war. So I fled Heidelberg – most of the scholars were already dispersed – but not before I had seen Spinola's troops stable their horses in the great library of the University, having flung the books out into the courtyard to be trampled and defecated on by the beasts. A fitting end to all that human endeavour.'

I helped him to another drink of water. 'I scarcely know how I lived, the next few months, but live I did,' he continued. 'In time, I came with some of my friends to Paris, and began to practise there. Then, in the year 1623 – eight years ago – there appeared, in certain places in the town, placards announcing the arrival there in secret of members of the Fraternity of the Rosy Cross. Soon after-wards, amongst pamphlets published in response to these placards, was one alleging horrible pacts, secret Sabbaths, between the fraternity and the Devil. A real fear and great suspicion of strangers swept the city. There was talk of witchcraft. Matthew Jack supped it as mother's milk. One Sunday, after I was leaving the service with some compan-ions, he came up to us and said he knew what we were about. He had seen my name on one of those pamphlets I had written years before, in Germany, entreating accept-

ance into the fraternity of the Rosy Cross. He said he was
going to expose me to the authorities as one of the in-
visible brotherhood. I did not wait to find out if he made
good on his threat. I left Paris that night and headed for
home. Eventually I landed back in Scotland, and made my
way north to join Rachel and her brother here.'

'You had been away from her a long time,' I said, carefully.

'I know, too long. I should have sent for her to join me,
but I had never managed to settle anywhere properly, to
build a practice on which we might build our life.'

'But you have managed to do that here.'

'Oh yes, all was well for a time. And then one day, two
or three years ago, I was walking up the street, and there
emerged in front of me, like a portent of every bad fortune
remaining to me, the form of Matthew Jack. I could not
believe it at first, and walked on without acknowledging
him. But soon I found the deacons of the kirk session at
my door, asking questions about secret societies, diabolic
entertainments. Thank God I had made my good name by
then, and the minister and session were no more inclined
to believe in Jack's tales than they would have a talking
donkey.'

'I certainly have no recollection of having heard anything
of those accusations,' I said. 'Why has he begun to haunt
you again now?'

'Now? He never really gave up. He just bided his time –
malicious looks here, snide remarks there – he was just

waiting for his opportunity. One day, late last autumn, Robert Sim came to see me. I knew him, but not well. At first I thought he had come for a medical consultation, but I soon realised it was something else. He told me that the library had just come into possession of a document he believed I might be familiar with, and which he was keen to learn more about: it was the *Fama* of the Rosicrucians. And that was how it began. I was reluctant at first even to look at the document again, but Robert was fascinated with it, and I found that I enjoyed our discussions on the matter, and indeed his company.'

I wondered if he knew that during this nascent friendship between him and the librarian, something else was being born between the librarian and his wife. I tried to ask but the words would not come, and he continued, unremarking, with his tale.

'We began to study Hermetic literature together, and, one evening, a debate on a point of theology arose which we found impossible to resolve. That was when Robert suggested we should invite John Innes to join us in our studies, and so we did. I wish to God we had not.'

'Why?' I asked.

'Because in John I saw reborn my young self of more than ten years before. The *Fama* lit a flame in him, and he was not to be dissuaded, either by Robert's arguments or my experience, that the brotherhood of the Rosy Cross was not real, that it did not, indeed, exist.' His voice fell. 'That it had never existed. John was eager that we should add to our number one more, that we might become four, as the original cells of the fraternity were thought to have been. For myself, and for Robert, our meetings had taken on the form of a society where we might discuss ideas, knowledge, questions other than the endless controversies over forms of worship that so exercise our Divines. And so we did invite another to join us, one whose knowledge of mathematics could help fill the gaps in our own.'

'Who was this?' I asked.

He shook his head. 'I cannot tell you.'

'But what harm can there be now?'

'Of the four of us involved in our society, one has been murdered, one driven to the brink of madness, and I myself, tonight, have been attacked. I will not endanger the last of our number by naming him, to anyone.'

'Then you are certain that Robert's death is connected to his involvement in your society, brotherhood, call it what you will. What did your society engage in here that you – and John Innes – believe has called evil down upon you?'

He said nothing for a moment and then, 'We used to meet in the house to begin with, but just before winter set in, Rachel decided we should rent out her brother's old masons' lodging to some family in need. I persuaded a friend to help me clear the place. It was only once we had done so and begun to sweep the floor that we noticed them.'

'Noticed what?'

'The markings on the floor.'

I looked on the floor but in the dim light of my small lantern I could see no markings but the scuff marks from the struggle that had taken place there earlier.

'Light the candles here,' said Richard Middleton, indicating a large church candle in an iron sconce above the door, 'and there, by the east door.' I had not noticed that there was another door to the lodging. I did as he suggested, and looked again at the floor, bringing my lantern closer to the ground as I bent down to examine it. And now indeed I did see something. Just a few inches in from the wall and going around the entire room was a line, formed by a very narrow, shallow trench, and filled in with chalk, perfectly straight where it followed the walls, perfectly angled where it must turn a corner. Apart from the indents at the doorways, the line was broken in only three places, below the windows. The first marking I noticed was on the ground in the north-east corner of the building – a representation of the sun. In the south-western corner was a marking like an arrow. I squinted at it a moment, not quite able to make it out.

Richard Middleton had somehow got himself to his feet. He shuffled over to me. 'Compasses,' he said. 'It is a set of compasses. And look there,' he said, pointing to a place on the floor below a window in the east wall. 'A square.'

Something had begun to nag in my memory, but still I could not quite see it. He pulled me by the sleeve and I went with him to the west door, by which I had come in. There, just inside the doorway, on either side, and unremarked by me in the face of the terrible sight that had greeted William and me as we'd entered, were two strange stones, almost identical to one another, hewn in octagonal columns. Like two small, squat pillars. The pillars to Solomon's temple. Jachin and Boaz. I knew it then, I heard it then in Sarah's voice: the Mason Word.

It was rumoured that the masons had a word by which they could recognise other initiates of their fraternity, be they working craftsmen or, as was said to be increasingly the case, gentlemen initiates, but Sarah knew that 'the Mason Word' was not one, but two words: Jachin in greeting, Boaz in reply. And because these words together had the power to reveal and identify members of this secret brotherhood one to another, regardless of their rank in life or where they came from, they were also the key to unlocking the whole corpus of Masonic learning to those who would be adepts. And so, 'the Mason Word' had come to stand for that whole body of esoteric knowledge.

I looked at Richard Middleton. 'This is a Masonic temple?'

'We are certain of it.'

'Are there really such places?'

'Come over here,' he said.

I followed him to the west wall and he showed me a stone in it which differed from all the rest. It was large, perfectly square and, he told me, went all the way through to the outer side of the wall. 'And there,' he said, 'you see the oval and there,' pointing to the ground to the left of us, 'is the square pavement.' And there was indeed a perfectly square slab of stone set in to the earthen floor. 'All Masonic lodges have these special stones: they call them "jewels"'.

'But what does this all mean?' I said.

'That is what we have spent the last few months trying to discover. The masons, like all the other crafts, have their secrets, their rituals. But unlike the other crafts, they claim old knowledge, old secrets going back to ancient times and enshrined in stone and hidden places by the architects and builders who made the great pyramids, the temple of Solomon, founded on the mathematical principles that govern the universe.'

Again the Hermetic quest, that of the alchemists, of the pretended Rosicrucians.

'And the men of such lodges seek out this knowledge?'

He shook his head. 'No. They do not seek out the old knowledge, the secrets of the ancients: they claim to have them. The men who lived here would have had them. Increasingly, we have made the ways of the masons our study, their use of the art of memory and the messages of the lodge itself.'

John Innes's interest in the Roman architect Vitruvius made a little more sense to me now. 'Have you approached the stonemasons themselves?'

'Yes, there was a newly apprenticed mason whom one of us had known when the boy was younger; we asked him if he had any knowledge of the workings of the lodge.

The boy almost vomited with fear and told us never to ask such questions. He has avoided the sight of us ever since.'

'Why so?'

'Because, they say, the masons have terrible punishments for those who reveal their secrets. We thought perhaps the boy had been frightened in his initiation by some older men going too far, so we approached one of the older masons who labour in my late brother-in-law's yard.'

'Did they tell you any more?'

'They laughed at us, and told us to mind our own affairs. But though they laughed, I do not think they were rightly amused that we had asked the question, and we did not repeat our mistake.'

'Richard, tell me, what do you understand by the Mason Word?'

He looked surprised that my knowledge extended so far. 'It is the name given to the whole body of secrets revealed to the initiates of the craft who have served their time and gone through the initiation of their lodge. It is, they say, encapsulated in two words given to these initiates when first they are received within the brotherhood.' He shrugged, then winced at the pain in his arm. 'We have not been able to discover what these words are. At least, we hadn't. But Robert had hopes . . .' A cautious comprehension spread over his face. 'That day I saw you at Robert's lodgings . . .'

'I think I found what you had gone to look for, what Robert had found: Jachin and Boaz: the Mason Word.'

He shuffled with difficulty towards the pillars just inside the doorway. 'How foolish we have been,' he said quietly. 'How blind not to see it!'

'I know those were the names given to the pillars at the entrance to Solomon's temple at Jerusalem, but why should this be of importance to the masons?'

He was running a hand over the top of the small pillars, transfixed. 'Because the knowledge of the ancients was inscribed in the stone of those pillars by Hiram, architect of Solomon's temple, the greatest of all the masons.'

His eyes were shining, and I thought a second time that his experiences of the night, and that the fever that was coming over him, had made him a little mad. 'You cannot think these lumps of stone here to be remnants of the temple of Jerusalem – they are rough-hewn granite quarried not three miles from this place.'

He looked at me almost scornfully. 'Of course I don't. But I cannot but believe that somewhere in this lodge we will discover how we might draw closer to that ancient knowledge, a connection . . .' and again his voice trailed off.

I got down again on my haunches beside him. 'Richard, these ancient secrets you seek, this search for that thing common to us and to everything around us, for the Mercury that will enable us to transform it, are not to be found in symbols, in mathematics, in stone, but in the gift of the Holy Spirit. The key is in your own heart.'

'I have tried to believe that,' he said quietly. 'But wait' –

he grasped my arm and forced himself to his feet once more – 'there is one more thing I must show you. It is something that excited us greatly when we found it, and which should have alerted us to the true nature of those pillars.' He led me outside, to a place a little more than three feet from the door, where the turf was covered by a long, mossy slab of granite. The dog was at my side, growling.

I held up my lantern but as it swung in the wind I could see no special markings on the stone. 'What is this?'

'They call it Hiram's grave. The architect of Solomon's temple was murdered by three masons who tried to extort the secret of the Mason Word from him. His body was found in a shallow grave like this, with a moss-covered slab over it. His secrets were buried with him. Every masons' lodge has Hiram's grave, the housing place of their secrets.'

'And what did you find in this one?'

'A skull – the bone box of the initiates – and housed within the skull, three sets of keys.' He waved a hand towards me. 'You wear one of them at your waist.'

I looked down at the set of keys that had been taken from Robert Sim's dead body and handed to me by Dr Dun.

Middleton carried on explaining. 'One fits the lock of the east door to the lodge, from the building yard, the other the west, which is reached by the garden. Robert had the set you now wear, the other two sets were given to others of our fraternity. A fourth set my wife already had – they had been her brother's and she did not know of any others.'

'And the fourth set is the one you now use?'

He nodded.

'Do you keep them – you and the others – about your persons, or do you have some agreement amongst you to return them to their hiding place when they are not in use?'

'We keep them; the skull is empty now, but we have left it in the ground, in the hope of returning some symbol of some deeper knowledge to it. I will show you, if you can help me.'

He bent down and tried to lift the edge of the slab with his one good arm. The dog's agitation was now extreme and I had great difficulty in getting past it to hand Middleton the lantern before moving him aside to heave the stone off. It was heavier than it looked, and it was not until the third great push that I felt it move across the turf at my feet. I leant forward to look into the shallow hole in the ground that was the grave underneath and in the short moment between the piercing of the night by a woman's scream and the crashing of the lantern from Middleton's grip to the ground, I saw the luridly gaping throat and astonished eyes of a murdered man.

FOURTEEN

The Clothworkers' Page

In the kitchen of the house, Richard Middleton had once more taken on the role of physician. He had helped his wife inside while I had hastily shoved the cover back on the grave. Rachel Middleton, now dressed in warmer, drier clothing I recognised as Sarah's, was sitting at the table, shaking. Fearful for his safety, she had refused to wait any longer at my house and had been making her way down to the lodge when she had come upon us at the Masonic grave. Her husband was trying to make her drink a glass of strong wine. I did not like leaving them, but I had no choice.

'The dog is guarding the grave. I will be back as soon as I can.'

I was halfway through the door, on my way to fetch the constable, when I stopped and turned back to them. 'Richard, do you know him? The man who lies out there?'

He shook his head. 'I have never seen him before in my life.'

I looked at his wife, who scarcely seemed to register that we were there.

'I do not think he was known to her either. Do you know who he is?'

'Yes,' I said, 'I do.'

At six o'clock in the morning, I was once again in the library. In my few restless hours of sleep, the face of the dead man as he lay in his shallow grave, his throat gaping and almost black with blood, had haunted my dreams. By the time the drummer went past our house before five I had at last remembered what had eluded my mind's grasp in the night, and indeed what had eluded me on the one occasion I had met the murdered man. For I *had* met him, only a few days ago, in the kitchen of William Cargill's house as he was about to leave with Elizabeth's lucrative linen order in his pack. I remembered where I had seen his name before. And here it was now before me, written in Robert Sim's hand, the last entry dated on the day of the librarian's death, at the bottom of the Clothworkers' Page of the Trades' Benefaction Book:

Bernard Cummins, Weaver, lately returned from the Low Countries, 4sh. 6d. to the box.

That was all, nothing more, but I felt that here at last was something which would, if I could but see it, begin to make sense to me.

My first act, after alerting the town authorities to what had been found in the Middletons' garden, had been to hammer on the door of the college gate house and have the porter fetch Dr Dun who had slept in his college apartments since the night of Robert's death. Despite the gate-keeper's protests and assertions that I had surely, at last, lost my mind, he had eventually done as he was bid and had soon returned with the principal, who had quickly dressed and gathered up his case of medical instruments. It was clear that his first thoughts on being roused were that I was in need of medical attention, and it took a minute or two to persuade him otherwise.

'I have been worrying about you half the night, Alexander. You did not look in your right wits when I left you with William Cargill last night, and the reports from your students were not good.'

'I am sorry to have caused you that concern. It was a brief lapse, and it is over now.'

He did not look convinced, but said nothing more on the matter, and had followed me quickly back to the Middletons' house. Her husband had by this point persuaded Rachel to her bed, and Dr Dun took some time in attending to Richard's wounds before going down into the backland to examine the weaver's body. He had been unwilling to say much to me in front of the baillie and town's officers and had taken little time in despatching me to my own home with a promise and tacit understanding that we should meet in the morning to discuss what we had found.

When I entered the college dining-hall in the morning, a bursar gave me a message that I was to go directly to the principal's private chamber. I could not tell whether Patrick Dun was dressed because he had risen some time earlier, or because he had not yet been to his bed. The greyness of his face, the tiredness in his eyes, suggested the latter.

I was ravenous, having not eaten a proper meal in two days, but the principal showed little interest in the food that was brought to us, and I began to see just how heavily the difficulties of the college weighed on him. 'Matthew Jack is in the tolbooth, of course. He would have done better to have left the town altogether when I him put from the gates, but he was determined that his malice should have its day, and it may cost him a great deal more than his post and his liberty.'

'You think it likely he will hang for the murder of Bernard Cummins?'

'I think it a possibility. His threats to Rachel Middleton and his attack on her husband so soon before Cummins's body was found on that very ground stand ill against him, very ill, and the baillie is satisfied the sheriff will not take long to be persuaded of the logic of that either.'

'But you are not so sure?'

He got up from the table to look out of the window towards the sea. 'I pray God that I am wrong, but I fear it will not be long before others make the connections I have been unwilling to make. It looks bad for Matthew Jack, I grant you, and I have no cause to wish him set at liberty, but it looks worse for Richard Middleton.'

I had half-expected him to say it, but still I wished he had not. 'I know.' The doctor's scalpel used to murder Robert Sim, his wife's adultery with the librarian, the location of the body of Bernard Cummins at a place where

Middleton, Sim and others had secretly met: all of these things pointed not to Matthew Jack, but to Richard Middleton as the likely murderer of one, and possibly both men. Yet it had been Richard Middleton who had insisted on opening the grave, and I could not believe that he was the man we sought. I told Dr Dun this.

'No more can I,' he said. 'But with Matthew Jack screaming his accusations in the tolbooth, it will not be long before the baillies are at the young doctor's door again. I begin to wonder if Robert's affairs may have extended further than we at first supposed. What you have uncovered here,' he said, indicating where Robert Sim had inscribed Bernard Cummins's name in the Trades' Benefaction Book, 'is a connection, on the day of Robert's death, between these two men, and I cannot believe that it is simply coincidence. I give you leave, if you will consent to take it, to look further into that connection.'

And so it was that I spent the next hour in the company not of Aristotle and a classroom full of young searchers after the truth, but down at Putachieside, by the Green, amongst the smell and the noise of the dyers and weavers, asking questions about Bernard Cummins. Little enough was known about him, he was so recently returned to the burgh after years abroad. He had had grand ideas, nothing that would trouble the trade of the greater number of his fellow craftsmen in the town. A landlady was mentioned, a sister too. Someone thought they had heard tell of the patronage of Sir Thomas Burnett of Leys, laird of Crathes. Shock at the murder was expressed. The iniquity of the times blamed.

I found his lodgings, eventually, near the bottom of Futty Wynd, and from his landlady learned a little more. He was burgh born, his father having been a weaver burgess of the town, but when his father died his mother had gone home with the children to her own people.

'Overseas?'

The old woman laughed out loud. 'You haven't even to cross the Dee to get to Crathes.'

'Crathes?'

'Aye, Crathes. His mother died a good few years back, but his sister is there yet, at the castle, in service to Sir Thomas Burnett of Leys.'

'So it is true that the laird of Leys was his patron?'

'Oh, it was true. He it was that first saw the boy's gift, and put him as apprentice to a weaver there in the mill-town. Then he paid for him to perfect his craft abroad, under the best masters. I wondered that he had ever come back, but he said the laird had called him back, and he was bound in thankfulness to come.'

She let me see his room, but I had little luck there, for the baillie and his officers had been there before me, and the old woman had already packed up Cummins's belongings and cleaned out his chamber.

'There was little enough in it. He had only been here a few days, and was only waiting to conduct some business in the town, and for the arrival of his loom and other things from Rotterdam. His plan was to set up his workshop out

at Crathes. He had work on hand for the laird. The baillie
is sending his belongings on to his sister.'

'Was there anything strange amongst his belongings?'

The woman considered. 'His clothes were a little
strange – in the Dutch fashion, you know.'

'What about books, papers?'

'Books he had, with foreign writing on them. Huge books,
with pictures and patterns in them. I took a look once, but
could make neither head nor tail of the half of them.'

'And papers?'

'Receipts, bills, an order book, I think. All of these things
the baillie took to look through, and then they are to be
sent on to his sister.'

I tried another tack. 'Did he have any visitors here? Any
friends?'

'Friends, I do not think so. He told me he had left the
town as a young boy, and had still been not much more
than a lad when the laird of Crathes sent him overseas. But
he was a likeable enough man, with a good manner to him.
The making of friends would not have taken him long. As
to visitors, none, other than the occasional servant on business to him from their master or mistress.'

'Can you remember who any of them were?'

She pursed her lips. 'Someone from George Jamesone,
the painter's house. And one from that lawyer – William
Cargill.' Just business then.

'And what about Robert Sim? Was he ever here? Did
Bernard Cummins ever mention him?'

She eyed me sharply. 'The college librarian. Him that
was murdered too? No, he was never near the place and I
never heard Bernard mention him. Now, I have work to
be getting on with.'

She began to turn away, but I put my hand on her arm
to stay her a moment. 'One last thing. Were Dr Middleton
or his wife ever here?'

She shook her head. 'No, they were not. And I told the
baillie that too.'

Those last words repeated themselves in my head as I
walked up Futtie Wynd in to the Castlegate. The clatter
and clamour of the market, of people coming from the
tolbooth, or going down alleyways to the lawyers' chambers or the sheriff court, of visitors calling at the grand
houses that lined the square and of servants hurrying back
and forth down the pends between them, all that was
drowned out by those last words: *And I told the baillie that
too*. I had only spoken with Richard Middleton twice in
my life – last night, and on the day after Robert Sim's body
had been found – but I thought I had begun to see in him
a man whose friendship would be worth the having, and
whatever his wife might deserve, I would wish to spare her
what might be coming to her, for my dead friend Robert's
sake and for her own. I knew, in the ebb and flow of the
burgh's prejudices and fears, if the law did not satisfy itself
that Matthew Jack was the murderer of the librarian and
weaver, it would not be long before it had found another,
or others, to replace him in the tolbooth.

Sarah was alone with Deirdre when I walked back into our home. The baby was sleeping, the house quiet and still and showing no signs of the drama of the previous night. Sarah, though, was tired, pale and drawn under her tanned skin. We had not been able to speak to one another since I had left in the middle of the storm to go to Richard Middleton's aid. I looked at her for a moment, searching for the words that would put things right, but they would not come. Sarah put down the yarn she had been winding and stood up.

'Alexander, we must talk.'

'I know, I know,' I said. I sat down in the high-backed chair opposite hers and rubbed my face in my hands. 'But this is not the best time, Sarah.'

She lifted my face, forcing me to look at her. 'There will be no best time. Before we ever get to that best time, there will be nothing left to say to one another, and I have much I wish to say.'

I was too weary to argue any further, and gestured with my hand in acquiescence. She sat down by the hearth in front of me and took my hands in hers. The warmth of them, the tenderness in her face was all I had wanted these last days and her next words tore at the very heart of me.

'Do you think that I hold myself so cheap that I would give myself to another man, when I have you?'

I shook my head but I could not speak. How could I tell her 'Yes, I do'? How could I tell her of the imaginings that had been tormenting my every unguarded moment?

I did not need to; she read it in my eyes and let go my

hands, appalled. 'You hold me so cheap? Alexander, for God's sake, tell me what I have done.'

'Andrew Carmichael,' I said, the words barely audible even to myself.

She looked at me in disbelief. 'This again? Oh, please, not this again.'

I clenched my fists until my nails dug into the flesh of the palms. 'Remember? I saw you, Sarah. On Tuesday afternoon, at the Snow Kirk. You were with him.' I felt my voice, hoarse, crack. 'I saw him stroke your face.'

She looked as if she had been caught, frozen in a moment, and then she began to shake her head slowly. 'No, Alexander, no . . .'

I stood up and pushed my chair away so that it banged against the fireplace wall. 'Do not lie to me, I saw you.'

'No, Alexander. What you thought you saw you did not.'

'It was you, and him. I know.'

'Yes, it was. But it was not as you think. Please, sit down and listen to me.'

I did not know that I wanted to hear it, but I straightened the chair and, drawing a cup of water from the jug on the table, remained standing.

'I did go to see Andrew Carmichael on Tuesday. I had sent a message to the King's College, asking him to meet me at the Snow Kirk as soon as he might be able. Zander was at school, and I left Deirdre with Elizabeth. He came in the afternoon, when his students were engaged in private study. I asked him to meet me round the back of the church because I did not wish to be seen, and I could not think of anywhere else in or between the two towns where we might escape notice.'

Her candour was making me sick to the stomach, and it showed on my face.

'No, Alexander, you still do not understand. I asked Andrew Carmichael there because I was almost out of my senses with worry for you.'

'For me? What gave you cause to worry about me, and what in God's name made you think that Andrew Carmichael was the one you should turn to, rather than William, or Dr Dun, even?'

'It was what you found in Robert Sim's room and brought home to this house in your pockets. The Mason Word.' Her eyes were beseeching me to understand, but still I could not.

She drew some water for herself and continued. 'Andrew Carmichael mentioned to me once, in that time when you were away in Ireland and he started coming to William's house, that his father had been a stonemason. It was a passing remark, and in truth I think he wished he had never made it, for he was less inclined to speak of his family than I was of mine.'

Sarah's own parents had died of a fever when she was no more than five years old, and she had been brought up by her mother's sister, a poor, weak woman who could not stand up to a cruel and brutish husband. I had more than once thought that everything she did in her determination to make our family the best that it could be was done in an effort to erase the scars her own childhood had left, and to heal the wounds she had suffered when she had become a woman. And this, indeed, was the point to which this conversation was taking her. She had been sent from what passed for her home into service in Banff, in the house of a master stonemason, a drunken and violent man who had taken her against her will and who was Zander's natural father.

'When George Burnett was very drunk,' she went on, 'sometimes he used to frighten me with tales of what happened in their masons' lodge, of how apprentices seeking to be made masons would be scared half out of their wits into keeping their secrets. He would describe the horrible trials, the humiliations they would be put through – he would threaten to do the same to me. And once, when I was trying to fight him off, he gripped hold of me – his face was contorted with malice – and he whispered in my ear the Mason Word. And then he told me the punishment for any who revealed it.' She shook her head. 'I will not tell you. He thought to control me that way, with fear.'

She came over to me and I could see in her face the pain of remembering things she had fought for five years to forget. 'When you came home from Robert Sim's lodgings with the Mason Word in your pocket, after what had happened to him . . .' Her voice broke off and she rubbed the heel of her hand over her eye. 'I was in a terror at what you had begun to meddle in, and at what might happen to you. I could not think where to go for help. I could not go to the stonemasons and reveal what you now knew, for fear of where that might lead, and I could not think where else to turn. But then I remembered what Andrew Carmichael had told me, so long ago, and so I went to him.'

'But to what purpose, Sarah?'

'I wanted him to talk you out of continuing down this path, to leave off this search into Robert's past, and let the baillies find what they might. Robert is beyond your help now, and I do not care a jot for the name of the college – Dr Dun had no right to ask this of you. I wanted him to explain to you the dangers in which you enmesh yourself, for I knew you would not pay any heed to me.'

Sarah was not a woman to let her mind be overrun with groundless fears, and I could not question what she had learned at the hands of George Burnett. And Andrew Carmichael had mentioned his father to me too, as we had admired the sundial in Dr Dun's garden. But there was one thing yet that none of this could explain.

'Sarah, I saw him rest his hand on your neck and with the other stroke your face.'

She cast her eyes down to her hands, and then up to me again. 'I know; he should not have done that. I had been weeping. He put his arm around me to comfort me, to reassure me. And then for a moment, just a moment, he lifted his hand and stroked my face. I knew he should not have done it and so did he.' She looked away. 'It will never happen again.'

I sank my head in my hands and she rose and went quietly up the stairs to bed.

★

The grave had not been deep, there had been deeper graves. He had looked into deeper graves and wished with every fibre of himself that he could wrench the shrouded corpse from it and breathe life into it once more. But not this one, not this last grave. There had been no shroud and the blood had been warm and wet on his fingers as he had dragged the stone across it.

The other graves had upon them names. His own name, twice. Twice he had watched and mourned as his own name, chiselled into stone, had been set above the clods of dirt and the cold corpse. The dates, the mason's marks telling the truth, and the lies, of his life. A hammer, a chisel, a square, a skull. Beneath them the bones of those he had loved. But this last grave, most sacred of all the masons' graves, bore no marks, and it was empty now. In the whisper of the wind, he thought he could almost hear soft footfalls on the ground as the shades of the dead rose to pursue him to his own earthly tomb.

FIFTEEN

Crathes

The next morning, Dr Dun readily agreed to my absence from the college, and from the town, for the next two days, and furnished me with a letter to present at Crathes Castle, in the expectation that I would gain an audience with Sir Thomas Burnett.

'You may be right,' he said. 'The heart of this thing may lie with the weaver, and not in the town at all. I spoke privately with the sheriff last night, and I do not believe the law will pursue the matter of Cummins's death to Crathes – the town's officers are convinced they have the killer here, in the tolbooth or outside of it, but they have no interest in looking further afield than this burgh. They have sent Cummins's clothing and papers to his sister, but do not intend to seek her out themselves. I have said nothing to anyone outside the college about Malcolm Urquhart.'

It was when the dead weaver's landlady had been telling me about his childhood home, and the patronage of Sir Thomas Burnett of Leys, laird of Crathes Castle, that I had remembered that Malcolm Urquhart, the student who had fled past me down the library stairs on the day of Robert Sim's death, also came from Crathes. The boy's subsequent disappearance from the college would allow me to pursue my investigations there without raising undue notice.

'I have written to the laird on the matter of young Urquhart, and you can rely on his hospitality and assistance. You will have little difficulty in your dealings with the boy's older brother: Patrick Urquhart is a quiet-living, honest man whose gifts should have taken him further than a parish schoolroom. He should have had a glittering career abroad, but was called back after only a year to bring up his younger brother after the deaths of their parents. And now see how that younger brother has disgraced him.' The principal's voice was bitter; little angered him so much as wasted talent.

It was not yet nine when I set off out of town across the Den burn and down the Hard Ward towards Rubislaw and the road that would take me, in time, to Crathes. I did not want to be away from Sarah just now. I had waited, the previous evening, until I was certain that she was asleep, before finally going upstairs and getting into bed. I had held her to me through the night and slipped quietly from the bed early in the morning, leaving her only a brief note about where I planned to go today.

The walk was pleasing, and aside from the occasional stop by a burn to refresh myself, nothing hindered me on my way. It was early in the afternoon when I came to

Crathes. The Burnetts had clung to a boggy island fortress nearby on the Loch of Leys until the need for such places was long past, but in the last century the lairds had built for themselves this stately house, a tall tower of stout walls and few windows built storey upon storey towards the heavens, and capped with towers and turrets there as much for whim and fancy as to defend against the hostility of neighbours. I wondered about the many stonemasons who must have worked on it, men who must have lived in humble lodges such as that we had found at the bottom of the Middletons' garden, and yet could partake of the vision, comprehend the geometry, make real the designs of the finest of architects, to produce such places as this. Forty years since Crathes had been completed. The masons who had worked on it, like the lairds for whom they had toiled, were probably all dead by now.

Men, women and children were busy at their labours as I passed the brewhouse and bakehouse, and few paid any heed to me as I went to the front door of the castle, a small, arched entry set into the thick wall. I took Dr Dun's letter to Thomas Burnett from my satchel and rapped three times on the door. The man who answered was, I saw, well-armed.

'Yes?'

'My name is Alexander Seaton. I am here upon the business of the Marischal College of Aberdeen and would seek an audience with Sir Thomas.'

He sniffed, before standing aside to let me through, taking

care to bolt the door again behind me. 'You and half the country round. Today is court day and you will have to wait your turn. Sir Thomas is in the Long Gallery. Stand a moment.' I did so, and was not altogether pleased to find myself being searched. The guard indicated the knife at my belt. 'I'll have that and you can get it when you leave.'

I covered the handle with my hand. 'I am a teacher, not an assassin. I bear nothing more threatening to Sir Thomas than letters from Principal Dun.'

The fellow was unimpressed. 'So you say, and that may indeed be the case, although you do not look altogether like a teacher,' he said, surveying for a moment the scars on my forehead and at my neck, 'but that place is full of picklocks, swindlers and drunkards, who might take their chances at flight if they thought they could get their hands on a pistol or a blade. You'll hand over your weapon or you'll not take another step inside this house.'

I held up my hands and allowed him to take the knife. He gave me another doubtful look and then told me to go up the stairs in front of him. I ascended the narrow stone turnpike as it twisted for several storeys, passing doorways, all closed, all silent.

At last we reached the top and I was standing in the Long Gallery, and the barony court of Burnett of Leys. The gallery ran the length of the top of the house, and was well lit by tall windows at either end and down the southern side of the room. At the far end, behind a heavy oak table, Sir Thomas Burnett of Leys was in the act of passing sentence on a small, scrawny man, manacled at the hands. The judgment pronounced, the fellow was shuffled past us, a bitter look on his scabrous face, to spend a night in the castle jail before being transported the next day to the stocks in Banchory. As the stair door closed behind the offender and his guards, Sir Thomas stood up and stretched back his arms, letting out a great sigh. I had seen him before, of course, riding through town, at graduations and assemblies at the King's College, and from time to time, at divine service in St Nicholas Kirk, but had met him only once. He must have been about fifty years of age but looked, despite his fatigue at this point in a long day, to be a man full of health and vigour. He was soberly dressed, in a fashion even the most vehement of our ministers could not take exception to, but all the same a man completely in place with the grandeur of his surroundings. Sir Thomas Burnett did not need to prove his standing to anyone.

The laird looked up as the door of the gallery closed behind the thief and his attendants. 'Well, Robert, is this another recalcitrant you have brought to me – I had thought we were finished.'

'I couldn't say for myself, sir: he claims to be a teacher in the new college, but you may judge for yourself.'

I stepped out of the shadow of the doorway and a broad grin swept the laird's face. 'That's all right, Robert, you may leave Mr Seaton here with me, I think I'll be safe enough.'

The guard grumbled and he set off down the stairs again.

'Aye, well sir, if you're certain, but I'll just hold on to his knife.'

The laird gestured to a chair across the broad oak table from where he himself had been sitting. 'Take a seat, Mr Seaton. I'll be with you in a minute.' He checked the entries his secretary had made in the court book and then shook his head. 'Time and again, the same faces, the same crimes. And yet we must labour, must we not, Mr Seaton?'

It pleased me that he should remember me from the one time we had met at Dr Forbes's house, in Old Aberdeen.

When he had finished putting his papers in order, and after dismissing his secretary, Sir Thomas turned his attention once more to me. 'You are here on the business of the college, no doubt?'

'I am, sir,' I said, and handed him the letter from Dr Dun. As he scanned the contents, the face that had greeted me in so friendly a manner only a few minutes ago became grave. 'I see you are not here to bring me any better news from the town than I have already had today.' He glanced at the clock on the mantel-shelf. 'I have no doubt that Malcolm Urquhart will have sought refuge with his brother in the schoolhouse at Banchory, but Patrick will be at his duties in the school another four hours yet. If Dr Dun can spare you, you'll have my hospitality tonight, and I'll send word for the pair to come here when the school is done with for the day.'

'Dr Dun will spare me, and I thank you for your kindness, but I fear Malcolm Urquhart will abscond again if forewarned of my presence here.'

The laird shook his head. 'Malcolm Urquhart will go nowhere, for he has nowhere left to go.' He appeared to consider this a moment. 'But if it makes you more easy I will see to it that my message is delivered to Patrick, and not to his younger brother.'

I thanked him.

'Now, I have not eaten since I left Dunottar, and I'll wager you could manage a bite yourself after your journey here. Did you ride, or come on foot?'

'On foot. It was a fine morning, and I had not the time to arrange for a horse.'

'Then surely, you are famished! Come down with me and we will get them to feed us.'

Sir Thomas led the way through a different door from that I had come in by, and down another spiralling set of stairs. I remarked upon the silence of the house, and he told me that his wife and children were away. 'And I am truly glad of your company, Mr Seaton, for I received some dreadful news today.'

The room into which he led me was a room in which a man might make himself comfortable. It was a small hall with a broad flagstone floor and a high arched plasterwork ceiling. The chimney piece was simple, but the fire that burned within it gave off a welcome heat, for little sunlight made its way into the place despite the warmth of the day outside. It was a plain room, I thought, for a house I had heard of as a delight to the mind and senses, but in the whirl of duties and responsibilities Sir Thomas faced, a plain room perhaps afforded his mind the quiet it required.

He pulled a sash above the fireplace and very quickly a young girl appeared in a doorway. 'Bring some meat and drink for myself and Mr Seaton, will you, for we are both half-starved.' She bobbed her head and turned to leave. 'Oh, and Mary?'

'Yes, sir?'

'How is Marjorie Cummins?'

'The housekeeper has sent her to her bed, Sir Thomas. She is not fit for work today.'

'No,' he nodded. 'She will not be.'

Once the girl had gone, and we had taken our seats at either side of the fire, the laird said to me, 'The brother of one of my servants, a young man in whose life I took some interest and for whom I had great hopes, was murdered in Aberdeen the night before last.'

'Bernard Cummins, the weaver,' I said.

He looked up from the coals he'd begun to rake at. 'The news did not take long to travel the town.'

'Such news seldom takes long to travel, but' – I took a breath, not sure how he should take my role in the thing – 'I did not need anyone to tell me of this; I was amongst those who discovered his body.'

The laird exhaled slowly as he held me with his gaze. It was a gaze under which I could not have sat comfortable for long. 'And this then is why Patrick Dun has sent you to Crathes this day.'

'Not only this . . .'

'Do not try and tell me that with little more than a week until the graduations the Marischal College can spare its most able regent for two days over an absconded student. I suspect it was not really Malcolm Urquhart, but the other matter that brought you here to Crathes.'

'I fear the one will be shown in time to be entangled with the other.'

At that moment, the girl returned with our food, and only once seated at table did our conversation resume.

'Tell me what you know, Mr Seaton. I counsel you to search your heart that you leave nothing out.'

And so I told him of the death of Robert Sim and of Malcolm Urquhart's flight from the college after arguing with him in the library. I told him how my investigation of Robert's death, coupled with rumours William had heard around the burgh courts, had led me to the Middletons' house. I told him of Rachel's frantic call for help in the night, and of Matthew Jack, my disgraced fellow regent's attack on her husband. And then I told him of the discovery, in the Middletons' garden, of the body of Bernard Cummins. Finally, I told him of the last entry Robert Sim had made in the Trades' Benefaction Book, on the day of his death. What I did not tell him, in spite of his injunction, was of the lodge, or the secret fraternity that had met there. Something of the fears of John Innes, and of my own wife, had begun to take hold in me, and I realised that no more than Sarah did I want my researches into the masons' lodge in Aberdeen to become widely known.

'And what, precisely, did the entry in the Trades' Book say?'

'It was simply a record of Cummins's first contribution to the guild benefaction—'

The laird cut me short. 'I did not ask what it *was*, Mr Seaton. I asked what *precisely* it said. What were the words?'

I thought for a moment, pictured the page from the ledger in my mind's eye. 'It said, "From Bernard Cummins, weaver, lately returned from the Low Countries, four shillings and six pennies to the box." That was it, that was all.'

'And yet perhaps that was enough,' said the laird. 'If I had never called Bernard home . . .' He paused.

'It was you who called him back to Scotland?'

'Aye, and I who sent him to the Netherlands in the first place. He was a good lad, an able lad, from the time he could walk and talk. His gifts were not of an academic nature, but from an early age he showed himself adept with a bit of yarn or a needle. It was evident to me that he should be apprenticed to a weaver, which he was, here, for a while, and as soon as he was old enough to leave his mother, I had my brother find a place for him in the Netherlands, where he could hone his skills to something finer than can be got here in Scotland.'

'Your brother, sir?'

'Aye, my younger brother John is Scottish factor at

Campvere. He found Bernard an apprenticeship with a master weaver near Bruges, and there Bernard perfected his trade.'

'Why did you want him to return?'

Sir Thomas got up and washed his hands in an earthenware bowl the girl had set on the sideboard and indicated that I should do the same. 'Let me show you something.'

I did as I was bid before following him back up the stairs towards the Long Gallery. He stopped short of the top and opened the door in to a room I had heard others speak of. He stood aside to let me enter and left me a few moments to slowly walk the length of the room, looking upwards.

'Well, Mr Seaton?' he said at last, with a smile.

'It is . . . magnificent.'

The room of the nine nobles, it was called. Painted on the plaster ceiling, between the oak beams, were full length images of heroes from all the ages before our own: Hector, Julius Caesar, Alexander, King David, Joshua, Judas Maccabeus, Arthur, Charlemagne, and Godfrey de Bouillon the great crusader, rendered magnificently in blue, black, red, and gold. Each was accompanied by his coat of arms and a banner telling of his heroism and achievements.

'My father had a great love for the decorative arts. Each figure is a topic on his own, in which many arguments for valour, nobility and honour have their seat. Each image brings to mind the deeds of the man it portrays and the lessons to be learned and moral to be drawn from them.'

Images, topics, seats of arguments: a visual rhetoric. 'The art of memory,' I said.

'If you like, it may be seen in that way, although I believe the true practitioners of the art of memory involve themselves in much greater complexities than these simple decorations.'

'I have never learned it,' I said. But others had – Robert Sim, John Innes, Richard Middleton and the others of their fraternity. 'Such ideas are frowned upon in my college as tending to Hermeticism, to secret knowledge.'

'Perhaps some of my generation and my father's have gone too far in probing the possibilities of art. But these are brutal times, and you must forgive us if we indulge ourselves in the search for something finer. You will be wondering what this has to do with Bernard Cummins, though.'

I waited.

'Bernard was no simple journeyman weaver – he was a master. He had a gift, an eye for colour and design that cannot be taught, and the ability to transfer what he saw in his mind's eye or in the pages of a pattern book to the threads, the cloth he was working on, and render it something exceptional.' Sir Thomas lifted his hands towards the plastered wall. 'I know that arras hangings are not so much to the taste of wealthy men and women in our times as once they were, but to me they give a warmth and a depth and a texture to a tale that a painting cannot match. You are a Banffshire man, are you not, Mr Seaton?'

'I am,' I said.

'Have you ever perhaps been to Lord Deskford's place, at Cullen House?'

'Only as a boy, once, when my father was called to the fitting of his lordship's horses.'

'Ah. And I do not suppose they let a curious young boy up to see the Long Gallery?'

'They had better sense, sir. I was kept out in the yard where I could do less harm. But I know of it.' Archie Hay, wide-eyed with schoolboy excitement, had told me of it many years ago, for he had seen it; painted on the wooden boards of the Long Gallery at Cullen House, where the walls sloped to meet the roof, was the siege of Troy.

Sir Thomas Burnett broke into my memories. 'It is a magnificent piece. A man can look on it and feel the heat of the battle, hear the clash of the swords. It is that that I wanted Bernard Cummins to do for me, in threads rather than paints, but truer to the tale as Virgil tells it. It was because he was at last ready to begin this great work that I called him home. And now he has paid for my rich man's vanity.'

It was not my place to contradict the laird, and he did not look for comfort. I indicated the painted ceiling above us. 'Better that the rich man should commission work such as this than sit by a candle and count his gold.'

We went down again to the Stone Hall, where the laird called for Marjorie Cummins to be brought to talk to me, if she was fit to come.

A few moments later, a young woman appeared uncertainly at the door. She looked ill, and her eyes were red-rimmed with weeping, but she was enough alike the weaver that I knew this must be his sister.

'That's all right Marjorie, you just come in. Here, take a seat by the fire.' She held something white, a piece of linen, clutched in her left hand, and with her right hand she appeared to stroke it, again and again.

'This is Mr Alexander Seaton,' the laird told her. 'He is a teacher at the Marischal College in Aberdeen. He – knew – your brother and he is here for information that might help bring his murderer to justice. Will you help?'

She looked up momentarily and nodded.

At first I was not sure how I should begin. I leant forward in my chair and touched her hand.

'I am sorry, I am truly sorry, for the loss of your brother.'

She lifted her head a little. 'Did you know Bernard?'

'No, in truth I did not. I met him once, very briefly, but I did not know him.' I took a deep breath and continued. There was little point in putting off the moment with niceties. 'What have you been told of his death?'

She passed the piece of linen through her hands. 'That he was murdered. That his throat was cut and that he was left in a shallow grave in a wealthy woman's garden. They say his body was found there two nights ago, by the woman's husband.' A thought struck her and she looked at me directly for the first time since she had come in to the hall. 'Was that you?'

'No, it was not me, but I . . . I was with him. The man is a doctor, Richard Middleton, and his wife's name is Rachel.'

Her eyes were dull. 'Did they kill my brother?'

'I do not think they did. There is another man, already in the tolbooth, whom some suspect: his name is Matthew Jack, also, until a few days ago, a teacher at the Marischal College. Do you know him? Did you ever hear your brother speak of him? Or of the Middletons?'

She shook her head. 'I never heard of any of them until yesterday. I cannot tell you if my brother knew them or not. But you must know this man, Jack. Did he kill my brother?'

Again I had to tell her I did not know.

She said nothing for a moment and then looked directly at me. 'Then what is your interest in this matter, Mr Seaton?' I could almost have felt the laird at his window behind me smile.

'My interest is that a friend of mine was murdered, in the same manner as was your brother, only six days ago. His name was Robert Sim, and he was the librarian of the Marischal College. One of the last pieces of work he did was to write your brother's name in to the Trades' Benefaction Book held in the college library. It is not a connection the burgh authorities have made, but they may do. What I would know of you is whether you can tell me of any connection between Robert Sim and your brother. Did Bernard ever speak of him?'

She shook her head, frustrated almost. 'Bernard knew almost no one in Aberdeen; he has been away overseas more than ten years, and returned home not two weeks ago.' She broke off, her eyes beginning to fill with tears. 'Two days he had. Two days home here, with me, before he went into the town. And now I will never see him again.' She pressed her face into the linen in her hands.

I waited a moment before proceeding. 'When was he here?'

'As soon as he returned from the Netherlands. He came here straight from the ship that brought him back to Scotland. He had some business with Sir Thomas, I think,' she added hesitantly.

The laird smiled encouragingly at her. 'Go on.'

'He was here two days, two nights, then he went to Aberdeen and took lodgings while he waited for his loom and other things to be shipped from Rotterdam. I visited him there only four days ago. He was so full of ideas, so full of plans, and now it has come to nothing.'

'This was to do with his work here for Sir Thomas?'

Her face lightened a little. 'Yes, he was greatly excited by it – he had been working for years on his ideas and had gathered many patterns and sketches for it. But he also had hopes of setting up in the burgh, in Aberdeen, and attracting the custom of the wealthier burgesses. He planned to use only the finest materials and the best designs. He was alive, Mr Seaton, and filled with the promises of life.'

I remembered the bright, assured man who had so

charmed my wife and Elizabeth Cargill and I could not help but agree with his bereaved sister: Bernard Cummins had been alive with the promises of life. I chose my words carefully. 'He had . . . no presentiment of danger? He spoke of no one with whom he had had some grievance? No fallings out, threats from fellow weavers?'

She thought hard and shook her head. 'No, there was nothing, nothing of that sort. But . . .'

She stopped.

'Yes?'

'It was something, a little strange. Not much more than a curiosity. I wish I could remember it properly.'

I could feel my breath coming quicker, but held back, for fear of dislodging the fragments of her memory further. 'He spoke of having met some person that morning, seen him in the street. Someone he was sure he had met once before, in his time in the Low Countries. He greeted the man by name, but the man affected not to know him, and denied being whom Bernard thought him to be. And yet Bernard was certain that he knew him, even to the voice.'

'What was this man's name?'

She closed her eyes and rubbed her hands down over them. 'I am sorry, I do not know. I should know, for he said it more than once. In fact, he told me he was sure he had mentioned the fellow to me once in a letter.'

It was a slim hope, I knew, but I thought it worth the asking all the same. 'Do you still have his letters?'

'I can write my name, Mr Seaton, but that is all, and I

cannot read. Bernard would send his letters to me by the schoolmaster, and old Mr Angus and now Mr Urquhart read them to me, and would write my replies to him.'

I could remember doing the same thing myself, but I had always given the letter back to its owner after reading it for them. 'What did you do with the letter?'

'Bernard said it would have been one he had written a good long time ago: I would have left it with Mr Angus. He liked to have the letters as an encouragement to his scholars, to show them what they might do, if they would only apply themselves.'

'And did Mr Angus take the letters with him when he left?'

'Mr Angus died. Mr Urquhart always returns the letters to me after he has read them. What has happened to the older ones, I do not know.'

I glanced at the laird and he spoke quietly from his place by the window. 'Will you give Mr Seaton the authority to ask Patrick Urquhart for these letters, and to read them, Marjorie?'

She nodded. 'There is nothing in them that can hurt my brother's name, or any other's.'

I asked her then about her brother's belongings, sent out to her by the town. Two packages had been brought by a carter about an hour before. She had been unpacking one of them when I had arrived. 'There is nothing in it but clothing. Some working clothes, a sober black stand of clothes in the Dutch fashion, two shirts with such finely worked lace at the collar and cuffs . . .' Her voice trailed off. Her brother had been bent upon making something of himself, and he had finished with his throat cut, lying in a hole in the ground. I gave her a moment before questioning her again.

'And what about the second package?'

'Oh, papers, tied up together – receipts and the like, I think. And some books – an order book and some pattern books.' She looked up at the laird. 'The ones he had out here before to show you, Sir Thomas.'

He glanced at me and then spoke to her kindly. 'I think it would be a help, Marjorie, if Mr Seaton and I could see these papers.'

She readily agreed and after she had left, Thomas Burnett took a moment to write a note for me to give to the young schoolmaster. 'I am telling him to bring his brother up here to me. I am also asking him to let you see the letters, and to have his dinner with us this evening. I trust you will stay the night here at Crathes? I would wager your researches into these deaths have not gone unnoticed, and I do not think it would be wise for you to journey alone at night.'

SIXTEEN

Letters

By the time I reached the schoolhouse at Banchory, the sun that had guided my journey to Crathes was but a memory and all signs of summer were gone, replaced by a grey chill wind more fitted for November. The church bell had just rung out for four o'clock, and I knew it would be two hours yet before Patrick Urquhart could release his charges for the day. Not willing to be drenched for the sake of a nicety, I walked up the short path that led to the squat granite building and rapped hard on the door. The hum of young voices reciting their catechism faltered and stopped, and the door opened inward to reveal a roomful of expectant faces, glad of the distraction.

Patrick Urquhart was a little shorter than myself, but so gaunt as to give the impression of height. He had tousled, ungoverned red hair and his skin was the colour of chalk. His face was so pale it might almost have been devoid of life, were it not for the intense blue of his eyes, where all the soul of him looked to reside. As they took in the sight of me, I thought he was a man less in a state of surprise than of fear.

'Mr Urquhart,' I began, 'my name is Alexander Seaton . . .'

'I know who you are,' he said.

'Forgive me for disturbing your class in its lesson. I am here on the business of the Marischal College. My business will keep until the end of the day, and if you will permit me to shelter an hour or two here from the torrent that will soon be on us, I will disturb you no further.'

He turned away from me. 'I cannot . . . I do not think . . .' Then he stopped himself, straightened his shoulders and turned to the class. 'A storm is about to break, children. Take up your things and get home as quickly as you can. You, Willie Slater, go through and light my fire, for Mr Seaton and I have matters to discuss.' He said my name very clearly, deliberately.

Within three minutes, there was not a child left in the place, and Urquhart had bolted the outer door of the schoolroom behind them.

'There was no need to dismiss them – I could have waited.'

He was taking some pains over the straightening of the small room's few benches and the stacking of notebooks and did not look at me. 'Some of them live far from the school, and have a great distance to walk before they reach home. I would have sent them away early whether you had come or not.'

His glance flickered for a moment to the as yet unshuttered window in the west side of the room and as my eyes followed his I thought I caught a movement past the window. In my eagerness to trace the letter of which Marjorie Cummins had spoken, I had almost forgotten about Patrick Urquhart's brother.

The habitation into which the young schoolmaster now showed me was scarcely larger than the chamber I had occupied when first I had taught in the Marischal College. The hearth was narrow and gave little promise of heat. A narrow bed was set into one wall of the room, a bench set against another, a small table with two chairs serving for all the other furnishing, save a wooden chest in the corner and shelves bracketed to the wall on which were ranged a goodly number of books, and cups and plate of little workmanship. It was the dwelling of a man on his own who had no great hopes of being otherwise, a man whose only companionship was in his books. And yet there were signs, in the greying light, that Patrick Urquhart had not been alone here. A bundle of blankets hastily pushed under the bench, not one but two bowls on the table bearing the traces of a shared meal, a door to the back yard that had not been properly shut. More than that, it had not the smell of a place that had been unoccupied for the last few hours.

'Where is your brother, Mr Urquhart? Where is Malcolm?'

Patrick Urquhart poured himself a beaker of water from a pitcher near the door, but did not offer any to me.

'I cannot believe that the college would send a regent all the way out here, in almost the last week of term, in search of an errant student.'

I had not yet shown him Sir Thomas's letter. I wondered what his brother had told him about why he had fled the college. 'Malcolm's disappearance is not as that of other scholars. Where is your brother, Mr Urquhart?'

He sat down on the bed and began to pull off his boots. 'My brother has gone, at my instance, to Crathes Castle, to seek the counsel and protection of Sir Thomas Burnett of Leys.'

'That is why you sent the boy through to light the fire – it was to warn your brother that I was here.'

'Yes.'

'But why?'

'Because he has been in a terror since Sunday evening, when the news first reached us here that Robert Sim had been found murdered in the library courtyard a few hours after you yourself had seen Malcolm running from that place. Whatever truth may lie behind that killing, I can tell you my brother had nothing to do with it.'

'You know that for a certainty?'

He looked me straight in the eye. 'I am as certain of it as I am that you are standing in front of me. My brother may be a fool, Mr Seaton, but he is no more a killer than I am.'

Urquhart was in earnest. He was drawn and weary, a man close to his limits; I suspected this was not the first time his younger brother had brought difficulties to his door. I took the laird's letter from my pocket and handed it to him. 'Malcolm has no need to fear me,' I said. As he read a degree of relief passed across his face.

He swallowed. 'I will fetch those letters.'

'Will you answer me some questions about Malcolm first?'

He waited.

'Why did your brother flee the college on Saturday, Mr Urquhart?'

'Why?' he almost laughed, and the smile brought a light to his face. 'Because, for all his schemes and wiles, he is nothing but a daft boy, impatient and impetuous and never stopping to think that others might not be so.' He came over and took the seat at the table across from me, a little more at ease. 'I am not a wealthy man, Mr Seaton.'

'I was a schoolmaster myself, not so long ago.'

'I remember hearing something of the sort. I was a student at the King's College when you took up your post at Marischal.'

I imagined the students of King's had heard much else about me besides, but neither he nor I were going to allude to that. 'Did you always wish to be a schoolmaster?' I asked.

'Does anyone? Did you? No, I did not always wish to be a schoolmaster – I do not mislike the task, but it is not what I once aspired to.' He drew his finger along a line of fine dust on the table. 'I had hopes of being a mathematician. After I left the King's College, I travelled to Germany and thought to study there. But less than a year after leaving our shores I received a letter telling me that my father was dead and my mother dying, and calling me home to the care of my brother. Without the good graces of Sir Thomas Burnett my brother and I would be destitute.'

'You gave up much for your brother's sake.'

'Sometimes we are not given the choice. And besides' – he indicated the books on the shelves – 'I have my books, and even in this far-flung corner of God's creation a man might find learned converse and the society of like minds.'

I would have known more of Patrick Urquhart, but it was the matter of his brother that had brought me here, and so I turned the conversation back to him.

'Nevertheless, it does you credit that you have done so much for your brother.'

'I could have done little enough for him on my own. Malcolm was not eligible for a bursary at either college. Even had I starved myself, I could not have supported him through his studies, and that is when Sir Thomas came to see me here. He offered help and I took it. He saw some worth in Malcolm's mind that he would not see wasted. And this is how he is repaid.'

'You talk of your brother's debts?'

'His debts and the scandals, the drunkenness, gambling and worse that have led to them. He can have no hope of graduating. I returned to Scotland not that I might pay for my brother's education, but that I might watch over and guide him in his life, and in that I have utterly failed.'

'Not utterly.'

He looked up at me, a man defeated. 'Not utterly? How can you say so, when Robert Sim, of all people, would not consent to help him any more? Malcolm knew the game at last was up for him, that he would be sent from the college in disgrace. He fled the college because he knew he had burned every bridge he had.' His voice fell. 'And what will happen to him now? Is he suspected of Robert's murder?'

I shook my head. 'Only myself and Dr Dun have made any connection between the two, and we have not made that connection known to the burgh authorities. Dr Dun is determined that the town will meddle in only so much of the college business as it needs to.'

He breathed a sigh of relief. 'We had expected a delegation of some sort from the college or the town, searching for him. When I saw you, I thought you were in the van of an arresting party. I had told Malcolm he should make for the castle and Sir Thomas's jurisdiction should anyone from the town appear.'

I might well have done the same myself, to protect a brother. 'I suspect the goodwill of Sir Thomas Burnett, if such your brother still retains, will do much in his favour. As to Malcolm being suspect in the murder of Robert Sim, it may be that his flight from the town on that day has done more than anything else to establish his innocence.'

'How so?'

And so I told Patrick Urquhart of the murder of Bernard

Cummins. I would not have thought it possible that Urquhart's pale face could become more bloodless, but as I recounted my tale to the point of the discovery of the weaver's body in the Middletons' garden, he blanched still further. I stopped talking a moment, not certain that he was still listening to me. 'Mr Urquhart . . .' I got no response. 'Mr Urquhart . . . Patrick!' At last he looked up. He was shivering, although the fire had begun to warm the darkening room. 'Patrick, do you understand what I am saying?'

At last he spoke, his voice a monotone. 'You are telling me that you believe Robert Sim to have been murdered by the same hand that took the life of Bernard Cummins, and that that should spare Malcolm suspicion of the deed, for he had left the burgh by the time of the weaver's murder.'

'And that is true, is it not? He was here with you by Saturday night?'

'Yes, and has been ever since, thank God. And Bernard Cummins had his throat cut, just like Robert Sim . . .'

'Yes.' I judged it best not to tell Urquhart of the lodge or the fraternity: I was coming to believe, like Richard Middleton and John Innes, that the fewer who knew of it, the safer the remaining members would be. 'And I think there is a connection between the two.'

I went on to explain about the entry of the weaver's name I had found in Robert Sim's hand in the Trades' Benefaction Book. Finally I told him what Bernard Cummins had told his sister about the man he had recognised in the street. 'That is why I need to see the letters the weaver wrote to his sister.'

Without a word, he went over to the chest in the corner. It was not locked, and it did not take him long to find what he was looking for under the layers of clothing and winter blankets. When he straightened himself and turned back to face me, he had in his hand a bundle of letters, tied up with a length of string.

'I had almost forgotten they were there. I have only read the ones she brought to me herself – I do not know what is in the older ones, but I doubt you will find anything in there that is worth killing a man – two men – over.'

I settled back in my chair and began to sort through the letters, searching for the name of a man Bernard Cummins had met once, in Holland, many years before. The letters covered a period of almost twelve years, and there was one written every three or four months. The oldest were written on the poorest paper, a little crumpled and torn in parts, the writing unsure. Starting from the beginning, I accompanied the young weaver on his travels from this little Scottish parish to Zeeland and the town of Middelburg, where he was met by Sir Thomas Burnett's brother John, Scottish factor there. For a month, Bernard Cummins had stayed in Burnett's household, learning what rudiments he could of the Dutch tongue, in spoken and written form, under the watchful eye of Mr Alexander MacDuff, minister of the Scots kirk at Campvere. Burnett had then accompanied the boy to a small town near Bruges, and the home of the master weaver with whom he would perfect his craft. Cummins was a story-teller of some talent, and I felt with him the awe and wonder of the nervous apprentice confronted for the first time with the great centres of Europe, with people who spoke in tongues that were not his own, and who lived by manners and customs that were new to him.

An hour passed, and I was only vaguely aware of Patrick Urquhart across the table from me, working at something with pen and ink, and a small set of sticks he seemed to examine very closely. Napier's Bones, a favoured tool amongst mathematicians. In time the schoolmaster brought a lamp, and I realised afternoon had passed in to evening. So engrossed was I in the life of Bernard Cummins, of his master's household, the news and scandals of the small Flemish town in which he lived, that I almost missed it; I almost missed the one piece of news I had been looking for.

It had been nearly nine years ago, in early September, just as summer was turning to autumn, and Cummins had gone with his master to Leiden, to sell cloth. On their second evening in the town, the master weaver had left his young apprentice to his own devices and gone to spend the evening in the company of some old acquaintances. Cummins had wandered the town, taking in its sights, and in very little time had found himself in the student quarter. Feeling hungry, he had taken himself to a nearby inn, the Fir-Cone, and with the guilders his master had given to

him for the purpose had ordered himself a dinner. The
name of the inn struck me, for it had been a favourite haunt
of William's in his Leiden days. The young weaver had not
been halfway through his *hutsepot*, however, when he was
joined on his bench by a trio of English students with
nothing in mind but to dose themselves quite thoroughly
on brandy-wine before they should be tracked down by
their censorious professor. At least, he had thought at first
that they were all English, but after a very few words had
realised that one of them, the quietest and most sober of
the three, was a Scot. This young man soon left his companions to their drinking and fell to talking with Cummins of
their homeland, and any news either had of it. He told
Bernard he was a student at Franeker University, in Friesland, even further to the north. He and his fellows lodged
in the home of their divinity professor, Dr William Ames,
a fervent adherent of the views of Calvin with strict ideas
on discipline and morals. They had come to Leiden with
Dr Ames on a book-buying expedition and were to make
for Amsterdam the next day, from where they would take
ship across the Zuiderzee and back to Friesland. It was a
great boon to Cummins to converse in his own tongue after
so long a time away from home. The evening had been
brought to an abrupt ending by the outraged divinity
professor who after much searching had tracked down his
errant scholars before marching them from the inn with
little ceremony and no little prophesying of the punishments to come, in the next world and in this. Bernard

Cummins had ended his letter with the words, 'I was sorry to see the end of an evening of such good conversation and great cheer, and I hope that, whether here or in some other place, I might one day again come upon my countryman, Nicholas Black.'

I read the line again, and all the pleasantness of the last hours disappeared. I pushed aside the letters I had already read and started frantically to scan through those that remained. Almost nine years of letters, but Cummins had written less frequently to his sister as the years had gone by, and the number of letters sent across the sea had dwindled with time. Fortunately, his small, neat hand was familiar to me now, and I could run my eye down the pages at some speed, without fear of missing anything I might wish to see. This change in my behaviour did not go unnoticed by Patrick Urquhart who looked up from his work to observe me.

'What are you looking for?'

'What?' I said, distracted.

'What are you so desperate to find in those letters that you were not in the former?'

'A name, a man's name,' I said. 'I am looking for Nicholas Black.' There was no particular alteration in his face save a heightened curiosity. 'The name means nothing to you?'

'I do not think I have heard it before. I do not recall even seeing it in any of the letters Marjorie brought me.'

No. It was not in any of the letters Marjorie Cummins had brought to the schoolmaster to read to her, for her brother had mentioned the man only in that one letter, written long ago, when Patrick Urquhart himself had been but a schoolboy. I thought of the dangers of travelling alone at night, and wondered how far Nicholas Black might have gone in pursuit of Bernard Cummins. As I looked out on the rain that was now beating down on the ground with all the fervour of a foe too long thwarted, I was glad that I had Patrick Urquhart to accompany me on the unfamiliar road back to the castle.

We dined in the High Hall. The laird and Patrick Urquhart exchanged a smile at my evident awe on first stepping into the room. Every inch of ceiling, from window soffits to central boss, had been painted, decorated in blue, green, red and gold. The red berries and glossy green leaves of the holly, the family's recurring motif, sent tendrils out across the plasterwork, everywhere linking symbols, signs, messages. Had Bernard Cummins gazed on these, I wondered? He must have done. Had he understood them? Better than I. It was with difficulty, as we discussed what was to be done with Malcolm, that I managed to stop my eyes drifting too often to the mysteries above. Once we were agreed on how to proceed, the boy was summoned.

Within a few minutes he stood before us in the High Hall. Malcolm Urquhart was well-made, handsome, and with something in his bearing that Patrick had not. Indulged by over-fond parents and then left to be managed by the brother who should have been able to lead a better life, he had an opinion of himself that would not be curbed by the discipline of kirk or college. And yet, when he raised his head to look at us, I saw not the sullenness, the defiance I had expected, and indeed seen in him before, but the face of a frightened child.

I looked at Patrick, whose knuckles were white and looked as if they might crush the stem of the glass he held. It was Sir Thomas who spoke, and he did not play with his words.

'Well, Malcolm, you have disgraced yourself, shamed the memory of your parents, and thrown in his face every kindness, every sacrifice your brother has made for you. And now, to crown all, you have brought the authorities of the Marischal College to my door.'

The boy opened his mouth to speak, but the laird was in no humour to indulge him. 'I will not ask you the cause of your debts – there will be nothing edifying in what you have to say, and I have heard bad enough already in this hall tonight. I will tell you this, and this one time only, that I will pay your debts to the college, and you will finish your education. And if you do not make yourself the man that God gave it to you to be, you will have no further sanctuary in this house. Mr Seaton, on behalf of the college, has agreed to it. You are a young man who might offer much to the world, or be a blight upon it. It is for you to choose which it is to be, and you will make that choice tonight, and keep to it.'

The boy was flushed, and, perhaps for the first time in

his life, chastened. He scarcely lifted his eyes as he spoke. 'I will give you no cause to regret your kindness.'

The laird nodded. 'See that you do not. Now, there are some other matters touching the college that Mr Seaton must discuss with you, and I caution you to answer him straight and fully, or it will go the worse for you. Afterwards, you will stay here.'

Malcolm Urquhart might have been of a mind to protest, but he evidently thought better of it, and turned to listen to me. He made no effort to deny his presence in the library, nor his argument with Robert Sim on the day of his death. I asked him whom he had seen when he was there, and apart from my student Adam, to whom I had already spoken, the only other person he had seen had been myself.

'You did not go back to the library again, after you had passed me on the stairs? You did not return later to speak to Robert Sim one more time?'

His face was whiter than his brother's and he shook his head. 'I give you my oath, Mr Seaton: I did not go back; I wish that I had done.'

'Why so?'

'To say that I was sorry. Mr Sim was never anything less than kind to me, and my parting words had been ungrateful and harsh. I was angry that he wouldn't even put down the old set of theses he was reading to listen to me properly. I pushed the volume from his hand and left. All I wanted was to get away from the college, away from the town. I gathered my belongings and was over the Den Burn by three and back here at Crathes in time to have my supper with Patrick. And ruin his evening, too,' he added almost inaudibly.

I raised an inquisitive eyebrow at the older brother, but he continued to stare stonily ahead of him. The boy went on, 'He spent most of the evening trying to persuade me to go back and cast myself on the mercy of Dr Dun.'

'But you did not return on Monday?'

He looked at me with a flash of the old defiance in his eyes. 'I could not. By the evening of the Sabbath the news had reached here that Robert Sim had been found dead in the library close. I knew I would be suspected of the crime and I could not return.'

There was little more to be said – I believed him, and he had told me everything he could on the matter, which, I had to concede, on its own would hardly have merited the trip to Crathes. The laird sent him down to the kitchens to be fed, and Patrick Urquhart and I remained to take our dinner with Sir Thomas.

Most of our talk was on the condition of the country and the ceaseless feuding, the internecine slaughter between the landed families all around, the roots of which had been lost to memory and buried in time, to send up endless poisonous shoots of vengeance and retribution. Reprisals were swift and brutal, and grief inflicted that was beyond satisfaction by the law. Everywhere in the High Hall of Crathes we were surrounded by the trappings of civility: from fine delft tableware to the intricately carved chairs on which we sat. And yet, in rooms like this, all over the north, men of wealth, education and good-breeding could barely restrain themselves in their schemes of slaughter and desire for revenge.

'We know what it is, the world we should make, but our nature, it seems, revolts against it.'

'Not our nature, sir, not our true nature. If we could but isolate its essence, we might be in accord with all that is good in God's creation and the works He has enabled us to create.'

Patrick Urquhart's words pulled me right back to Richard Middleton and his lodge, dabbling in some Rosicrucian fantasy. I looked at him stupidly, but the laird's mind was quicker than mine. 'Spoken like a true mathematician, Patrick, although you should take care your words do not tend too much towards the excesses of the alchemists. Mr Seaton and, to a lesser extent, myself, are men of learning, but after the dislike of the king's late father for the subject, there are those who might choose to misunderstand what you say.'

Patick Urquhart swallowed and looked at the table. There was a slight tremor in the hand that returned his goblet to the tabletop.

'In fact,' said the laird, looking at me now as well as at Patrick, 'the messenger who brought news from the town today bore with him a tale of accusations in that vein.'

The schoolmaster opened his mouth to speak but the laird had not yet finished. 'Matthew Jack was dismissed by

Dr Dun from his regency in the Marischal College for brutality against the students, was he not, Mr Seaton?'

'He was.'

'And now you tell me that Matthew Jack is in the tolbooth, on suspicion of the murder of Bernard Cummins?'

I nodded.

'Bernard Cummins whose body was found in a grave in a garden belonging to the the man whom Jack has been proclaiming to have been involved in secret societies, alchemy, the pursuit of – what should I call it? – dark magic.'

Patrick Urquhart groaned. 'Oh, God.'

'You neglected to tell me, Mr Seaton, that Rachel Middleton was the sister of the stonemason Hugh Wardlaw and that Bernard Cummins's body was found at the door of the masons' lodge.'

I looked across at Patrick Urquhart who now had his head in his hands, and I knew what I should have guessed sooner: the identity of the final member of Robert Sim's fraternity.

Within an hour Thomas Burnett had been told more than I knew myself of the Rosicrucian fraternity that had gathered at the lodge in Aberdeen and who had begun trying to unravel the secrets of the masons who had occupied it before them. With greater coherence than either John Innes or Richard Middleton had been able to use, Patrick Urquhart had related for me the role of each of the four in pursuing the ends of their brotherhood. He himself had instructed the others in the intricacies of mathematics, the functions and possibilities of geometry, the dangerous, tantalising assertions of an astronomy that with Kepler, Copernicus and Brahe challenged to the point of annihilation the old certainties of Ptolemy, Aristotle and others. As I knew already, Richard Middleton had pursued the ends of the Swiss physician Paracelsus, in progressing from new methods of diagnosis and treatment of the ill to a deeper study of the alchemy that was medicine; Urquhart confirmed that Middleton had not been greatly interested in travelling further down the road of many other alchemists in seeking that ultimate repository of knowledge, the Philosopher's Stone. Robert Sim's special interest had of course been in the books.

Urquhart had relaxed a little and was warming to his theme. 'Robert tracked down the books. Occasionally, something of interest would come into the library's possession through a benefaction, or with money at the college's disposal, and Robert would bring it to our gatherings and see to it that no notice was taken of its absence from the library. He made it possible for us to purchase books ourselves occasionally – books that might have aroused suspicion had we bought them publicly, as individuals. Few booksellers would question the requests of the librarian of the Marischal College.'

'Had he found anything of interest lately, mentioned anything he was expecting to arrive in the college?' I wondered.

Urquhart shook his head. 'Nothing. Although there was something Richard Middleton had asked him to try to find, but I am certain he had ordered that through Melville, the bookseller – it was not something he had in the library.'

'Can you remember what it was?'

'I wish I had paid more attention. But the book was not something to assist us in our studies; rather it was something Richard thought might help John, cool him a little.'

The laird interjected. 'John Innes? Why should he need "cooling"?'

Urquhart shifted a little uncomfortably. 'Because he had been taking things too far. His enthusiasms were becoming dangerous for us and for himself, and were in danger of drawing attention upon our studies.'

I chose my words carefully. 'He took a special interest in the Cabbala, the guidance of angels, did he not?'

'Yes, and who is to say there is not a place for that? For myself it holds no interest, but John wished to delve further and further into things esoteric. Where Richard, Robert and I sought knowledge, John sought secrets. He believed every word of the Rosicrucian myth, and was becoming more and more obsessed, unsettled, by his pursuit of their "secrets". Richard had promised to show him that a myth was all it was; there was a work he knew of in the Czech language that he had been trying to obtain, to translate for John.'

I remembered John the last time I had seen him – distracted, rambling, terrified, mad – and I could feel a real anger rising within me, for there had been no guiding angel in that shuttered rank room from which he'd pushed me, none with him but some handmaid of the Devil that these studies had called forth. I had to push down bile, the anger in my voice, before I could continue.

'And you do not know that Robert had managed to obtain it, this book of which Richard Middleton spoke?'

'I never heard that he did,' said Urquhart. He was tired now, weary of talking, but the laird had not finished with him yet.

'Tell me this, Patrick, how much of the knowledge, of the secrets of the masons did your brotherhood unravel from what you found in their lodge?'

'Little, very little. We educated ourselves in the art of memory, but I am not interested in their secrets. What I would learn is their knowledge, what ancient knowledge they have of the geometry that frames our world. For that, I would give much.'

'Perhaps Robert Sim did,' I said.

'Did what?'

'Give much. Perhaps he gave all.'

SEVENTEEN

The Talk of the Town

I had lain, sleepless, thinking of Sarah through the few dark hours of the night at Crathes, filled with anxiety that what I had damaged between us could not be repaired. Being away from her could only make things worse, and I was up at first light and on the road back to Aberdeen before five.

It was another day of hazy heat, and I was a sorry sight of dust and sweat by the time I tramped in to the court-yard of my own house. I heard my daughter before I saw her, squealing as she chased a butterfly from honeysuckle to rose and failed to catch it. Seeing me, she stretched out her arms and as I bent to lift her I heard a sound that had been absent from our home too long – the sound of Sarah's laughter. I held the baby to me. 'Who is it, my pet? Who is in the house?'

'Jaffy,' she said, wriggling down after the butterfly once more.

She repeated the name and my heart lifted as I straightened myself to be greeted at the door of my home by my oldest and dearest friend, Dr James Jaffray. In a moment he had me in his ursine embrace before holding me away from him to cast his eyes over me.

'Tell me, Sarah, have you been feeding this fellow at all? He is a more scrawny sack of bones than many I have closed the eyes on. Though you are little better yourself. And tell me, does the sun never shine on this wretched town? I don't know which of you is the more deathly of pallor. To think that I thought to make a holiday of this jaunt, and now I see I will spend the whole time tending to the sick and sickening.'

'I had not thought to find you here, Doctor,' I said when at length I managed to get in to the house. 'The graduations are not until next week, and we had not looked for you until then.'

He raised an eyebrow. 'Well, there's a fine welcome to ease my weary bones. It is fortunate indeed that I am staying with William Cargill, where at least I will be made welcome.'

'You are welcome here, James. You know that. Always.'

'Aye, I know that, but William has the room for me, my boy, and you do not. And you are right: I had not planned to come to town for a week yet, but there has been an outbreak of good health in Banff and I thought I would get out of the place before it came to an end.'

'Then I am glad to see you. When did you arrive?'

'Late last night. I came round here early this morning,

hoping to find you at your breakfast, and Sarah has been kind enough to put up with me since then.'

'There is no kindness in it, Doctor,' she said. 'We miss your company as no other's. But I must go to Elizabeth's now, to help her begin planning for Monday night.'

'What is happening on Monday night?' I asked.

Still she didn't look at me. 'William is giving a dinner to welcome the doctor back to the burgh. We are invited, and others too.' She lifted a clean apron from the back of the door and went quickly past me to gather Deirdre from the yard.

The doctor was the first to break the silence. 'And so, Alexander, are you going to tell me what is the matter here, or am I to go out after your wife and ask her in the street?'

'The matter? It is nothing. It is . . .' I saw that would not do it. 'Och, just that I have been away too much on college business, and she does not like the nature of it. It will pass.'

I turned away from him to look for a clean shirt in the press by the door. When I turned back, he was still watching me. 'Do you think to fool me with such nonsense? Do you think I have not known you since the day I first skelped your backside and handed you to your poor, exhausted mother? You could never carry off a lie, Alexander Seaton. Do not seek to do it now.'

I opened my mouth but he held up a finger to silence me. 'I did not come fifty miles on the back of an old horse to hear the first story to come into your head. I came because William Cargill wrote to me three days ago, saying that you had had a lapse into your old ways and would not be helped, and that Principal Dun himself had fears for your health.' He laid a clenched fist on the mantelpiece. 'I will not see you fall again as you did before. You will tell me what is the cause of this concern, and why your wife looks ill near to collapse.'

'Sarah?'

'Who else, man?'

'But she is not ill.'

'Not ill? Did you even look at her?' His angry frustration became something else, and his voice which had been rising, became softer. 'No, I know you did not, no more than she did at you. Alexander, what has happened between the pair of you? Is it something to do with the child?'

'The child?' I looked at him, surprised. 'Do you mean Zander or Deirdre?'

'I mean the one she is carrying just now,' he said quietly, his eyes never leaving my face.

I looked at him, stupefied. And then it was a moment before the roar within my own head subsided enough that I could hear his words, for they had begun to enter my mind before they had left his mouth. I clattered against the table and knocked over a stool as I rushed for the door, just in time, to vomit in the yard. I retched until there was nothing, beyond nothing, left inside, and slumped down the wall, crushing the honeysuckle that grew there. In time, I felt the strong, familiar hand on my shoulder and accepted the ladle of cool water the doctor held to my mouth.

'You did not know,' he said flatly.

I shook my head.

'She is near enough four months gone, I would say.'

'She told you?'

He sat down beside me, avoiding the pool of vomit. 'Oh, not in so many words. But I know a woman with child when I see one. I had been about to ask her outright when you arrived in the yard.' He offered me his wetted handkerchief. 'This is not as you were when you heard that she was carrying Deirdre, or the next one, that she lost. I never saw a man with greater joy or love in his eye than in those days, and I do not see that now.'

I said nothing, but looked at the ground.

'You cannot think it is another man's child that she carries.'

His words twisted whatever was left inside me. I tried to speak but my heart was racing and I found I could scarcely breathe.

He gripped my arm again. 'Hold steady, hold steady, it will pass. Now take a breath with me. Are you listening to me? Good. Take a breath with me.'

When he was satisfied that my crisis had passed, he gave me another drink and then lifted me to my feet.

'Let us go back into the house,' he said, and I let him lead me through my own door and sit me in my own chair, as if I were some sick child or aged soul who could not shift for itself. He drew his own chair close to mine and studied my face. 'Tell my why you think this terrible thing, boy.'

And so I told him of the scene I had witnessed between Sarah and Carmichael at the Snow Kirk, and what her explanation had been. I told him too of the rumours I had started to hear, a little over a year ago, of Carmichael's attempted courtship of her before our marriage, when I had been in Ireland, and of the admission by William Cargill and indeed Sarah herself that this had been the case.

'That is it?' said the doctor.

I nodded.

'And when you returned from Ireland, how long was it before she agreed to be your wife?'

I remembered it well. 'Three minutes,' I said. 'Five, perhaps, until she stopped crying and beating me, until her rage, despair, subsided and she finally trusted herself to me.'

'Three minutes, perhaps five,' he repeated. 'And yet you doubt, and still you doubt. Alexander, I begin to wonder if it is Sarah that you doubt.'

I looked up at him. 'What do you mean?'

'That you are a man, and a man who cannot trust a wife who has given him no cause to doubt her may have secrets of his own. Is it Katharine Hay? Do you still harbour thoughts of Katharine Hay?'

Katharine. I had scarcely thought of her in all of this.

My dead friend Archie's sister. The girl I had loved with a love that had changed the course of my life, and hers. The girl I had turned my back on, in a moment of madness that had sent her hundreds of miles, a world, away. 'No, it is not Katharine Hay. That was a lifetime ago. I would not abandon Sarah for Katharine.'

His words came slowly. 'No one has spoken of abandoning Sarah. What have you done, Alexander?'

I took a sip from the beaker of water he had given me. 'I have . . . it was in Ireland. It was one night, that was all. A girl that should have married my cousin. One night.'

'I see. Did you love her?'

'Love her? No, I do not think so. Not the Alexander Seaton that is sitting before you here. But in Ireland – no, I did not love Roisin O'Neill even there, but it was a different place, and I a different man.'

'And do you hanker for it?'

'No, but there are times I wish I had never seen it.' I turned the beaker round in my hands. 'I saw another life there, James. Another life that had no place for Sarah, for Zander, for the man who lectures in the college and reads in the kirk. I did not want it, I know that, but it is too stark a thing for me to know that while I had a choice, so did she – Sarah. She also might have chosen a different life, with a different man. And to know that he is a good and decent man as William and others never sicken of telling me, a man whose conversation is interesting and company worthwhile, makes it all the worse.'

'And yet she did not choose him, you know that, don't you?'

I nodded.

'Then tell her.'

'I try. Dear God, I try, but I find I am taken over by a poison that goes from my heart to my mouth, and I can do nothing but accuse her. I will drive her to him. Perhaps – the child – perhaps I already have done.'

He stood up abruptly and took his hat from where it lay on the table. 'A word more of that and I will pack up her and the children and take them to him myself.' He shook his head at me in disgust. 'That girl has looked shame in the face and not been broken by it, she has given you everything a woman has to give – the care of one child, she has borne you another and lost a third, and by God, Alexander, I wept with you then. But I swear to God, I will be His agent in taking from you that which you do not deserve and leading it to one who does, who will cherish and care for her, if ever I hear you speak one word more against your wife.'

In all the time I had known Jaffray, through all my worst days, he had never before raised his voice to me. Before I could muster a reply the door had banged shut behind him.

It was early afternoon that, washed, changed, and in full control of myself, I descended the steps from the principal's rooms and crossed the courtyard of the Marischal College.

Dr Dun had been called out to Belhelvie, where the laird's daughter had fallen ill with a fever, and he was not expected back until the evening time. I had left him a note, sealed, detailing what I had learned from Malcolm Urquhart at Crathes, and also what I had learned of his schoolmaster brother. I looked in briefly on my class who were being led out by John Strachan with their bows for an afternoon at the butts. I promised him and my slightly wary looking scholars that I would return to my duties the next morning. I wanted to go to Sarah, but what I had to say to her could not be said in the midst of someone else's kitchen. No courts sat today, so instead I turned my steps to the Castlegate and sought out William Cargill in his rooms.

His clerk had me wait ten minutes or so while William had a deed and its copy notarised. He looked up when I entered. 'I hear you were out at Crathes. What called you there?'

'Perhaps we will talk of Crathes later. I arrived home late this morning to find Jaffray in my house.'

William coloured, but only a little.

'Your behaviour – I had never seen you like that before, Alexander, but I knew Jaffray had. I was concerned for you, and did not know where else to turn.'

'I gave you cause to be, and I am sorry for it, but I will give you no such cause again.'

'And is all well with you now?'

'It will be. The doctor has addressed himself to my ills quite thoroughly, and shown me the remedy. There is no other who could so hold a glass up to my face and force me to look. You did well to send for him.'

'Then we need talk no more about it.'

'No.'

'Good. And now,' he said, reaching for his wine bottle and two glasses, 'tell me what took you out to Crathes.'

When I had finished my account he was thoughtful. 'And so Patrick Urquhart was the fourth member of their fraternity. Why did Middleton make such a mystery of it?'

'Because he was convinced that some harm would befall Urquhart if his identity became known. Hardly surprising, given what has happened to the others. But he has not fallen victim to violence, or begun to slide in to madness.'

'I am glad of it, but how could he have joined in their fraternity, when they met at the lodge and he was out at Crathes?'

'The minister there takes the school on alternate Saturday mornings. The children are free to play on a Saturday afternoon. That allowed Patrick to travel into town on a Friday evening and return to Banchory on the Saturday night.'

'So that is why they held their convocations so late at night. It is little wonder then that Rachel Middleton became the object of the burgh gossips, or that Matthew Jack began to suspect something sinister of these gatherings. Rumours of dark practices at the lodge have begun to circulate the town, and I'll tell you this, Alexander, the masons do not like it.'

'The stonemasons?'

'Aye, the stonemasons. Theirs in an honourable craft, with its secrets, as all crafts have, but they do not like this calling down of attention on themselves by what happened at the Middletons' lodge, or the interference in their practices of those who have never raised a hammer. There is a feeling building in the burgh against the Middletons, and soon it will not need Matthew Jack to feed it.'

I knew it. Accusations, insinuations, that the physician had dabbled in the darker side of the alchemical arts would not be long in losing him what patients he had, and the rumours that had begun to abound about his wife were not those that a woman such as she could long survive.

'It does not help that they are strangers here, with no kin and few friends.'

'I would be their friend,' I said at last.

'And I also. And in pursuit of that cause, Elizabeth has invited Richard Middleton and his wife to join with us on Monday night, to meet the doctor. George Jamesone and Isobel are to be there too.'

My painter friend and his wife always made for entertaining company. 'It will be a night of good cheer, then,' I said.

'Yes, that is what I intend. And . . .' He seemed unsure as to how to proceed.

'And?'

'I have also invited Andrew Carmichael, in the hope that he can bring with him John Innes. John has not been seen outside the King's College since he heard the news of Robert Sim's murder.' He was watching me carefully. I was not sure that I was ready to face Andrew Carmichael after the thoughts that had rampaged through my head and emptied my stomach only a few hours before, but I knew that if I was truly to excise the canker of suspicion and distrust within me, I must.

'It will be a good thing if he manages to get John down out of the Old Town.' I was glad to have managed this, and it seemed to satisfy William, too. That achieved, I was keen to change the course of our conversation. 'Has any fresh evidence come to light in the burgh in the case of the two murders, any witnesses?'

'Nothing, nothing at all. The baillie and his men are circling Richard Middleton like vultures round a dying beast. They cannot see beyond the rumours about Robert and Rachel and the killer's use of a doctor's scalpel. As to the death of the weaver, much though many would wish to see Matthew Jack found guilty on that charge, no connection can be found between him and Bernard Cummins other than the Middletons' garden. The weaver was so recently returned to the burgh that his connections here were very few indeed.'

'I do not think it is here that the connection is to be found. Tell me, William, in your days at Leiden, you never came upon a Scot, a student at Franeker, by the name of Nicholas Black?'

William thought for a moment and then shook his head.

'It is not a name I recall, although I never went to Franeker, you know. There was little to recommend it for a lawyer, and the climate was more miserable than I had a mind for. Why do you ask?'

'Because Bernard Cummins did come upon him. One evening, about nine years ago, when in Leiden with his master, he met Nicholas Black at the Fir-Cone inn. And he met him again here, in the street of this burgh, not a week ago, but Nicholas Black denied the fact, denied the name, and claimed never to have met Bernard Cummins before.'

William's eyes grew wide. 'But how do you know this?'

'Bernard Cummins, like Malcolm Urquhart, came from Crathes. His sister told me of it, and I read the weaver's account of his meeting with Black in a letter almost nine years old in the schoolmaster's possession. I do not think we will find the killer of these two men until we find Nicholas Black.'

William thought a moment before he spoke. 'But you know as well as I do, Alexander – there is no scholar in Aberdeen by the name of Nicholas Black, not in either burgh. Surely, after nine years the weaver was mistaken?'

'His sister said he was not, that he was sure of it. For want of an option, I am determined to find him.'

'And where do you propose to do that?'

'I had thought to begin with Matthew Jack.'

He was incredulous. 'You are not serious? You and I were the last people to have seen Robert Sim alive, and you it was who found him dead. And then you discovered Bernard Cummins's body also. How long do you think it will be until it occurs to Matthew Jack to turn his bile on you?'

I could not argue with what he said, for I knew Matthew Jack had no love for me. 'I have no other option,' I said.

William was silent a moment. 'You have another option, you know.'

'I would be glad to hear it.'

'The masons.'

I shook my head. 'That lodge has been out of use for years. Richard Middleton took me over every inch of it on the night we found the weaver's body. There are no secrets there worth killing a man – two men – for.'

'I tell you, Alexander, the lodge the masons seek to protect is not a lodge of stone, but of the mind, and it is in that lodge that Robert Sim and his companions had begun to dabble.'

'And Bernard Cummins?'

'The laird of Crathes's father was much in the company of his kinsman, the late Chancellor, who was known to have taken some interest in the practices of the masons. His house at Pinkie was more adorned with emblems and symbols even than Crathes. He made no secret of it, and I never heard a word of the present laird involved in anything sinister, but if Cummins was studying and executing designs for his project in the castle, then . . .'

'Then?'

'Then you should tread warily, Alexander, that is all I am saying.'

'I will, but I cannot leave the matter as it stands. The faces of those dead men haunt me, and I fear they may not be the last.' I got out of my chair. 'I am going to the tolbooth.'

William shook his head. 'You cannot. There is to be a hanging on Tuesday morning – they will allow no visitors over the door until that is safely done, for fear of an escape. Go home, Alexander, take your rest in the tranquillity of the Sabbath, and leave this for a while.'

I told him I would go home, and had intended to do so, but my footsteps took me instead down past the Guestrow and eventually to the house at the top of Back Wynd that just two nights ago had been a scene of horrors. Not wishing to be seen knocking on the street door, I went down the vennel to the backland of the house. The door to the kitchen was open but there was no sign of Rachel Middleton, and no response from inside when I called out her name. It was only as I was turning to leave that I heard her voice.

'Mr Seaton!'

She was coming around the corner from the lodge, a bunch of marigolds and daisies in her hand. 'Is it Richard you are looking for? He is sleeping.'

'I hoped you might have a minute to talk to me.'

'I have many minutes. Very few seek out my company.'

She sat down on a stone bench by the side of the lodge,

below the north window, and invited me to join her. The garden was very different place from the dark and rain-lashed scene of two nights ago. Rather than the stench of blood, the smell that reached me now was of sweet aniseed from the rowan in flower above the bench. Along the south-facing wall of the house were pots of chive, mint, parsley, rosemary and sage, and the pathway from the flag-stones at the back door down to the lodge was fringed with lavender. Behind the lodge was a tangle of raspberry bushes. Kale, carrots, peas and onions grew in orderly rows, and in a bed, carefully strewn with straw and covered with netting, strawberries were coming forth from their flowers. The heavy hum of insects was cut through occasionally by the song of blackbird or thrush. Only the sound of the sea in the background, and the occasional caw of a gull spoke of a world outside this garden.

A bee, busy at a yellow rose, held my attention.

'It is untroubled by the cares of man, is it not?' she said, also watching it.

'There is perhaps a lesson there we might profit from. God's crucible is around us, in the quiet industry of His creatures, working in harmony in the earth He created. What your husband and his friends sought in their studies and experiments in the lodge was to be found not there, but outside, here.'

'It is not as it seems,' she said quietly.

I turned to her. 'How so?'

'Can you have forgotten? Two feet from where you sit

a murdered man was laid in his grave. Wickedness, evil, has reached into the heart of this garden and made it rotten.'

'The evil was in the man who came here; it is not here now.'

'Is it not? Richard, Robert and the others called it here, and I don't know if it will ever leave. But we will.'

'You are leaving?'

'We have no choice. You must have heard what people have begun to say, about me, and about Richard too. There is no safety here for us. Richard has his medical degree. It will take him anywhere. I will go with him, where we are not known, and we will start again.'

'You will remain together? After everything?'

She regarded me for a moment, weighing something up, it appeared. 'You know some of what has passed in our life, but that is only a small portion of what you would call "everything" means. We will remain together. Always.'

I was uncomfortable and I think she may have intended to make me so. I turned the conversation back to the question of her husband's career. 'Richard's degree – his medical degree – where was it conferred?'

'Heidelberg. But he travelled and studied widely after he fled the city in the face of the Imperial forces – up into northern Germany and Poland, then down through the Netherlands to Paris.'

'Where in the Netherlands?'

'Groningen, I think. Why?'

'You do not recall if he ever mentioned meeting a young Scottish weaver?'

She shook her head. 'He spoke of his friends, his studies, and something of the towns and peoples he came across, but he never mentioned a Scottish weaver. He told you himself: he never met Bernard Cummins, either in the Netherlands or here. He is in no doubt upon that point.'

'And you?'

'I?'

'Did you know Bernard Cummins?'

'I did not know him, but I knew who he was. I had heard him being spoken about, seen him pointed out – he was the kind of man women noticed. And then I saw him one day – the day before his murder – in David Melville's shop.'

'The bookseller's? What was he doing there?'

'He was talking about pattern books – there was a Dutch name, I think.'

'Did he speak to you?'

She shook her head. 'I do not seek the conversation of men I do not know.'

'I am sorry,' I said, and after an awkward moment, 'Who else was in the shop at the time?'

'No one. There was no one but me, Bernard Cummins and the bookseller.' Then she understood what I was asking. 'Do you think the weaver was followed around town before his death?'

'All I know is that nine years ago, in Leiden, he met a

Scottish student by the name of Nicholas Black, and that he met him again in the streets of this burgh only days before he was killed.'

'I know no one of that name.'

'Nor I. The man denied to Bernard Cummins that he was Nicholas Black or that he had ever seen the weaver before.'

'And who did he claim to be?'

'That, I am afraid, I do not know.'

EIGHTEEN

Jaffray's Dinner

The Sabbath passed without incident and a thorough testing of my classes on the Monday showed them not to have suffered during my latest absence, but left me with no leisure to visit Matthew Jack in the tolbooth.

Sarah was waiting for me when I returned from the college. She had left the children upstairs and come down to change out of her everyday gown in to a finer one of crisp grey cambric that in summer she wore on the Sabbath. With it she wore a simple white tucker and cuffs with the merest run of lace where her sleeves met her bare arms. She was standing before the old looking glass on the wall, her hair pushed to one side as she tied at her neck a black velvet ribbon I had brought her a year ago from Edinburgh, from which hung a small stone of agate, the best that I had been able to afford. I promised myself that one day, somehow, I would see her dressed as other women were.

She did not turn when she heard me come in, but continued to stand with her back to me and began slowly to pull the brush down through her hair.

As I watched her, and I took in her whole form, I saw what I should have noticed days, perhaps weeks ago. I saw what Jaffray had noticed in minutes: a slight broadening of her hips, a swelling below her waist. I went across the room and saw the brush go loose in her hand. She scarcely moved as she waited. I put my arm around her waist and my face into the back of her neck. Her hair was soft against my cheek and I felt the warmth of her, and of that other life, my child, under my hand.

'Why didn't you tell me?'

'Can you even ask?'

'Forgive me,' I said.

'It is forgiven.'

I turned her around and lifted her face in my two hands. 'You do not know what there is to forgive. Sarah, I have to tell you . . .'

She shook her head. 'No.'

'In Ireland.'

She threw down the brush in frustration, tears trimming her lashes. 'Do you think I do not know what happened in Ireland? Do you think I do not know you? When I see you sometimes, caught in one of your dark moments, as if the world you see is not the one I look upon, I know you have gone there in your mind.'

'You are wrong, Sarah, I seldom think of it, still more seldom of . . .' I stopped.

'Of her?' she finished for me.

'Sarah . . .'

'Don't, Alexander! I *know*, I have *always* known, that there was a woman. But that was before, before you ever asked me to be your wife, before I became your wife or bore your child. I can live with that, as I must, but I will not hear you speak her name.'

I took hold of her wrists in my hands. 'It was not love. I knew it then and I know it now, here. I know love, and it is you. It is you, Sarah. And the fear of losing you to another man has almost driven me to despair, to seek refuge in the worst of myself.'

'You will never lose me to another man, can you not see that? Please, Alexander, let us leave the names of others unspoken, in their own places, and let us be what we are, here.'

I held her to me, held my child to me, and if I could have done, I would have built a wall around our house, stone upon stone, so high that none could breach it.

We arrived early at William's house. I left Sarah with Elizabeth and went up to the parlour. The fire there had been lit for cheer as much as warmth, and William and the doctor were seated at either side of it, bent over a gaming board where William's walrus ivory chessmen were locked in combat with one another. Neither man looked up as I came into the room. 'Your bishop is in peril, Doctor,' I said.

'The bishops will be in more than peril if the king doesn't stop his meddling,' retorted the doctor, swiftly capturing William's rook with an unremarked pawn.

William shook his head, smiling. 'I am too trusting, but tomorrow night, I will be ready for you, Doctor.'

'We shall see, we shall see,' said the older man. Still he did not look directly at me, merely raising an eyebrow in my direction as he ranged his captives. 'Sarah is here I hope?'

'She is,' I said.

'And I will have no further cause for regret that I did not drown you at birth?'

'None, James. I give you my word.' I saw by William's face that I had been the subject of some earlier conference between the two, and that my appearance at the evening's gathering had been no certainty in their minds.

'Take a seat, Alexander, and I'll help you to a glass.' William went to the French carved oak cabinet in which the best glassware was kept, and produced a bottle of the finest Venetian glass into which he had already decanted what looked to be a substantial claret. He poured out three glasses, and I noticed that until that point, he and the doctor had been drinking ale from his favourite Bartmann jugs. I squinted at the jug in Jaffray's hand. 'You know, Doctor, were it not for the beard, I would say that fellow had been modelled on yourself.'

Jaffray held up the jug to his own face the closer to examine it. 'You may well be right, Alexander, and a good stout drink he holds too. I will sample your claret all the same, William.'

'That is very good of you, Doctor.'

William stood against the great sandstone over-mantel

into which his and Elizabeth's initials, with the year of their marriage, had been intricately chiselled. Jaffray, of course, sat in the master's chair, high-backed oak with two stout arms. He took a sip of the wine, and savoured it a moment before speaking again.

'William has been telling me about the terrible things that have been happening here in the town. The news of Robert Sim's death reached Banff the very next day, and I and others were sorry to hear it: he was a fine man, and knew his books. I know also that you counted him a friend, both of you, and a friend is a loss not easily made up. But William is concerned, and so am I, that Dr Dun asks too much of you in setting you to look for this killer – that is a job for the town, not the college, especially now with this second murder.'

I sought to reassure him. 'Dr Dun merely asked me to look into Robert's life, and matters in the library, in so far as they might affect the college.'

'And that has taken you already to the grave of another man with his throat cut, and away from home, to Crathes, has it not? To look into the life of a murdered man may well bring you into the path of his killer, and this is not what Sarah needs, not now. You have enough on hand at home, boy; can you not content yourself with that and leave the justice of the realm to those who are called to enforce it?'

'But there are connections that I am beginning to make that others would not see—'

Jaffray broke in, jabbing a practised finger at me. 'This arrogance is a fault in you, Alexander. "Connections!" That the weaver's name was written in the Trades' Benefaction book? So is that of practically every craftsman in the burgh of Aberdeen. Are we to fear they will all be found in shallow graves? And this foolishness of secret fraternities and the masons – I would counsel you strongly not to enmesh yourself with that. Once a man begins to believe he sees secret signs and connections, he will see them in everything.'

'But Doctor, I have a name for the man I believe murdered Bernard Cummins. If I can find that he also knew or was known to Robert Sim, all I have to do is find him. All I have to do is find Nicholas Black.'

At that moment a sound of familiar laughter reached us from the corridor and the door was opened by our friend, the painter George Jamesone, who was followed by Richard Middleton and his wife.

The doctor greeted Jamesone warmly, and waited to be introduced to those he did not know.

'This,' said William, indicating the young woman, 'is Rachel Middleton, sister to Hugh Wardlaw, the stone-mason, some of whose work you will have seen at Craigston Castle.'

'Indeed, indeed,' said the doctor. 'I took my dinner there with Urquhart only last week. The corbelling and ornaments are very fine. Very fine. And so you are a friend to Elizabeth?'

'We have not known each other well, but she has been kind enough to ask me here tonight . . .'

'And then you will be friends, do not doubt it. And this, I will wager, is your husband.'

Richard Middleton nodded his head to the older man. 'I am very happy to make your acquaintance, Doctor. You are much respected in our profession hereabouts.'

Jaffray laughed. 'I hear good things of you too, and that the burgh is fortunate to have so well-qualified a young man. You were at Basel for a time, I hear. It would have changed greatly since my day, I'm sure, but tell me, did you ever meet . . .' and he had his arm around the younger man and was leading him over to the fireplace, where he had soon placed him in my seat the better to question him about his own old faculty and the town where he himself had been so happy, over thirty years ago now.

'I fear your husband's company will be monopolised for the rest of the night.'

Rachel Middleton turned her eyes on me. 'It will do him good to be out in company, to remember happier times.'

'And you too, I think,' I said.

She looked away from me, brushed an unseen speck of dust from her dress. 'I am stronger than Richard is, and I can play the part required of me better.' I could not argue with this. The care she had dressed with was evident – a fine cinnamon-coloured satin gown, embroidered in a way that spoke of a degree of wealth that was something above comfort, an intricate silver clasp that held her chestnut hair in a manner that suggested it might tumble free at any moment, but which I suspected she knew would not, a hint of the scent of roses. Nothing to surprise in a woman of means still young enough to know that she was desirable. But any who looked more carefully, as I did, would see a slight looseness of the dress on a figure that had once been fuller and shadows under fine eyes that had slept too little and wept too much.

I was still trying to find a response when the parlour door opened once more, and Sarah entered along with Elizabeth and George Jamesone's wife, Isabel Tosh. Sarah stood next to me and I felt an old thrill, as in the days of infatuation, as her fingers played their way into my hand. 'It is good that you are here, Rachel,' she said. 'We should have been friends before now.'

'The fault lies with me.'

William's voice travelled across our heads to his wife, who was in conference with Isobel Tosh. 'Are we all here now, Elizabeth? Should we take ourselves to table?'

'We wait only on John Innes and Andrew Carmichael.'

It was not long before Elizabeth's expectations were shown to have been in vain. A knocking on the door downstairs was answered by William's steward's slow trudge and in a short time Andrew Carmichael stood before us, alone, his hat in his hands and his boots dusty from the walk down from the Old Town. 'He would not be persuaded. I had the Devil's own job to get him to open the door to me.'

'Is he still as bad?' I asked.

Carmichael rubbed a hand over tired eyes. 'Worse,' he said. 'He has not taken a class in days, and I do not know that he has eaten in as long either. Principal Rait is concerned about him, and I think his patience is close to wearing thin.'

'Has he seen a physician?' This from Jaffray.

'He will let no one near . . .'

'I have been to see him,' said Richard Middleton. 'But I have not been able to go to the Old Town since the night of Matthew Jack's attack. Rachel will not let me out of her sight.'

'And quite right she is,' said Jaffray. 'Have you let anyone else have a look at that wound?' Even in the candlelight, Richard Middleton was as white as alabaster, and the short journey from his home to the Cargills' had evidently exhausted him.

'Dr Dun has been over to the house every day.'

'Then I shall not meddle in his treatment of you, but mind what your wife says – the King's College would be too long a walk or ride for one in your condition. As to John Innes, I do not like what I hear. I know enough about young men who shut themselves away in their rooms with a mind to have no more to do with the world. You will take me up to him tomorrow, will you not, Alexander?'

'Gladly, once my morning classes are finished.'

The last of the introductions were made – Jaffray had met Andrew Carmichael once or twice before, at William's house and elsewhere, but Carmichael and the Middletons did not know each other. We were soon seated around the long refectory table to which a great quantity of food had been brought. There was the commotion usual to such gatherings over the matter of seating, although I knew from experience that Elizabeth would have a firm plan in her mind which we would all eventually be brought to adhere to. However, her plan on this occasion was set awry at the last minute by George Jamesone, too busy running an eye over a majolica bowl William had lately bought in Edinburgh to pay proper attention to where he sat. 'You have taken Sarah's seat, George,' Elizabeth gently chided him.

'Oh, have I?' he said in his good-natured, absent way. 'You know, this really is a marvellous bowl.' He continued to turn the piece in his hands and unconsciously settled himself all the more in the place where my wife should have been seated.

Elizabeth opened her mouth to remonstrate with him more firmly, but Sarah, sensing that the issue was already drawing more attention than was comfortable, indicated by the slightest movement of her hand that she would take the place that should have been Jamesone's. I felt the familiar hard tug in the pit of my stomach, that I had so promised myself I would master, to see her sit down at Andrew Carmichael's left hand.

The first course was dealt with with some gusto, and before we set to the fish, Elizabeth handed round a tray of sherbets.

The doctor beamed like a child. 'Truly, Elizabeth, you

turn the simplest of fruits into something beyond my powers to describe. You are an alchemist.'

'I am but a mere housewife,' she said. 'It is Dr Middleton here who is the alchemist.'

Interested, Jaffray shifted his attention to the young man directly opposite him. 'Is it so? Do you follow the method of Paracelsus?'

'Certainly, as a physician, I employ the method of Paracelsus where I can.' He leaned forward, that Jaffray might hear him better, and winced as a dart of pain shot through him.

'Please, do not trouble yourself,' said the old doctor.

'No, no, I am fine,' Middleton replied, 'and it is pleasant to talk on matters that interest me. Rachel has forbidden all mention of my old interests until I am recovered . . .'

'See the pass they have brought you to, these "old interests", your "fraternity",' said his wife with more scorn than she may have intended. 'You and others.'

Jaffray feigned an ignorance I knew he did not have. William had apprised him fully of the nature of Robert Sim's activities and interests before his death. He could play the part of the old man well, when required. 'A fraternity – I well remember some of the fraternities at Basel and Helmstedt. I could not stomach half the food or a quarter of the beer now that we did then, and it seems to me looking back that we did not sleep at all. Your wife is right, Dr Middleton: such fraternities are not good for your health.'

'It is quite another fraternity of which my husband has been part,' said Rachel quietly. She looked around the table. 'I would ask you to join with me in begging him to have no more to do with the activities at my late brother's lodge that have already led to the deaths of Robert Sim and the weaver Bernard Cummins.'

George Jamesone looked up from his meat, frowning. 'Your brother the stonemason? I had thought the lodge disused.'

'It had been so, for years,' said Middleton. 'But last winter I uncovered some signs of what I suspected were its ceremonial uses from the time when my brother-in-law lodged his workers there. The discovery reawakened my interest in Hermetic knowledge, and I was not long in finding others of a like mind. We began to pursue our studies together, rather than individually. The lodge made for an appropriate meeting place.'

Jamesone shook his head. 'For the pursuit of secret knowledge. No, secret places are not where secret knowledge is to be found, but in the open. Take yourself to the Castlegate on market day, to the kirkyard after the sermon, to the harbour when the merchants are waiting for their cargoes to come in. Look in the faces of men and women – watch their eyes, the glances, the small movements of their hands. Who do they hate, fear, love? I tell you, you need not an alchemist's laboratory or a hidden lodge – this town is a crucible of secrets, and those secrets are to be found in the faces of the men who keep them.'

'You misunderstand me,' said Middleton. 'The alchemist seeks to isolate the essence of the object of his study, so that by knowing the essence, he may also find the agent of change, which will redeem corrupted matter and restore it to what God intended it should be.'

'I think we take too much upon ourselves,' said Andrew Carmichael quietly, 'if we claim to know the intentions of God. The wrong agency, the wrong element, will corrupt just as the true one will redeem.'

'Indeed,' said Jaffray. 'But you and I will talk of this again, Dr Middleton, for it is an interesting subject, and I would know more of how you have been able to apply your findings to your work.' He turned kindly to Rachel. 'Your husband and I can have our talk some time when you are not present, my dear, for I see the subject has set you ill at ease.'

'It is just that I have heard too much of this talk already, from Richard and from Robert, too, and I fear that that talk has already cost them much, or will call attention on us that will do us little good.'

It was a little after this that Jaffray inclined his head towards me and muttered, more audibly than I felt was comfortable, 'That fellow is giving me the evil eye.'

I held my glass up to the side of my face and brought my own voice to a considerably lower level. 'Who? Middleton? Carmichael?'

'What?' He frowned in exasperation then suppressed a rumble of laughter. 'No, not them, the fish. That fellow there on the wall,' he said, helping himself to another slab of salmon from the platter in front of him. 'I feel he is threatening revenge on my every mouthful.'

In the dim candlelight, I had not noticed the painting on the wall opposite me. Everyone now looked to see what the doctor was talking about.

'Oh, that!' Elizabeth spoke with disgust. 'I can scarcely look at it – that is why I have the room so badly lit on that side.'

I could not but agree with her that the painting, however fine the brushwork, was indeed an ugly thing. The carcass of what had once been a trout lay, butchered, on an earthenware platter. On the slab beside it were two smaller fish and fresh cut slices of raw salmon. Hanging on hooks above the grisly tableau were ready-gutted flounders. The baleful dead eye of the trout did appear to favour Jaffray, and it would not have shocked me greatly to learn the next day that he had been ill half the night.

'To think,' Elizabeth continued, 'of all the times you have travelled to the Netherlands and I have pleaded with you to bring back something pleasing, some study of fruit and flowers – for Isobel tells me they are much in vogue amongst the Dutch – and at last you bring back this.' She waved her hand in disdain at the gilt-framed canvas on the wall.

'Mind you,' said the doctor, 'I have seen worse. On a window of the St Janskerk in Gouda, in size and colour quite horrible, is depicted the whale disgorging Jonah. I could scarcely look on the thing. Have you seen it, William?'

A shake of the head.

'I was never that far north,' said Carmichael, 'but I have heard that is a prodigiously ugly beast to be found adorning a kirk.'

And so the evening went on in companionship and increasing good humour, and as was so often the case on such occasions, conversation eventually turned to reminiscence and to tales of William and me in our younger days, a favourite topic of the doctor's. He recounted fondly the difficulties of William's courtship of Elizabeth, and the loneliness of their separation for the four years of his law studies in Leiden.

'Now *there* was a place where such matters were dealt with more efficiently,' murmured William, passing a bottle down the table. 'A courtship of nigh on eight years would not be heard of in the Netherlands: there is an anxiety on the part of Dutch mothers to get their daughters off their hands that is altogether commendable.'

And so the company fell to discussing Dutch practice, and the women became more and more outraged as William, Richard Middleton and Andrew Carmichael outdid each other in the telling of raucous tales. Stories from Schermerhorn of the collusion of the community in plying young girls with intoxicating beverages that they might look the more kindly on potential bridegrooms, or Schagen, where the young women themselves paid for entrance to a field where they were enclosed for inspection like cattle at a mart, were as nothing to Carmichael's recollection of a night he had spent in the home of a friend on the Frisian island of Texel. We listened with increasing disbelief as he told of the family's acquiescence in their daughter's suitor's breaking into the girl's bedroom in the dead of night. They had then invited Carmichael to join them in listening at the bedroom door as the lover pursued his quarry. Only when the young man's ardour became too great would the girl summon her family's assistance by beating ferociously with a pair of tongs on an iron cauldron set by her bed for that express purpose. Andrew was a born story-teller, and revelled in the telling of the tale, but he could hardly get to the end of it as William and the doctor were by now laughing uproariously, and Rachel and Richard Middleton were not long in joining them.

Then Jaffray began to reminisce, with much embellishment of his difficulties, on his courtship of his own late wife, and as he did so I watched my own. There were no tales I could tell to amuse of the days before Sarah had become my wife. There would be little joy for either of us in my relating the indecision and uncertainty that had cost me two years with her, her visceral grief when she had thought I was dead, and the spectres of that time that I had allowed to haunt our marriage since, one of whom was sitting across William's table from me, and could have no comfort in his own reflections on courtship. I caught him, in an unguarded moment, looking at her, and then he looked to me, and in that look was a final admission of defeat.

Talk turned then to other strange customs of the Dutch, including the new fashion there for the drinking of tea.

Jaffray shook his head sadly. 'Indeed. I heard only last week from Webster in Haarlem that it is the foulest concoction of herbs he has ever been forced to swallow, and should be kept for the sick bed and that alone. He has utterly forbidden his wife to have it in the house.'

'I fear the gentleman will be in the minority, Doctor,' said Andrew Carmichael, 'for Dutch matrons have developed a great liking for it, and it is commonly said, "*Buyter en Brae en t'zijs goe Huwsmanne spijs*" – butter, bread and green tea is a good houseman's food.'

'Then I can only thank the good Lord that He did not make me a Dutch houseman,' replied the doctor, shuddering as he swallowed down another glass of wine.

As time wore on, fatigue became more and more evident in Richard Middleton's face, and despite his protests, the urging of his wife and of Jaffray prevailed. Jaffray promised to visit his younger colleague in the morning, and William helped him on with his cloak. 'I will see them safe home,' I heard William say to Elizabeth as the Middletons made their final farewells.

In the brief silence that followed, Sarah yawned and Andrew Carmichael was on his feet in a moment. 'I too should be leaving. I will hear overmuch about it from the porter if I am not back within the gates of the King's College soon.'

'Will you at least not wait until William returns, and have one last drink with us?'

Carmichael smiled his appreciation but shook his head. 'I fear Alexander's wife has been tired out by all of this, and I would not be the cause of her discomfort.' Then he bade us all a good evening, her last of all. 'Good night, Sarah,' he said.

'Goodnight, Mr Carmichael.'

Elizabeth persuaded Sarah to lie down in her old room, where our children were already sleeping, and then retired with Isobel Tosh down to the kitchen, to show the painter's wife a crewel-work hanging they had been working on together.

'I should have come with you,' I said, when William returned at last.

He held up a hand. 'No need. I helped get Richard to his bed and then I went around the place – that damned lodge too – to check that all was locked and secure. Rachel Middleton's fears grew with every step we made closer to the house.'

'How far was she involved in this . . . "fraternity"?' asked Jamesone.

It was a question I had been beginning to wonder about myself. 'All she knew was that her husband and his friends met in her brother's old lodge to talk and study together. The rest she has learned since.'

'You believe her?'

'I see no reason for her to have lied about it.'

Jamesone raised his eyebrows but said nothing more.

'Mathematics and theology leading to alchemy and Cabbala.' Jaffray sighed heavily. 'I have never understood why men have endlessly sought God and the right way of living in His world in secret books, arcane symbols, when it is made so freely available to us all, in the one Book.'

'Not all men see so clearly, Doctor. They must always convince themselves that there is something hidden.'

'And they believed the keys to this hidden knowledge were somehow to be found in a stonemasons' lodge?'

'They are not alone in that,' said Jamesone, 'and that is my concern for the three who are left, and for Rachel Middleton.'

A thought struck me. 'You too are an adept?'

The painter smiled and shook his head. 'Not in the manner of these young men of your fraternity. But I am a painter, a simple craftsman. My first training, like that of any painter, was not in how to paint a duchess's face, a bowl of fruit or flowers, or, with respect to our host's impeccable taste, a dead fish, but a wall. Plain and simple. And what gives a craftsman his strength – the protection of his craft from interlopers, untrained charlatans, those who would undermine his living? What gives the craftsman his voice, his public face in burgh and kirk?'

'The guild, of course,' I said.

He nodded. 'That's right, the guild. And yet, there is no painters' guild.'

William was beginning to smile. 'I had forgotten, but I remember now. George is a mason, Alexander. Like the plumbers and the carpenters, the painters are part of the masons' guild.'

I stared at him. 'So you know the secrets of which we speak? You know what it is they are looking for?'

'I know the symbols and the words, I can walk through the house of memory as any mason must do and unlock for myself the meanings of what I find in the rooms of that lodge of the mind. Ultimately, it is the lodge of the mind that holds the secrets of the architects of the pyramid, of the builders of Solomon's temple. Richard Middleton and his friends may root around in their lodge for many a long year, but they will not find the knowledge they seek there.'

'I think they had begun to,' I said.

'What do you mean?'

There were only four of us in the room now, all good friends, all of whom I would trust with my life. And so I said, out loud, Jachin and Boaz, the Mason Word.

Jamesone's face blanched. 'Alexander, where did you hear that?'

'I found it, written down, hidden away in Robert Sim's room when I searched it after his death.'

'Do you think he had told the others?'

'No. Certainly neither Richard Middleton nor Patrick Urquhart had had it from him, and as for John Innes – well, I have not been able to ask him.'

I could see Jamesone's mind was working away at something. 'I wonder if he mentioned it to Rachel?'

'She did speak tonight of having heard more of the fraternity's business from her husband and from Robert than she wished to.'

Jamesone was pensive. 'It makes me fear for her. She should be careful to tell no one else that Robert had begun to make her privy to his discoveries, and I think she may need greater protection than her wounded husband can afford her.'

'Is it really so dangerous?'

'I hope to God that it is not. The men of my lodge are good and honest, and hard-working. They tolerate me for my craft's sake, although I move in circles now that most of my fellow painters in the town do not. But they know that I am a craftsman, and not some gentleman dilettante such as those that have begun to infiltrate the lodges around Edinburgh. They will not like this meddling in their business by this so-called fraternity.'

My throat was becoming dry. 'What might they do?'

'A quiet warning, if anything at all, would be in the nature of the men I know. They would have no truck to do with the other things.'

'What other things?' asked William gravely.

Jamesone looked in to his wine cup and then set it aside. 'The punishment promised at the initiation ceremony to those who give away the Mason Word is that they will have their throat cut from ear to ear.'

NINETEEN

Scotsmen, Rats and Lice

It was with a pounding head and a mouth as dry as a haystack in August that I entered the lecture room the next morning. The college well was rank and scaly in the summer months and best avoided. I asked a bursar to bring me a jug of ale from the college brewery, but could not look at it when it came. My enthusiasm for discussing my thoughts on Aristotle's *Ethics* or Aquinas' exposition of them was only marginally less than that of my students, who were buzzing with talk of the hanging that was to take place that day, and the prospects of its being followed by that of their erstwhile tormentor and former regent at the college, Matthew Jack. After struggling through the first page of my lecture notes, I gave up, and set them a proposition to argue amongst themselves instead. I took myself to the back of the room and a place out of the sunlight, where I lay down on a bench behind my scholars and hoped for rest.

I heard some sniggering from those closest to me. 'It is the heat,' I heard one say to another. 'It is sending them all to the Devil. Not just Mr Jack – may Beelzebub welcome him with open arms – but the rest of them, too. John Innes at the King's College has gone mad.'

'Mr Innes? The one like a monk? No – he has not the capacity.'

'I tell you he has. I had it from my cousin who is in the first class there: he has barred himself up in his room and shrieks about devils and angels.'

'Do you think it is him?' hissed another in a loud whisper, clearly thinking I was asleep.

'Who? Mr Seaton?'

'No. Mr Innes.'

'Him what?'

'Killing people. The librarian and that weaver.'

'No,' came another. 'It was a doctor. I heard one of the college servants talking about it. Both of them. With a scalpel.'

'Maybe it was Dr Dun!' More sniggering.

'Don't be daft.'

I hauled myself up and roared at them. 'One more word of this and you will all be in the tolbooth yourselves. *Nicomachean Ethics*. Book Five: *Justice*.' And I marched up to the front of the class, reinvigorated, and lectured them without pause for the next hour and a half.

By the time we reached the dinner hall, I think my scholars were as convinced that I was fully as mad as they believed John Innes to be. In the course of ten days they had seen me gradually – or perhaps not so gradually – transformed from a careful and diligent teacher to one who could disappear from the lecture room for hours or indeed days at a time, and on each return to them have become something else: a dejected creature, a misanthrope, a raving drunkard, a disciplinarian of so little cheer that it would have put Matthew Jack to shame.

'You are preoccupied, Alexander,' said Dr Dun as I took my seat beside him at the top table.

'What? Yes. I think I have not been the best of teachers to my students of late; they deserve better of me, but I am not certain how I can give it.'

'They have not been neglected in your absences – John Strachan has done well by them, and besides, it is well known you had taken your scholars through their courses by the end of May and spent the last month rehearsing with them what they have already been taught.'

'It is not that that concerns me. You have told us often that we regents and professors are *in loco parentis* to these boys. What has happened here these last days has affected them more closely than I had troubled myself to consider. They know so little about what lies behind Robert's death . . .'

'As little as we do ourselves.'

'Yes. And they fill their ignorance with wild imaginings – and who can blame them?'

'Not I,' sighed Dr Dun, 'and not some of their parents either. Look around the tables.'

I did so, properly, for the first time in days. The tables occupied by the lower classes were much more sparsely occupied than was usual.

'Their parents have been calling them home. It is perhaps a blessing – although not a blessing we would have looked for – that Robert's murder and the derangement of Matthew Jack have occurred now, so close to the vacation. Had so many of our students begun to desert us in the middle of the year, we might have had to close our doors, and as we know from what has happened in the German lands, colleges and universities so forced to close their doors might never open them again.'

I knew it well. 'I have become too concerned with things that have happened outside these walls to the detriment of those still within them.'

'The fault is mine,' said the principal. 'I have asked too much of you, these last weeks, and our friend Dr Jaffray is of the same opinion.'

'Jaffray?'

'I spent a pleasant hour with the doctor this morning. Your health—' the principal's hesitation as he searched for the last word suggested to me that 'state of mind' was more likely to have been Jaffray's phrase – 'is of great concern to him.'

'It need not be,' I said. 'Besides, he shouldn't bring his fears over me to you – you have enough to occupy yourself here and at the King's College without taking thought over me.'

Dr Dun smiled. 'But I do, Alexander. I value the counsel of my old friend as much now as I did twenty years ago. If James Jaffray brings his concerns over you to me, then

I am duty bound to listen to him.' He cleared his throat. 'We can do nothing more for Robert now, and we must leave the burgh and the forces of the law to deal with what does not concern us. The matter of Malcolm Urquhart has been happily resolved by your visit to Crathes. I am grateful for what you have done in attempting to uncover Robert's killer and to protect the college interest, but it has gone far enough, too far for you.'

'Dr Dun,' I protested, 'I wish to finish what I have—'

He held up a hand to silence me. 'No. You are finished with it. See to your scholars. See to your health and to your family.'

'But . . .' I was almost at a loss. 'This afternoon I am to go with Jaffray to the King's College to see John Innes. John has not been well, he—'

Again he stopped me. 'Jaffray has told me all about it. I am Mediciner of the King's College, and I have known that boy for years. *I* am going with Jaffray to see him this afternoon. You are to stay here and to concern yourself no further in these matters.'

I opened my mouth but was not permitted to speak.

'Look to your students, Alexander.'

His meal scarcely begun, Dr Dun wiped his hands on his napkin, pushed back his chair and, to the mild curiosity of the rest of the teachers ranged along the table, left.

It was two o'clock before I had gone round my whole class and checked their notes of the morning's lecture. I took time to discuss with each of them, in small groups of two or three, any misunderstandings they might have. By the time I released them to go to their chambers and study what they had learned I felt that at least some of the damage caused by my erratic behaviour of the last week had been set right, and I promised myself that I would scrape together whatever Sarah and I could spare to provide a supper for them in the graduation week. Checking that at least one of my fellow regents would be remaining in the college for the afternoon, I passed out of the gates, telling the porter that I was going home, and should be returned before five o'clock. Once out of sight of the college gates, I turned not right, to the close that would take me to my own home, but left, and cut through a long vennel joining Netherkirk-gate to the Shiprow. From there, safely hidden from the view of any gateman who still might have an interest in me, I strolled casually up to the Castlegate and across to the tolbooth, where my college robes gained me access, without over-much questioning, to the cell in which Matthew Jack was held.

The place was strangely silent today. On my previous, rare, visits to this stinking place, usually to stand caution for a student caught with a harlot or in a drunken brawl, the grille at every cell door had been filled by the sneering or broken faces of those behind it whose manacles gave them the freedom still to walk. Today, there were no faces at the doors, no snarling insults or desperate pleas for money or for justice, instead just the occasional cough, groan, or shuffle of feet and clink of chains against the stone floor.

'What has happened?' I asked the guard who was leading me up the turnpike to Jack's cell.

'They are always like this on these days. Gives us a bit of peace for a while.'

'What days?'

'What days?' He turned to me in astonishment, his lamp swinging above me on the narrow stair as he did so. 'The hanging days.'

I had forgotten. The servant of a landward laird had been hanged for the murder of another. 'Makes them all realise that God's judgement is closer than they thought. They soon forget, mind you. Not your fellow, though. God's judgement is never off his lips. I've slept through shorter sermons in the kirk, and better ones, too, than I've heard from that quarter. The other prisoners would rather hunker down six to a cell than share one with him.'

We had come to a small door at the end of a short corridor on the topmost floor of the tolbooth. As he pulled back the bolt the guard said, 'We have him bound to the gad, hand and foot, but I'll stay in with you if you like. I wouldn't be alone two minutes with that fellow for all the harlots in Aberdeen.'

'It's all right,' I said. 'I have no fear of Matthew Jack.'

The man looked at me a moment as if I had said I had no fear of the Devil, then shrugged his shoulders and told me to shout for help if I needed it, before turning back down the stairs and taking with him his lamp.

I pushed open the door carefully, and took a moment before stepping into the place to let my eyes adjust to what light there was. I had never been this far up the tolbooth before. The smell as I had come up the stairs had been bad enough – it had worsened with every step that took me from the doors at the bottom and the occasional draught of less putrid air it allowed in from outside – but what assailed my senses now was rank beyond belief. The straw piled on the floor was thicker than any I had seen in other cells, caverns, dungeons in this place or elsewhere – so deep my foot sank to ankle level when I first stepped upon it and when I lifted it again, such filth clung to my boot that I would not have expected had I stood in a drain in the tanners' yard. I realised that the extra depth of the straw here was not for the comfort of the prisoner, but because the guards never cared to spend long enough in this cell to lift it. The worst of the smell came from a pot in the corner that had been over-turned to send its noxious contents seeping into the sludge on the floor. I could barely hear the screeching of the gulls in the marketplace below for the buzzing of flies. And in the middle of it all, looking more as if he belonged there than any other human creature could have done, was Matthew Jack.

I swallowed, trying not to gag on the air as I readied myself to speak. But Jack was accustomed to his own

surrounds and needed no such preparation. He greeted me
with a guttural laugh.

'Alexander Seaton. Patrick Dun's lackey. What pleasure
it must give you to see me here.'

'To see a man reduce himself to a level worse than the
beasts? You have brought yourself here, and it gives me no
pleasure to see that, for I know what has been suffered by
good men and women, boys too, that brought you to this
pass. I would see you walk free on the streets and spare
them the harm you have done them.'

'Harm? You speak of harm? I have been cleansing them,
cleansing them of their looseness, their backsliding and
depravity. You look on me and see me in filth, but I am clean,
Seaton, clean. It is this town, *your* college, that crawl with dirt,
that suppurate with the sores of sloth and immorality. You
stand there in your regent's gown, as if that will protect you
from the infection, the noxious spores that pass through the
air from one to another of the citizens of this cesspit. Look
at your fine collar the whore your wife thinks so white – the
smudges and smears of the Devil's fingers have wrung it out
for her. Feel the cut of the good black stuff of your jacket. It
crawls with the beasts of the midden you walk through every
day. The worms are in your skin, they penetrate your skull
and feed on the rot of your mind. Do you feel them writhing
there, Seaton? Do you long to gouge them out?'

It was only with the greatest effort that I could keep my
fingers from going to my head to relieve the intense itch
that had started to creep under my hair.

'You are sick, Jack,' I said.

'Then take care you do not become infected.' He turned his head from me and began to pick at a sore on his arm. After a moment, he looked up. 'Still here, Seaton? What do you want?' Then a slow smile spread across his face. 'I know what you want. You want to know what I know.'

I pushed the door to behind me, and took a step further into the cell, provoking creatures in the matted straw to scuttle to an even darker corner. 'Yes, Matthew, you are right. I want to know what you know about Nicholas Black.'

He raised his eyebrows in surprise – genuine or otherwise, I could not tell. 'Nicholas Black? Now why should I know anything about Nicholas Black?'

'Because you know about everyone, every Scot who went to Europe from the time you left Edinburgh to the time you appeared here. Fifteen years later. No one has been safe from your insinuations, your sly hints as to knowledge of their past. Everyone knows that there is not a university town in reformed Europe that has not seen you in its lecture halls, had you in its kirk.'

'You misrepresent me, Seaton.'

'Do not belittle yourself, Jack. No one that has returned here from the continent has escaped the poison of your innuendo.'

'Oh, I do not belittle myself – you have misunderstood me, *Mr* Seaton. You talk of fifteen years. A minor detail, but inaccurate. After I graduated from the town's college in Edinburgh and set sail for Danzig, I was away from Scotland thirteen years. True though, those thirteen years I took note of everything, everything, there was to be known of my fellow countrymen abroad. Not simply those that were there when I was, but those who had gone before me and left something of their story behind them. And there were so many.' He laughed to himself and then caught me with his direct look. 'You know what the Poles say, don't you, Seaton? About finding Scotsmen, rats and lice the world over? Well, every louse-ridden inn I stopped at, every barn I slept in that had rodents scuttling in its rafters, had a story for me of some fellow Scot who had been there before me. For years, Seaton. Years.' Such was the venom in his voice now that he almost spat the last words. 'Our sainted principal, Dr Dun – I could tell you of him at Heidelberg.'

I sought to forestall his malice. 'Dr Dun only stayed a very little while at Heidelberg.'

He leered through the dim light. 'Have you ever wondered *why*, Seaton? And your dear, dear friend Dr Jaffray – so tragic that he could never father a child on his wife, when there is more than one bastard in France with the look of a Banff physician in his eye.'

'You lie.' My mouth was dry and the words would hardly come from my throat.

'Do I? Ask him. You are so well acquainted with the sons of whores yourself, it should give you much to talk about.'

I thought I might kill him. Had he not been bound, hand and foot to the iron gad that ran the length of the room,

I might have killed him. Instead I walked to the one small aperture in the wall, blocked by two iron bars, that allowed a breath of air, a glimpse of light into the place. I gripped one of the bars, my fingers so hard and fast around it that my nails cut in to my own palms.

'Tell me about Nicholas Black,' I said through gritted teeth.

He affected an airy disappointment. 'Oh? You do not wish to hear of the associations of our venerable advocate, William Cargill, so respectable now? Or of the pastimes of Andrew Carmichael at Breslau, Frankfurt and elsewhere, before he took ship for Aberdeen, to practise his continental manners on your wife . . .'

Before I knew I had moved, my hands were round his throat. 'Tell me about Nicholas Black,' I said again, 'or I swear before God I will strangle you with my own two hands and save the hangman a job. What do you know of Nicholas Black?'

He managed to make some sound escape his throat that suggested he would co-operate, and I loosened my grip enough to let him speak. It was a moment before he could. 'All right, all right, I will tell you.'

I let go his neck and went to stand in front of him. 'Well?'

He put a manacled hand to his throat and rubbed where my fingers had left their imprint. He swallowed and it gave me some pleasure to see that it gave him pain.

'It was only once, at Rotterdam. I had gone there to hear the minister preach on—'

'I am not interested in the sermon. Tell me about Nicholas Black.'

Jack gave one more meaningful rub to his neck. 'All right. Let me think then. It was eight, no, nine years ago. I had left Leiden and was making my way down through the Low Countries to Paris. While I was in Rotterdam I went by the Scots factor's office, to send some letters back to Edinburgh and to see to a transfer of funds. The factor's office was thronged with Scots booking passages home, or arriving and waving around their letters of commendation, seeking to find others who might be travelling their way. Nicholas Black was there. I caught his name as one who had given up his place on a ship bound for Leith, and was ready to sell his passage to another. A young physician returning from Montpellier paid him well for his place.'

'What did he look like?'

'Black?'

'Of course.'

'Like one who did not need the money. The young physician was clad in threadbare robes and patched breeches, while Black was finely dressed: he should have given up his place for free.'

I almost spat in exasperation. 'Not his clothes, man – his hair, his eyes, his stature.'

'Ah.' Jack paused so infuriatingly that I thought I might set my hands to his throat again. He caught the look in my eye and thought better of his play-acting. 'He was of middling height. Small, perhaps, but of stocky frame. Fair hair, cut short, and a close-trimmed beard. As to his eyes, I cannot tell you. We were not so close as I would have noticed.'

'His age?'

'He would be yours now, though better worn.'

I whirled the description through my mind, but it could have been anyone or no one. 'Have you ever seen this man in Aberdeen?'

'Never.'

'And the physician who bought his place?'

'Never. And before you ask it, I do not know his name.'

'Where did Black go after he gave up his passage?'

'I heard him laugh and say it was to Franeker. A suitable place, no doubt, for a rich man's son. Known for the licentiousness of its students. There were riots among them a year later. No doubt he was amongst them.'

I saw now that Jack was reverting to his favoured pastime of malicious speculation, and that I would get little else of use from him. But there was one more thing I wished to know.

'And you, where did you go then?'

He raised his chin, a hint of triumph glinting in his eye. 'Surely your good friend Dr Middleton has told you that.'

'To Paris,' I said.

'Indeed. Middleton and his associates had no time for the acquaintance of one such as I. But I returned their gracious friendship, in kind.'

'You accused them of witchcraft.'

He affected a hurt expression. 'Indeed, I did not. But imagine my surprise a few months after my arrival to hear rumours of a secret brotherhood come to the city, travelling in disguise. A Rosicrucian fraternity. Now, the good citizens of Paris did not like the sound of agents of the dark arts moving around their city in disguise. They began to fear very greatly what evils the sorcery of such agents might procure. I felt it only my duty to inform them that in their midst, a practising physician, and one following the alchemical practices of the order, was one who had openly professed himself a Rosicrucian in Heidelberg several years before. That the citizens of Paris did not like this, and that your friend Dr Middleton decided to flee rather than persuade them to his case, is none of my affair.'

It dawned on me then that Jack knew nothing. He spoke only in malice and built great edifices of vitriol and innuendo from the few scraps of information he could scramble together. And he had been doing this for years. I had been wasting my time, and I told him so. This time, a look of real hatred replaced the habitual sneer. 'I know nothing? I know things people would not have me know. You think alchemy is the only unnatural practice Richard Middleton indulges in?'

His laughter followed me as I went to the door and shouted for the guard. Even after the door had been bolted behind me, I could still hear him. 'You will be sorry, Seaton. You and your college and this whole accursed town – you will be sorry you did not listen.'

Once down the stairs and out at last of the tolbooth, I leant against the wall and took lungsfull of air. Never had the air of the Castlegate, with its mixed odours of seaweed, fish, spices and cheeses, vegetables warming in the afternoon sun, and the constant throng of people, tasted so clean and sweet. I pushed my way through to the apothecary's shop and bought a packet of lavender which I crushed in my hands and rubbed all over my skin and clothes. And then I went home, to try to wash away the traces of the dirt, the infection that was Matthew Jack.

TWENTY

The Devil's Angel

Dr Dun was not in his usual place in the dining-hall for supper, and I did not see him return to the college until I was leading my scholars into the common school for evening prayers. His shoes were dusty and his face flushed, and I guessed he was not long returned from his visit with Jaffray to John Innes at the King's College. I tried to move quietly towards him as the youngest bursar read from the first book of Kings, telling of the building of Solomon's temple, and Hiram's casting of its pillars. Where, where in the Word did it speak of secret knowledge in these pillars? Nowhere – a distraction, an invention of man. I had begun to wonder if that was what all this talk of the masons' lodge was – a distraction, a stone that instead of revealing the truth, was placed to obscure it.

'Well, Alexander,' said the principal as I reached him by the door, 'this afternoon has passed without incident, I hear. Perhaps our college life is returning to what it should be.'

'It can hardly do that, while Robert's killer might still walk amongst us.'

'No,' he conceded, 'but as you yourself have said, over-much dwelling on the events of the last week is not good.'

'You have seen John Innes?'

He pursed his lips. 'I have, and it is not a sight such as I hope to see again within the walls of either the King's College or this one.'

'He is no better?'

'I do not know how bad his condition was when last you left him, but it can hardly have been worse than what Jaffray and I found today. It should have been dealt with before now, long before now.'

His tone left no doubt that he held me complicit in the state John Innes had been allowed to fall into, and I could argue nothing in my defence: all my interest in John had been in what he could tell me regarding Robert Sim. Had I gone to him in any other circumstances and found him as I had done, I would not have left off until I had seen him get the help he evidently needed. I struggled for a response that would not come. The porter brought some message and it was too late, the principal was gone.

It was after eight by the time I left the college, but I was not ready to go directly home. Instead, I let my steps take me down to William's house, where I found him by the empty hearth in his study, deep in conversation with Jaffray. The doctor looked weary, and something in William's face told me he was glad to see me.

'Alexander, we had not looked for you tonight.'

'I wanted to speak with the doctor here before I went home, to ask after John Innes; the principal told me little, other than that he was in a very bad state.'

'Take my seat here then,' said William, 'and I'll get you a glass.' My friend nodded in the direction of a thick brieve lying on the table. 'I have to look that over before tomorrow. I will be in the parlour. Call upon me before you leave.'

'Tell me what you found,' I said, as he left and I took his seat opposite Jaffray and filled both our glasses.

Jaffray took a long drink before he spoke. 'I have seen many men, too many, near to the end of their wits and beyond it, but few in as bad a state as John Innes. He would not let us in at first, though Dr Dun pleaded and then ordered him too. Andrew Carmichael came, and tried to persuade him, but to no avail. Eventually Carmichael went for another regent and between them they broke the door down. And then the stench, Alexander, the stench – as bad as I have known in the meanest hovel. There had not been a breath of air in the place for days. I do not know when he last ate – Carmichael says the trays he has left at the door the last two days had gone untouched. There was rotting and mouldering food on the floor of the place, flies, maggots. The only water was in a jug of brown stuff, warm and brimming with insects. I think he had taken some ale. The skin was hanging from his bones, and the clothes we took from him were only fit for burning.'

'He let you undress him?'

'He would hardly let us look at him to start with, never mind come anywhere near him. He was shrieking about black magic and agents of the Devil, calling on his angels not to abandon him.'

'The Devil's angels?'

Jaffray shook his head and swallowed down more of the wine. 'No, his own. He had become convinced, we gathered at last, that his every movement was guided by angels, but that they would only talk with him while he was alone. When we got some light in the place we saw scattered everywhere books and tracts on the Cabbala. Symbols, words he thought his angel words were scrawled in ink on the walls, in the dirt on the floor. He thought they would protect him.'

'From what?'

'From whatever – and he was very clear it was a "what" and not a "who"– had killed Robert Sim. Robert had not followed the Cabbala, had not trusted in the angels you see. They had spoken of it, it would seem, on the morning before Robert's death . . .'

'In the library,' I said. 'John had been in consulting a work on Vitruvius. I had thought his interest was in architecture.'

'His interest was in everything, and that was the trouble.' He looked up at me. 'Your friend John has not had an . . . eventful life, has he, Alexander?'

'Eventful? No,' I said, 'I would not call it eventful.'

'He arrived in the King's College, Dr Dun tells me, at the same time as you yourself did.'

'Yes, and William too. But I do not follow you.'

'Unlike the rest of you, he has never left it. Now, I know as well as you do yourself, that your fortunes have not always been what they are now, that you have known disgrace and failure. You have lived; you have loved. John has never experienced loss because he has never had love; he has never known failure because he never aimed at success. He has known nothing of the world not bounded by the sea and the two rivers that encompass these two towns of Aberdeen. This fraternity, this study – call it Rosicrucian, call it Hermetic, call it dabbling in the secrets of the masons – call it what you will, it opened doors of wonder and possibility to him. And so he lighted like a sparrow on one topic before flying to the next, trying to encompass it all and in the process understanding very little. The others took seriously their study for that study's sake, but John believed every word of promise, of the fantasy of the *Fama*. And then he kept rambling about a book.'

'A book?'

'He was very anxious about it. We could get very little sense out of him. All he would say at first was, "She hasn't brought the book; she said she would bring the book and she hasn't brought the book."'

'Rachel Middleton?'

The doctor nodded. 'Eventually we got out of him that

Rachel Middleton had been to see him on the day after Robert's body had been discovered and he had asked her for it. There had been some book Robert had promised to show him, and Rachel had promised she would find it and bring it to him. It was only after we had got Strachan and Carmichael to carry him – for he was not fit to walk – to the Mediciner's manse . . .'

'Dr Dun has taken him into his own house?'

'Yes, he did not think it wise to leave him in the college where he might upset the scholars and be a danger to himself.'

'I see. Go on.'

'It was only after we had settled him in the Mediciner's manse and sent the two others to clear out his lodgings that we could get more sense about this book out of him.'

'What was it?' I asked.

'Something that Richard Middleton knew of, that Robert had promised to obtain, that would show John Innes the errors of the *Fama* and its followers, and point him in a better way.'

'I remember now – Patrick Urquhart mentioned it to me when we were at Crathes. He didn't know the name. Did John tell you what it was called?'

'That I cannot tell you. I doubt the poor soul knows himself. But he is settled now, and will be looked after by Dr Dun and his daughter. She was preparing a decoction of camomile when I left, to calm him. I think in the greater scheme of things, the title of the book is of little importance.'

'I think you are wrong, Doctor.'

He put down his glass and summoned up a warning look I knew well. 'Alexander, if you are even thinking, even *thinking* of questioning John Innes further on this book, still less trying to find it, I utterly forbid it. Utterly. The boy must be helped to forget this whole episode. If you seek to pursue this matter of foolish books about secret societies, I will personally see to it that Dr Dun allows you no access to John Innes at all.'

'Peace, Doctor, peace,' I said, laughing. 'I am not as callous as you evidently think me. John Innes will hear not one more word of this book from my lips. But I fear I must find it out, for I believe it is the book Rachel Middleton went to Melville's bookshop looking for, on the day she saw Bernard Cummins there. If this book is in some way the connection between the two murders, it may help me track down the killer.'

The doctor frowned. 'It is a very slight connection, Alexander.'

'But you will admit it is one?'

'I admit nothing.' He had roused himself from his earlier weariness. 'Go to Melville if you must. The man never forgets a book or who bought it. And I will come with you – that way you are less likely to land yourself in trouble.'

★

All was in darkness. Four hours of the night before daylight would start to send its specks of grey and blue so that a movement sensed a moment before in the dark would become an object, a man seen.

He turned the key, locking the door of the lodge behind him. He had wondered, all these days, why they had never thought to ask about that key. So taken up with other matters, they had simply forgotten it. Thank God. His search of the lodge had revealed nothing – he had looked in to every hiding place, every nook they knew about and those they did not, but what he sought was not there. She must have it in the house. Sim must have brought it there. She could not have looked at it yet, of that he was certain, but how long could he trust, believe, that she would not open the volume, turn the pages and find the name that would lose him all he had, and lead him to the hangman's rope?

At the other end of the path, the kitchen door was locked, of course. He slipped the chisel from his pocket and wedged its edge between door and jamb. A few moments' careful work, and he had the thing open, the final splinter startling a rat from the midden and out under the pend gate.

There was no noise, no movement in the kitchen, save his own breathing. He went to a drawer in the kitchen table and found a knife. He lit a candle he found from the embers in the hearth and looked around the room. There was nothing in here that might not be found in any kitchen, nothing save a doctor's bag, and he had seen enough of those. A door near the bottom of the stairs was partially ajar, and he pushed it a little further open. A figure lay in the bed, breathing steadily. He took a step in and lifted the candle a little. It was Richard Middleton, beside him an empty glass. He ran his finger around the inside and tasted: some sort of sleeping draught. Good.

He crept back out of the room and set his foot on the stair. The step gave a light creak under his foot. He stopped and listened: nothing. Another step, and then a third, making noise he knew could not be put down to the light wind rustling the branches of trees in the garden. Upstairs there was the sound of someone stirring, and her voice, tremulous at first and then crying out, louder, 'Richard? Richard, is that you?'

In a second he had his hood up and was bounding up the stairs, three at a time. Casting aside the candle, he crashed through the door at the top and threw himself at the figure just sitting up in the bed. The woman went down with a scream beneath him, and he flung her over on her face, pushing his knee into her back as he bound her wrists behind her with one of her own stockings. Next, as she struggled and squealed beneath him, he pulled the cover from her pillow and shoved it over her head, tying it at her neck. He felt her pass out beneath him, whether from fright or lack of air he did not care. All the while he said not a word. He found the candle again and struck flint to light it. Aside from the bed in the middle of the floor and the prostrate form of the woman in it, the room was practically bare. His eyes swept over what there was to see. On the table by the window a hairbrush, a bottle of rose-water, a looking glass. Not as much as a jewel-box. But he had no time or interest for jewels in any case. He threw open the doors of the wall-press. Bare, save for one simple grey linen dress hanging there. A shawl lay over the back of a chair, a pair of shoes beneath it.

But then he saw the chest. At the other side of the bed, away from the window. A large oak chest, almost too big to fit through the door, he would have thought. But he had no need of taking it through the door, for what he sought would fit in his pocket. The key was in the lock. She could not know its contents, or she would have taken greater care. He turned the key and opened the lid. Dresses, linens, undergarments, a jewel-box. He flung them aside, sending a locket and rings from the jewel-box skidding across the floor. And there, at the bottom, at last, were the books. A man would have packed them at the top. A man with nothing to hide. He rifled through them – a book of receipts for the preparation of stock, the making of custards, the pickling of fruit and the drying of peas and beans. He tossed it aside in disgust. Something smaller – a woman's book filled with scrawls on the uses of herbs and the preparation of simples and poultices. That too was discarded in frustration. His hand came to rest on the last thing in the chest, a small, octavo volume. He lifted it carefully, opened the ties on the cover, and there, before he saw the title, his eyes fell upon the name of Robert Sim, and a dedication written in the librarian's own hand, a commonplace book for his love. His eyes flicked over the notes, the favoured excerpts, the copied verses. It was not here, what he sought, and yet he read on, to the last page.

It is said these words were found amongst the pages of Sir Walter Raleigh's Bible at his death. My name will not be known, as his is known, I will not be mourned, as he was mourned, but I take comfort in these words, however small and mean my life has been, that my Redeemer shall not treat me differently from him.

And below, the librarian had copied,

> *Even such is Time, that takes in trust*
> *Our youth, our joys, our all we have,*
> *And pays us but with earth and dust;*
> *Who in the dark and silent grave,*
> *When we have wandered all our ways,*
> *Shuts up the story of our days;*
> *But from this earth, this grave, this dust,*
> *My God shall raise me up, I trust.*

What he searched for was not here, amongst these lover's notes. He had tried to take the place of time, to 'shut up his story' in another man's dark and silent grave, but he knew now that that was not his to do: God was raising that other's shade from its grave, its dust, and it would be silent no more. He picked up the candle and went down the stairs, without bothering to close the door behind him.

TWENTY-ONE

A Visit to the Booksellers

The next morning, after lecturing them for an hour, I set my class to composition in Greek. 'A eulogy to our founder and Maecenas, the earl Marischal, father of our current patron.' The class groaned as I would have expected them too. 'An exemption from dining-hall duties for a day for him whose composition I judge the best.'

This was met with more enthusiasm. 'But who shall fill their place?' from one of the perennial strugglers.

'He whose composition I judge to be the worst,' I said, before leaving them and going to seek out the principal.

Dr Dun would generally have given me leave to go out in to the town for half an hour without question, but I knew that he was determined I should not re-embark on my researches, and was not surprised that he questioned me closely as to my intentions in town, and how long I expected to be out of the college.

'Not half an hour,' I said. 'I need to go down to David Melville's for a book.'

'Which book?' he asked, more than a hint of suspicion in his voice.

I had not expected this level of interrogation, and mentioned the first title that came in to my head.

He raised his eyebrows. 'Scot's *Apparatus Latinae*? I would have hoped any regent in this college might have been able to struggle his way through the works of Cicero without that to hand.'

'There are sometimes points of debate amongst the students . . . it is useful for settling them. My own copy is so dog-eared now. I thought to get another while they are quietly occupied . . .'

This seemed to satisfy the principal and he asked me to check on the college orders while I was there. Like a young scholar caught in some minor misdemeanour, it was with some relief that I left his room and descended the stairs into the relative freedom of the courtyard.

Jaffray was waiting for me out on the Broadgate, caught up in conversation with an elderly merchant of his acquaintance. I waited while they finished pronouncing their doom on my backsliding generation, then hurried the doctor along to the Castlegate.

'Dr Dun only has your well-being at heart, Alexander,' Jaffray said, when I complained about the principal's new surveillance of my movements. 'He much regrets having involved you in this business at all. Had I been here when Robert's body was discovered, I would have counselled him against it. But I was not, alas, and now he knows for himself.'

'Knows what?'

'That you have not the capacity to observe matters affecting your fellow man without involving yourself in them.'

I was stunned. 'You have spent as many years as I can remember exhorting me not to stand on the edges of the pool of life, but to immerse myself in it. How can you now criticise me for doing exactly what you have so long urged me to do?'

'I have never said to you that it must be all or nothing. You either shun your fellow man, or entangle yourself entirely in his sufferings and his fears so that they become your own.' He stopped and threw out his hands in exasperation. 'For God's sake, man, you have a wife, and a family that is growing. Your health is no longer your own to jeopardise, nor your life your own to endanger. Patrick Dun is right to pull you away from further involvement in matters that have already set you in the path of madmen and murderers. If William's dog had not dealt with Matthew Jack as it did, Sarah might now be a widow.'

I opened my mouth to protest, but we had now reached the door of David Melville's booksellers, and Jaffray strode in, the unassailable victor.

Melville was just coming down the stairs from the printer's workshop above his own premises when we entered. He smiled broadly when he saw me, and even more so when he saw Jaffray. 'Mr Seaton. Doctor! It is a pleasure indeed to see you. You will be here for the graduations?'

'Indeed I am. I saw Paul Ogston into the world, I will see him walk out into the estate of man with the magistrand's cap upon his head.'

I had never doubted that Jaffray would be here to see the graduation of the Banff boy who would even now have been working with his father in the chandler's shop of that burgh had not his natural gifts been matched by the doctor's generosity.

Melville pointed towards the printer's workshop. 'Raban is railing at this new fashion for printed theses that has come across the sea to us, for all that it brings him much business. The students have him near enough run ragged with it; their dedications become ever longer and more ornate, and they will keep changing their minds.'

'Ach, he should indulge them a while, for so will they mark their youth and their friendships, for all posterity to see.'

'No doubt you are right, Doctor. Now, what can I do for you gentlemen today? Are you to take over from Mr Sim in library matters, Mr Seaton?'

'That will be a matter for the council,' I said, 'but for the meantime, Dr Dun has asked me to check on the college's order.'

Jaffray wandered over to a display of prints and woodcuts, and left me to talk to the bookseller in private. As the doctor had predicted, Melville remembered exactly what both Bernard Cummins and Rachel Middleton had wanted from his shop on the day before the weaver's death.

'What Cummins wanted had already been ordered and paid for on his behalf by Sir Thomas Burnett of Leys.'

'What was the book?'

'It was not a book as such, but a set of prints in the grotesque style, sixteen of them. Jan Vredeman de Vries was the artist. I remembered them from having supplied a set a few years ago to George Jamesone. Cummins could have got them himself in Antwerp, but he feared they would be damaged should he have had to carry them home himself, so he had arranged for them to be sent here. He checked each print, professed himself satisfied, and paid to have them sent out to Crathes direct.'

'And Rachel Middleton was in the shop all this time?'

Melville considered. 'Most of it, and she was certainly still here after he left.'

'Did she take an interest in what Cummins was doing, what he was looking at?'

'None that I could see. It is unusual to have a woman in my shop, and she did not seem altogether comfortable. She spent most of her time scanning the German books on that wall there.' Melville indicated the shelves nearest to the door. 'She only came over to me after the weaver had left.'

'Did she ask about him?'

'Nothing. All she was concerned about was a book Robert Sim had ordered. I took it from that that what was being said about the town concerning her was true – for how else should she know his business with me if he had not told her? She was greatly disappointed that I did not yet have it to hand, and besought me that I would not sell it to anyone else, but send word to let her know when it arrived.'

'What was the book?' I asked.

Melville turned to the shelf behind him and brought down a volume, considerably weightier than the Rosicrucian *Fama*, its title in German. 'Newly translated from the Czech,' he said, handing it to me.

I read out, 'Jan Amos Comenius, *The Labyrinth of the World and the Paradise of the Heart*.' I had never heard of it.

'Has she seen it?' I asked.

'It only came in last night, on Walter Anderson's boat from Rotterdam.'

I glanced over to the doorway, where Jaffray was now standing to examine some of the prints by the light from outside. 'Will you let me take it to her?' I asked quietly.

'She has not paid for it,' said Melville.

I rooted in my pouch and handed him more than the book could be worth. The bookseller counted out the money he was owed and returned the rest to me.

'What is the importance of this book, Mr Seaton?'

I had not expected his question, and scrambled in my head for an answer that might satisfy. 'Robert had advised its purchase for the library. Why it matters to Rachel Middleton, I do not know.' The easy lie recalled to me the other I had told less than an hour ago, and I was relieved that Melville had a copy of Scot's *Apparatus Latinae* to produce on my return to the college, should I find myself questioned by Dr Dun.

'Are you ready, James?' I asked when my purchases and enquiries were complete.

'A moment,' he said, holding up a finger, 'a moment. I have a fancy for something new to look at while I contemplate the pleasures of old age.'

'Not a medical tract then, Doctor?' said the bookseller. 'I have here . . . ' and he named a pamphlet by an English physician of some repute.

'Ach, I knew the fellow thirty years ago. I would not trust him to lance a boil. No,' he said, stroking his chin in thought, 'I was thinking of something like that.'

My eyes followed those of Melville to the large framed print Jaffray was looking at.

The bookseller went across and lifted it down from its place on the wall. '*Leo Belgicus*. Johannes Doetichum. A magnificent piece of work, Doctor, and as fine a map of those parts as I have seen; it would afford you many rewarding hours of study.'

It was indeed an impressive piece, a curiosity for anyone interested in those flat lands, run through with rivers that held the keys to all the wealth of the world and could ship it to our shores. All the provinces of the Netherlands, north and south, were delineated as a lion, the Belgian lion, three of its huge feet planted firmly in the ground of Northern France and Germany, its head turned eastwards and its tail flourishing over the North Sea. There were illustrations of the royal palace at Brussels, and the palace of the Counts of Holland, and the whole was bordered on two sides by

a series of portraits in miniature of the Spanish governors
of the Netherlands, and along the bottom with the
stadtholders of the Northern provinces, ending with
Maurice of Nassau, the Dutch military genius who had
'come, seen, conquered, restored liberty and governed'. It
was a thing of delight, and I knew it would be so to Jaffray.
Melville's offer to arrange for its transportation to Banff
with some other unwieldy items being shipped up to the
burgh was declined by the doctor, who would not entrust
his new purchase to the dangers of a sea journey, and so it
was that I left him, ten minutes later on the Broadgate,
happily directing the bookseller's struggling assistant in the
carrying of his prize down to William's house. Not wishing
to be found with Rachel Middleton's book, which I had
had the bookseller wrap for me, I asked Jaffray to leave it
off in my own house, and to ask Sarah to place it carefully
amongst my own small library. Thus happily displaying
Scot's *Apparatus Latinae* to any who might chance to glance
my way, I walked back to the college a little over half-an-
hour after I had left it.

TWENTY-TWO

The Labyrinth of the World

It was a beautiful evening as I strolled from the college through the streets to my own home. The sun was slowly dipping, but still sent out its rays over the town and the cold and darkness that were our lot more than half the year were things almost impossible to remember. People sat on benches outside their homes, working at small tasks and calling greetings to one another across lanes and vennels. Young men and women walked in groups together down to Futtie or the Links, from where the sounds of games with ball, bat and club drifted to the town. The warmth of the day seemed to radiate still from the very stones of walls and houses, and even the increased rankness in the air, of decaying food missed by the burgh cleansers, spoke to me of summer. Middens hummed, alive with flies and other beasts, and the gulls down at the quayside cawed endlessly over the trophies left them by the fishermen. It was not yet eight – there would be almost three hours left of daylight, and I looked forward to spending some of them with Sarah, reading to her in our backyard as I had done in the early days of our marriage.

I turned down the pend in to our shared close and stopped. Everything was strangely quiet. There seemed to be no movement anywhere, no face at corbelled windows of the house across from us as often there was, no hint of air stirring the herbs ranged in their pots on the forestairs, no rustling or scurrying of insect or animal in the backland and its gardens beyond. I put my hand to the door. It was locked. I could not remember the last time I had returned to find the door locked. Never. I brought out my keys, augmented now by those of Robert Sim which Dr Dun had never asked me to return, and turned the right one in the lock. Sarah was sitting alone at the kitchen table, looking worn out by anxiety. She stood up as soon as I walked in.

I closed the door softly behind me and went over to her, keeping my voice low so I did not wake the children. 'Sarah? What on earth is wrong? Why is the door locked?'

'The book,' she said, her voice scarcely audible.

'The book?' I repeated, not understanding.

In exasperation, she went to the mantelpiece and took a packet from it. 'This!' she said, brandishing the packet in my face. 'This book.'

I saw then that it was the package I had asked Jaffray to take home for me from the bookseller's earlier in the day.

'Why did the doctor say I should hide it? From whom? What have you brought into this house? After what happened to Rachel Middleton . . .'

'Matthew Jack is securely locked in the tolbooth – I have

seen him there myself – and Rachel is safe now, Richard too.'

She stared at me. 'Alexander, does nothing of the real world find its way within those college walls? Have you not heard?'

'What?'

'Rachel Middleton was attacked in her own bed last night.'

'For the love of God. Is she all right?'

Sarah looked away from me. 'She was tied up, gagged, near enough suffocated. Her attacker ransacked the room and left her for dead.'

'But she is not? Sarah?'

'No, thank God, but it was long enough before her husband found her.'

'Found her? Had he gone out?'

'No, but he has been sleeping in a room down the stairs since the night he was attacked, that Rachel might not disturb him.'

'Had he been bound too?'

She shook her head. 'There had been no need. Rachel had given him a heavy sleeping draught last night, to force him to rest. He did not wake until after ten this morning, and it was then that he found her. She had managed to work the pillowslip off her head but in the darkness she tripped on something and banged her head on the bedstead. She had lain there for hours before Richard found her. Elizabeth and I went to the house as soon as we heard. She is in terror and her husband near in despair, but they have been taken into protection at Paul Menzies' house on the Castlegate.'

'That is something, at least: no one will reach them at the provost's house.' I tried to think. 'You say the room was ransacked – was anything taken?'

'Nothing. Everything was thrown about but the books.' She thrust the package from the booksellers on to the table. 'He was looking for a book, Alexander.'

My hand closed over hers. 'I will take it out of here tonight, I promise you. I will get rid of it. Once I have read it, I will hide it out in the backland, in the woodstore, then I will take it to the provost's house for Rachel tomorrow.'

I had thought to reassure her, but Sarah's eyes blazed. 'You will do no such thing. If it is not out of this house and away from here in the next ten minutes, I will burn the thing to ashes myself.' I put a hand out to calm her, but she slapped it away. 'Ten minutes. Nine now. Get rid of it, or I swear before God, Alexander Seaton, I will make this the sorriest day of your life.'

'All right, but please, calm yourself – it cannot be good for you, or the baby.' I picked up the packet and my hat. 'I'll be away two hours, maybe three. Be sure to lock the door.'

I had hardly reached the pend to the lane before I heard the lock turn and the bolt pulled closed behind me.

It was a common enough thing, on an evening such as this, to see a man walking with a book in his hand, out to the Links or the Meadows. Few would wish to waste light so much better than could be had within thick walls, up narrow closes, through small windows. I myself occasionally struck out from the confines of the streets and lanes to the open spaces outside the burgh ports to read for simple pleasure. But tonight was not such a night. I did not know yet the nature of the volume I carried, but I could not risk meeting a friend or inquisitive acquaintance who might question me on it. The college library was the last place I was prepared to take this book tonight, and so I turned in the other direction, away from there and the Links and the Meadows, and went instead deeper into the heart of the town. I slipped out of Flourmill Lane on to the Netherkirkgate, and went as casually as I could through the port that straddled it, remarking to the gatekeepers on the fineness of the evening. I avoided St Nicholas Kirk where the session, I knew, was meeting tonight and turned down a lane to my right, from there joining Back Wynd as it descended steeply towards the Green. It struck me that Robert Sim must have taken this route often on his nightly journeys from the library back to his lodgings. I shivered a little, despite the warmth that still hung in the air, and hurried on down Aedie's Wynd to come out at last at the Green.

The weekly dairy market had been held that day, and a sour smell of curdled milk and butter gone rancid in the heat rose from the cobbles to mingle with the usual aromas of animal waste and rotting vegetables. People were about, boys playing at football near the Bow Brigg, others walking nearby. There was no private reading place here: I must go still deeper into the town.

I turned down Fisher Row and eventually found myself

in the precincts of the ruined place of the Trinity Friars, desolate for seventy years now, since the Reformation of religion in our land. Here at least, where the women of the street plied their trade amongst the sailors come on shore, I need not fear being approached or overseen by some well-meaning burgess, some respectable acquaintance, some curious friend. Here no decent man would be seen in the evening hours, or the night.

I stepped through the empty gateway, its iron gate long gone, and picked my way across the rubble of what had once been the friars' garden. Towards the shore end of the grounds was the remnant of a boatyard, in use after the friars had been hounded from this place, murdered or fled to safer foreign shores. It too had fallen into disuse and decay, its last boat also long ago launched on to the Denburn and thence out to sea. I found a spot against a pillar in a ruined section of the cloister walk, well lit from the west by the slowly dropping sun, but far from view of any passers-by on Putachieside or the Shore Brae.

And then I began to read, and as I read I remembered who Jan Amos Comenius was, for Jaffray had heard of him from a friend in The Hague, a Bohemian scholar who had suffered greatly following the fall of Prague and the depredations of the early years of the war in his homeland. *The Labyrinth of the World* was the book of hope of which Middleton had spoken, written by Comenius as he struggled free from his personal and intellectual despair. So I sat and I read, and I followed the story of Pilgrim, as he entered the

Labyrinth, not a house of memory but a city, where all the arts and sciences had their own quarters, every human calling and occupation its place. It should have been a Utopia, but Comenius's pilgrim found himself instead in a city where everything was wrong, where the streets led nowhere and endeavour was pointless. The arrival of the Rosicrucians with their promises of a sharing of knowledge, the way to the Philosopher's Stone that would cure the ills of the world, proved a cruel and empty boast, leaving their followers at last silent and in despair. I saw the mirror of Richard Middleton's life in the story. Worse was to follow when Pilgrim journeyed deeper into the city, down into the streets of religious sects, where he witnessed the toppling of a throne followed by brutality, bloodshed and death, from which he only narrowly escaped himself. Again, I saw the young doctor's life in the lines printed out on the page. Plague, famine, the relentless devastation of hostile armies followed and Pilgrim, distraught at the hopelessness and destruction, fled.

I held the book in my hands and looked out across the sea, out to the horizon beyond which lay the lands where such horrors had been and were still the lot of scholars and labourers, beggars and kings. I thought of Archie, my dearest friend and companion of my own young hopes, whose earthly time had ended amongst the carnage Comenius described. The sea was no longer blue, but golden, as the last rays of the sun spread over it from a sky the colour of a withered yellow rose.

The sun finally gone, I shivered a little in the cooler air, but there was light enough yet to return to my book, wondering what worse there could be to come in the few remaining chapters. At the last, as the depths of despair threatened to take him, Pilgrim was called to return to the 'House of the Heart' and there to shut the doors behind him. Answering the call he found himself in the company of the godly who were surrounded, not as he had at first thought by a wall of fire, but by thousands upon thousands of angels, each one a witness to the face of God, and the guardian of the human soul. Here, at last, the mysteries of the world, the mind of God would be revealed to those who sought them and had answered that last call.

I shut the book. There was in it a reassurance, I supposed, for the likes of John Innes who had hoped for great and impossible things from the Rosicrucian dream and found instead the festering corruption of man, but it told a lesson I had learned long ago, and there was nothing in it that I could see that would bring me closer to Nicholas Black, or he to me.

The sky had faded from a hazy grey to a pale blue which was deepening. I had no wish to be still in this place when darkness finally fell. The book had nothing sinister in it that I could see, but I would not break my promise to Sarah. I considered leaving it behind the pillar against which I sat, but the collapsed roof of the cloister left it no protection from the elements or from the rats and other creatures that made their home here. I went up the cloister and into the old friary church, its roof now also almost gone. Inside, the place had been stripped bare of anything that could be removed and used; anything that could not had been defaced or destroyed, and yet, as I walked the length of the nave to the choir, I felt around me something of the presence of those long-dead monks. I shivered and quickened my pace. In the back wall, behind where the altar had stood, was a small recess, the aumbry, its hinges still visible and rusted in their rotten frame. It was here that the priests of the order had kept their blasphemous host. I hesitated, then reminded myself that there was nothing holy in it now and never had been. The book fitted with ease into the space, and after casting around for a moment on the floor I found two stones that would fill the outer opening and hide what lay behind from predator or view. I would return early in the morning to retrieve it so I might deliver it at last to the Middletons at the provost's house. It would be for them to decide whether to take it up to John Innes. If it somehow reassured John, then so be it – I had found no harm in it.

There was something unsettling in the gradual creep of the sounds of the night over the burgh. There was a great evil, somewhere in this town, and I could almost feel its presence coming closer, watching me. I cast my eye around the broken walls and crooked graves, the trees bent by the wind into unnatural shapes. I was being foolish – there was no other being here but myself. And yet I felt fear, a strong desire to be away from this place. I made my way carefully out of the haunt of the dead friars and set off up Putachieside, for the safety and comfort of my home.

★

He had not even had the time to open it, so brief a moment had there been between Alexander Seaton leaving the place and the old drunken packman stumbling in to rest his head for the night. A tightly knotted thin leather cord held fast the oilcloth Seaton had covered the book with, and his fingers had been shaking too much to work it loose before the tinker had appeared. Now he would have to conceal the thing beneath his doublet and scurry home in the darkness, hoping to escape notice, he who had boldly walked down through the burgh in the light.

His neck ached and despite the mildness of the night he felt a chill from where he had crouched so long behind the remnants of a smashed grave as Seaton turned the book's pages. All the while he had watched him, watched his face in the failing light for any sign that he had come upon the thing that he so feared, but he knew, in truth, that the words that would condemn him could not be there, for they would have been right at the beginning. And yet he waited and watched as time passed and Seaton worked his way to the end of the volume. There would be no need, he eventually realised, for the rock he held fast in his hand. When he had set out tonight it had been for the purpose of a friendly visit to that house in Flourmill Lane, and he had had no weapon with him. He had passed the entrance to their pend, once, twice, hesitating, unsure. He had gone out onto the Guestrow and taken up a seat near the water-pump, in the shade of an overhanging apple tree. There had been nothing remarkable in him being out for a stroll away from the concerns of his day on this fine summer's evening. When he had seen Seaton arrive home, his courage had almost failed him, but at length he had persuaded himself that the thing could be done, and could be begun now. He had hardly risen from his seat when he saw him emerge again from the pend. He would have gone to him still, but then he noticed how Seaton looked about him, and how carefully he carried the package, evidently a book, under his arm. It was then that at last he knew that all his resolutions, his good intentions as he had left Rachel Middleton's house the night before, could not be.

Another man might have contrived a visit yet, a conversation, a look in the man's face that would have told him, in a moment, whether he knew, but all he could do was to slip out of sight and follow. Seaton had not made for the college, but deeper into the town. Just as he had begun to wonder whether he might be making for the docks, or thinking to jettison the book into the Denburn, he saw him turn into the friars' yards, and there he followed, to hide amongst the rubble and desolation of that once holy place, and watch.

He scarcely moved, in the near darkness, as the other man, his reading finished and his book hidden, passed within a foot of the grave behind which he sheltered. And then, when it was safe, he too went up the nave to the chancel where it was no great feat to retrieve the book from the aumbry. He too struck out for home, glad of the lanes and vennels, the high walls between backlands, all the secret ways he had come to know that would keep him from the sight of those whose interest it was to find him.

At last, in the quietness of the room he could call his own, by the light of one small candle, he cut through the leather cord and drew aside the oilcloth. He closed his hand over the book a moment before taking a breath and turning the page to look upon its title.

He felt winded for a moment and then laughed. Was this it, then?
The Labyrinth of the World? *He turned the pages a while.
They had been better to follow their talk of alchemy, of art, anything
but this nonsense of pilgrims and cities and angels, for the world
was not a labyrinth but a crucible: Paracelsus' crucible, where the
dark arts could bring the dead back to life. He was the alchemist
and this town his crucible, and if they truly believed this was the
book they sought, the book that Robert Sim had found, then he had
nothing more to fear.*

TWENTY-THREE

Secrets

When I had returned early in the morning to the Trinity Friars' old kirk in search of Comenius' book I had found the stones moved from the aumbry and the book gone. I had not puzzled long over this – some sailor or vagrant, adventuring schoolboy perhaps, must have found it and hoped to turn a penny by its sale. It was of little matter – there was nothing in it that could bring harm upon its reader, and little of comfort that the Middletons or indeed John Innes would not find, in time, elsewhere. I reasoned besides that the sooner all involved forgot about their Rosicrucian experiment the better it would be for their well-being and the peaceable life of the burgh.

And indeed, the town did seem almost to slip into a forgetfulness of the evil that had visited itself upon us for a while, to take comfort in the incarceration, and certain hanging to come, of Matthew Jack. For who could it have been who had cut the throats of these two men but Matthew Jack? It was increasingly said in the town that it was his malice, brought on by his lust for Rachel Middleton, that was at the root of both killings. It was not long before it was declared as fact that he had discovered the librarian's clandestine night visits to the doctor's house, and that the unfortunate weaver had simply found himself in the wrong place at the wrong time. The weaver had been left for dead in the Middletons' garden on the very night Jack had purposed to force himself upon her and then had been dragged, knife in hand, from her husband's very neck. Who would have had greater opportunity for the murder of Robert Sim, widely now declared to have been the lover of the physician's wife? Little wonder, they said, some other assailant had thought to try his luck on her – she had called such things down upon herself. There was little agreement on the wisdom of the provost in protecting the pair under his own roof, but perhaps it was as well to remove the woman from the temptations of honest men. Alexander Seaton, it was said, had been often at her house, but then his taste for a certain type of woman was known, was it not? Soon she was to be gone; as soon as Dr Dun declared her husband sufficiently recovered, they would both leave our burgh bounds and not return. All would be well, and life would continue as it had done before, the outsiders having played their tragedy before us.

In the college too, it seemed that all might, indeed, be well. Preparations for the graduations gathered their usual pace, and the days passed in a busy haze of heat, nerves and excitement. Dr Dun was evidently intent that I should have not a spare moment for further enquiry or search into the matter of the murders of Robert Sim and Bernard Cummins: when I was not taking my classes through the revision of their courses, I was charged with every petty task in the arrangements for the laureation that seemed to enter the principal's head.

Every bench in the Grayfriars' Kirk had to be inspected by me before and after it was cleaned, every corner of the common school of the college swept under my oversight, lest at the disputations or the ceremony after them some petty laird or aged doctor of divinity might find himself inconvenienced by the sighting of a cobweb. The porter and the other college servants were sick of the sight of me, although their disdain could not match that of the head gardener when I appeared in his domain under instruction to oversee the choice of flowers from the gardens that would bedeck courtyard and kirk. A man who had kept the college garden thirty years needed no advice from one who could scarcely tell a marigold from a dandelion, and he was not long in making this plain.

And so the days passed, and in truth I began to find that the shadow of Nicholas Black fell less and less across my mind. Gone was the jealousy and suspicion of the last weeks and months that had eaten away at all the good things that had come in to my life since I had met Sarah, and I saw clearly now what I had risked losing. The knowledge terrified me. Once Dr Dun or Jaffray or William Cargill had seen me into my own courtyard at night, my world was there and I had no wish to sully it by thoughts of other things.

'I do not know how you have put up with me,' I said
to her one night.

'No more do I,' she replied, without turning from her
inspection of Deirdre's old baby gowns to look at me.

I went to her and put my hands around her waist. 'I am
in earnest, Sarah. I could not have lived with the man that
I was becoming, I could not have lived with the bitterness,
the changes of mood . . .'

She turned now. 'We will leave aside the fact that I had
no choice, for whatever happened between us, I had no
choice. But had I been a wealthy woman of good family,
had I had no children, had I not been carrying your child,
I would have stayed anyway.' She put aside the gown she'd
been holding. 'I did not marry you because I needed a
home – I had one with William and Elizabeth, and would
always have had one there. I did not marry you because I
needed a father for Zander – has the boy not three god-
fathers of greater wealth and better standing than you?'

It was true. When Sarah's son had been born, she had
been reluctant to ask any to stand godfather to her bastard
child, but the matter had soon been taken from her hands
as William Cargill, Dr Jaffray and John Innes had stepped
forward to claim that role.

'And I did not marry you,' she continued, holding my
gaze in a challenge, 'because no one else would have me.'
I opened my mouth to speak but she had not finished. 'I
married you because I loved you, Alexander Seaton. I knew
from the first moment you bent down from your horse to

speak to me that I would love you. From the moment you put your hands at my waist to lift me onto that horse, I knew that I would never let another man touch me. Nothing you have ever done, nothing you could ever say can change that, and if you were to walk out of that door now and never come back, I would die never loving another man.'

'Nor I another woman,' I said softly. I bent down to kiss her, and felt the touch of her lips on mine with all the thrill, all the wonder, of the very first time.

All would be well, then. Sarah must have heard what was being said about me, but she never spoke of it — she had heard such things often enough before. My own sense of unease that Matthew Jack was not the man I had sought receded a little in the gathering excitement as graduation day approached. Principal Dun himself became somewhat lighter of spirit, and although he tended Richard Middleton each day, I felt he too would be happier to see his younger colleague gone from our horizon. While his vigilance over his patient did not waver, that which he had so carefully exercised over me began to relax its grip, and I at last found myself able to come and go, unattended, from the college as the occasion suited me.

I took the opportunity, whenever it might arise, to slip out and visit the Middletons for myself, or to find an excuse to go to the King's College in the Old Town, and call upon John Innes, who, under the care of the principal's daughter, in the Mediciner's manse there, seemed to strengthen a little

in mind and spirit by the day. He called less now on his
angels, and found some solace in quiet prayer, from the
spectres of devils that still beset him in the short hours of
darkness. I related to him, in as much detail as I could recall,
the experiences of Pilgrim in Comenius' *Labyrinth*, for the
book itself had never been found. To my relief, the tale
did not add to his delusions, but seemed to have a kind of
enchantment of truth and light for him, which had been
absent these latter weeks in the dark and stinking hermitage
of his college room. He followed the progress of Pilgrim
from day to day, and came with him to see the futility of
the Rosicrucian dream. At the end of each visit, I thanked
God that my friend, this kind and gentle man, had been
pulled back from the edge of the abyss.

The last day before the final examinations and laureation
dawned, a little hazy, but with promise of great heat. My
own scholars, in their third year and with no examinations
to face until our return to college in the autumn, had
finished their course and been ploughed through it again
by myself and John Strachan who had now proved himself
sufficiently that he was to have Matthew Jack's vacant place
as regent. As some went happily off to the Links to play
golf, and others down to the shops and booths of the Castlegate to fulfil some last commissions for their parents before
returning home to the glens of Aberdeenshire and the
scattered Highland settlements from which they had come,
I too left the college. As I made my way down the
Upperkirkgate, I saw, halfway down the street, a young

boy of about twelve struggling out of William Cargill's door carrying a large and vaguely familiar looking object in his arms. Dr Jaffray was following after him, his head turned towards William's manservant, standing in the doorway.

'Days of wickedness – you have it there, Duncan, you have it right. Days of wickedness. When a man such as David Melville cannot be trusted!'

I crossed over quickly, just as Jaffray's lately bought map was about to fall from the hapless boy's grasp. 'What has our good bookseller done to so incur your wrath, Doctor?' I asked, as I gave the grateful boy his penny and told him I would see to the doctor's errand.

'Good bookseller? Was there ever such a thing? A charlatan! A purveyor of fakes!'

'Come, you know David Melville is neither of those things. You have been buying books from him for longer than I have myself.'

'That is what makes it all the worse, that after all these years he should so abuse my custom and my trust as to sell me this.'

'The map?' I said, holding the thing at arms' length the better to scrutinise it. 'But it is a fine piece. There is no fakery here.'

'The map is wrong, I tell you. It has the Frisian islands too far to the north or Gouda too far to the south – it is one thing or the other.'

I looked again at the map. The geography and topography

of the Netherlands was not entirely unfamiliar to me, and it did not appear to me that anything was amiss.

'But what makes you think that, Doctor?' I asked.

Jaffray's response was lost as a great sound of shouting and commotion reached us from the direction of the Castlegate. A shadow passed across the doctor's face; all thought of maps was forgotten as he thrust the object back through William's still-open doorway and gripped my arm. 'Come Alexander; I have heard such sounds before and they rarely portend good.'

And indeed, it was nothing good that we learned even before we had breasted the Broadgate. Word was spreading through the streets that Matthew Jack had broken free of his gaolers whilst being transferred from the tolbooth to the sheriff court, and was loose somewhere on the streets. My first thought was of Richard Middleton and his wife, but a guard had been set on the provost's house as soon as the escape had become known. Every moment Matthew Jack was free, on the run, was a moment more for him to continue spinning out his web of malice. My mind worked quickly. Where was my wife? I could not remember what she had said that morning as I had left.

'Sarah!' I shouted. 'Doctor, is Sarah at William's house?'

My friend shook his head. 'I have not seen her there all day. There was something I think about her staying at home – some preparations she had in hand for your students' supper.' His face told me instantly that his fears mirrored my own, and for all his sixty years he had turned and was pushing against the crowd to get back across the street before I was myself.

I must have reached the pend on our lane in less than two minutes. Jaffray, breathing hard, was some way behind me by now. I ran into the courtyard shouting Sarah's name, and for the second time in recent days found the door to my own house barred against me. Before Jaffray had caught up with me, I had lifted the wooden bench from its place by the wall and begun to ram it against the door. The son of an elderly neighbour came running down the forestairs, shouting, until he realised who I was and joined me in my battering of the door. At last it gave way and I crashed in to find my daughter huddled in a corner, crying for her mother, and Sarah on the floor, lifeless but for the blood seeping from her head. Jaffray spoke quietly behind me. 'Good God, Alexander, can it be him?'

It was. The thing that crouched over my wife, a knife in its hand was more beast than man, filthy, matted, covered in sores.

'Have your brat cease its squalling, Seaton, or I'll skewer it from here.'

As I took a step towards him, the old woman from across the courtyard scurried behind me to sweep Deirdre from the floor.

I turned to fall on my knees beside Sarah.

I heard Jack suck at his teeth. 'She did not prove as accommodating as I thought.' He was rubbing at a livid scratch on his face. 'More feisty than the usual bitch in heat.' He nodded towards the scar on my own neck. 'Does she like to get it rough, Seaton? I can take her rough.'

Before I knew that the animal scream that filled the room was from my own throat, I felt my fist connect with his head. It was only with the first kick of my boot into his ribs that I heard the knife skitter across the floor, only with the second that I felt bone crunch beneath my foot. They had to pull me from him in the end and then they had to drag me from Sarah, where I held to her on the floor.

'Good God, the place is like a flesher's yard.' It was William, downstairs.

'I doubt it will ever clean,' came a woman's voice.

'They said in the chambers that he had killed him.'

I did not know. I did not know if I had killed him. I did not care. Everything, almost everything I cared about lay, swathed in clean white linen, on the bed in front of me, my marriage bed.

'Come away, Alexander,' Jaffray said gently. 'I must dress your hand.'

I shook my head. 'I will not leave her.'

'There is nothing you can do for her. Elizabeth will sit with her, will you not?'

They were treating me like a child. 'Yes, I will sit with her.' She smiled. 'Go with the doctor, Alexander.' And I went like a child.

I did not recognise the room downstairs in which I found

my neighbour on her hands and knees, scrubbing as if her last days depended on it. I tried to speak but I could not, dazed, not knowing if the blood on the floor came from me, or from him, or from my wife.

William sat opposite me, never taking his eyes from mine as the doctor carefully cleaned and bound my hand. He kept swallowing, as if trying to swallow down the question he must ask. In all the days I had known him, I had never seen my friend, the great lawyer, the master rhetorician, so lost for words. As his eyes brimmed with tears and he reached out a hand to take mine, I knew I had never loved him so well.

'She lives,' I managed to say eventually. 'She lives, William.'

'And the child?'

Jaffray's lips were bound tight. It was a moment before he spoke. 'The midwife is with her. We will know soon.'

Elizabeth sat through the night with Sarah, William, having seen the children safely into the care of George Jamesone's wife, with me. Jaffray tended to us all with the energy of a man half his age. I drank down everything he gave me, and slept for some of the hours of the night. In the morning, when at last she woke, her first question was of our unborn child.

'Jaffray and the midwife believe that all will be well, but you must rest. Is that not so, Doctor?'

'It is. The wound at your temple will heal in time, and

it will not spoil your pretty face, my dear. Though nothing can be done for your senses, I fear.'

'My senses?' she murmured dozily.

'Well, a bump on the head cannot put back what you lost years ago, to put up with this one for so long,' he said, indicating me with a tilt of his head. 'But truly, Sarah, you must rest. Elizabeth will not allow you across her door to do work, so you need not think of it, and Isobel Tosh will have Zander and Deirdre until you are well enough.'

'But they will need to see me, and oh – Deirdre.'

She was remembering now, the scene our daughter had witnessed in the room below.

'She is fine,' I said. 'They are both fine, and I will take them to you this afternoon. Deirdre knows the bad man will never come here again.'

The bad man would never be anywhere again, but the road from the tolbooth to the gibbet on Heading Hill. I had not killed him, William had told me late in the night after he had been out to talk to the sheriff and to see for himself that Jack was safely in chains once more. 'You didn't leave many bones in one piece, but you didn't kill him, more's the pity. Dr Dun went in there and patched him up sufficiently that they might set a rope round his neck to hang him.'

'Dr Dun?'

'It would not have been me, I'll tell you. But for all that it was he who dismissed Jack from the college, the principal still feels a Christian duty towards him that few others could muster.' William looked uncomfortable.

'What is it? There is something else?'

He drew a breath. 'Dr Dun got little thanks and much abuse for his troubles. Jack raved at everyone and everything that came near him. The townspeople who could get into the building, and the guards, thank God, jeered and spent their effort on heaping abuse on him rather than listen. For had he spoken in a clear calm voice, had they listened as I listened, they would have heard, amongst the ravings, what I heard.'

'What did you hear. William?'

And he told me.

Had it not been so late, had my wife not being lying, insensible, in the room above us, we would have gone then to warn them, but as it was, we could only leave it until the morning.

Richard Middleton's face was white, whiter even than it was after he had been attacked in the masons' lodge by Matthew Jack.

It was his wife who spoke. 'How did you know?' she asked.

'Matthew Jack,' William said. 'I think you must leave, now, before anyone else takes a moment to listen and understand what he is saying.'

The young doctor looked up at his wife. 'Rachel, I am so sorry. I never meant to bring you to this. You do not deserve this. I will go alone. People will accept you for your brother's good name and your own; they will soon forget about me.'

'If I have not you, Richard, I have nothing. What is there here for me? I took your name years ago and discarded my own. And when I die, that name will be on my grave. The provost will not detain us, and what belongings we will need are already packed up. We can be gone by tomorrow.'

'That is good,' I said, 'but you may have a little longer before another listens to what he says; it may be that all he says will be discounted as the mad ramblings of a mind lost.'

The young woman looked at me steadily. 'But you did not discount them so, did you?'

I looked away a moment, ashamed almost. 'No. I had begun to – to suspect.'

How long ago had I begun to suspect? At the very beginning, I think, when first Robert Sim's landlady had told me of his night-time wanderings, for in all the time I had known him, Robert Sim had never once sought the company of women for anything other than their domestic aid or their conversation, never once. And for all Sarah and Elizabeth had discoursed on his need for a wife, I had known he would never take one. And when William had repeated to me the words that had tumbled forth from Matthew Jack's mouth in all the filthy torrent of his invective, I had realised at last what were the unnatural practices of which he had spoken to me that night in the lodge: when Robert

Sim had come alone, in the night, to the Middletons' house, it had been to spend the hours of darkness not with the young woman, but with her husband.

Dr Dun's face was grave. 'You realise, do you not, Alexander, that this must be reported to the session. The crimes of Richard Middleton are an offence against God, and he must answer for them.'

I had rehearsed what I would next say carefully, for it had not been likely that the principal would accede to my request at the first time of asking, and I could not see how the thing was to be done without him. 'He will answer for them, at the Day of Judgement. But others should not face the discipline of the kirk, and all that you know would follow, for things they have not done.'

'You talk of his wife? She was complicit.'

I shook my head. 'I talk of this college.'

Patrick Dun's face darkened and his nostrils flared as he took in breath. 'What are you telling me, Alexander? What are you telling me has been going on here under my very eye?'

'Nothing, I think. I never heard a word, a whisper, about impropriety, or indeed much converse between Robert and the boys, and Richard Middleton was never in this place amongst them.'

'Then why should anyone here be brought before the kirk?'

'Because of Matthew Jack,' I said. 'He knew Richard

Middleton in Paris, when he was newly qualified and thought to set up in practice as a physician there. Jack thought the coincidence of their shared nationhood would give him access to the circle of his fellow countryman and his friends, but his overtures towards them were rejected. Jack saw to it in time that he was hounded from the city. When Matthew Jack eventually came to our college, and discovered Richard Middleton living in this burgh, he again sought revenge, but his old tales of secret, malign brother-hoods held little favour amongst our burgesses and so he waited, and he watched for something else. For years, Richard gave him nothing, no scrap of scandal that he could fix upon, lived quietly, built his practice and did not much seek the society of others. And then, his curiosity about what he found at the masons' lodge took him to our library and Robert Sim. Whatever care they took, it was not enough, because Matthew Jack began to suspect the true nature of their association.'

'That I can believe, but it still does not excuse Richard Middleton or – or Robert Sim,' he added. 'And I still fail to see how it threatens others in this college – your fellow teachers or the students under our care.'

'Do you not remember the threats Jack flung at you, at this place, as he was put from its gates? Did you not hear what William heard last night, as you tended to Jack in his cell?' In my frustration my voice was rising and I was speaking to the principal as I had never before done.

He started to shake his head slowly. 'I paid no heed to his ramblings – I was tending his wounds.'

'He made good on his threats, Patrick, as you set his bones and cleaned his sores. Amongst the garbled filth that poured from his mouth was that the Marischal College was a cesspit of sodomy. He was jeered and shouted down by the rabble down the stairs and outside who could not discern what he said, but if you yourself were to bring Richard Middleton before the session and accuse him of unnatural acts with Robert Sim, who was our own librarian, there are few within these walls who would escape the finger of suspicion, and no decent father would ever put his son here again. Boys who huddle together under a blanket through the winter nights in their chambers would find themselves accused of heinous crimes against nature and against God.'

The principal sat at his desk with his head in his hands. 'And even should they not be found guilty, their names would be blighted by the rumour of filth. And all under my care.' I waited, conscious of the sound of my own breath. At last he looked up. 'All right, Alexander, I will do as you ask.'

Within ten minutes, I was loping down the stone steps from Dr Dun's chambers to the college courtyard, his letter attesting to the good repute of Richard Middleton and his fitness to practise as a physician grasped firmly in my hand. It was a letter without which the Middletons' hope of a new life, far from here, would have had little success.

★

'And do you think they will be all right?' Sarah squinted a little in the sun that came streaming through the small window of our chamber.

I sat on the edge of the bed, softly stroking her hair. I did not really want to speak of this. 'I don't know. Rachel is determined that they will be, and she is a strong woman, very strong. They have enough money to last them a good while, and when Richard's arm is properly healed and his strength restored, he will be able to begin in practice again. The letters of recommendation from William and Principal Dun will open doors for them with the burgesses of Glasgow, and, in all, it will be a sort of homecoming for them.'

Sarah was silent a moment.

'What is wrong?' I said.

'All these years she has been here, she must have been so lonely, and I never thought to offer her friendship. I thought she kept herself aloof, and all the time it was not for lack of friendliness on her part, but for fear of discovery. I never even considered where she had come from.'

'It seems she travelled around a good deal with her brother before he settled here.'

'And all that time Richard was studying, and beginning to practise on the continent. She had sacrificed so much for him, but for what? To wait all those years for your husband's return and then to discover that it was hardly a marriage, that you could never be a proper wife nor bear children? She has had her good name maligned, been accused of things she has not done, all for his sake. And now instead of freeing herself from him, she goes with him.' Her face was almost bitter. 'I do not understand it.'

'It is because she loves him.'

'But how can she love him, after he has so deceived her?'

'He never deceived her, Sarah.'

She sat upright and regarded me with something approaching contempt. 'Never deceived her? Alexander, the man is a sodomite.'

'But he never sought to conceal the truth from her.'

'He . . .' She stopped. 'What?'

'Rachel knew it from the start.'

And so I told Sarah what Rachel Middleton had, haltingly, told me, as her husband looked on with a degree of love in his eyes that few men could match. She had first met Richard when a Lanarkshire minister known to her father had brought to their home in Glasgow a beautiful, sullen-looking boy of fourteen. It had been agreed that the boy should lodge under their roof while he studied at the town's college, the University of Glasgow. Money changed hands and admonitions were given, and the minister departed, leaving the boy at the stonemason's house. He had stood there, she recalled, like a scared animal with nowhere left to go, and she had sworn in that moment that she would be his sanctuary, she would be his place to go. And so, almost four years later, it had proved, and he had become her sanctuary, too, when her father, noticing that she had attained to womanhood, decided she should become another man's burden. The son of a plumber was found, an apprentice, to take the girl off his hands, and both fathers were well-pleased with the arrangement. She had protested that she did not love the plumber's boy, did not know him, but no one paid her any heed. And then, one night soon afterwards, there had been a great banging on her father's door, and demands from the college authorities for Richard Middleton to be produced before them, that they might enquire into allegations of lewd and unnatural converse with another scholar. Richard had been brought from his bed and had not known what to say as the regents had accused and her father thundered. But she had known what to say. Richard Middleton had smiled at the memory as he recalled her very words for William and me,

"'You are poorly informed gentleman, and Richard maligned, for he has promised to marry me.'" As the men stared and her father blustered, she had looked at Richard and seen in his face that, yes, they would be a sanctuary to each other.

Her father had thrown them from the house, and they had gone back to that parish whence he'd come, and the minister there had married them, persuading himself that what he had suspected of the boy all those years ago could not be true after all. Richard had been permitted to take his final examinations and to graduate, but there was too much rumour, too much insinuation, and they could not stay in the town of Glasgow. And so Richard had gone abroad, to further his studies and become a physician, and

Rachel had taken refuge with her brother, by then a master stonemason on his own account, and waited for her husband to come home. And he had done, when the hounds had found and started to haunt him in Paris, and now they had followed him here.

'They will not have him,' she had said defiantly to us that afternoon. 'I will die before I let them have him.'

TWENTY-FOUR

Laureation

As had become our custom, I joined with my fellow regents and the professors of mathematics and divinity to watch from the casement windows of the principal's chamber as the courtyard filled up below us. Parents, friends and dignitaries from the town and further afield thronged through the archway to greet or avoid one another, to parade their finery and observe others do likewise. The talk amongst us watching was of plans for the summer vacation, grumbles at the tardiness of the council in paying stipends, and covert hopes that amongst the great and the good beneath us, a generous patron might be found. Nobody mentioned Matthew Jack. The determination not to mention him on this day was thick in the air. As for Robert, our librarian, our friend, I surveyed the men around me and it appeared that by some silent agreement from which I had been excluded, they had truly forgotten him.

'We have been blessed in the day, Alexander.' Dr Dun was watching me carefully. I suspected I had not been able to mask my unease.

'Yes,' I replied. 'I pray it will continue so.'

'You fear it might not?'

I indicated the throng now filling the courtyard. 'One amongst those, walking freely beneath us, or somewhere out in the streets of this burgh, conceals a murderous heart. And we do not know who he is; we may never know who he is.'

Dr Dun kept his voice low. 'After all that has happened, you still do not believe Matthew Jack to be guilty of the crimes with which he is charged?'

'Of the killings, no.'

'Why not?'

'Because Matthew would have taken great joy in exposing Robert for what we now know of him. He would have taken great pleasure too in tainting the college with the association.'

'And the weaver?'

'The weaver's death, the concealment of his body, was a careful thing, a thing premeditated, not an act of passion and rage like Matthew's attack on Richard Middleton or my wife. And Matthew Jack would not have known of Hiram's grave.'

The principal regarded me carefully. 'There are many in this college and this burgh who would not be sorry to see Matthew Jack called to account for past misdeeds and malevolence. Of all men, I had not thought he would find a champion in you.'

'It is Robert, my dead friend, that I champion. May God

forgive me, but you, sir, know I will happily see Matthew dance from the gibbet for all he has done, but I know he did not murder those men.'

'How can you know, Alexander? How can you be so certain?'

I turned away from him and looked again down onto the courtyard. 'Because the name of the man who murdered the librarian of this college and the weaver Bernard Cummins is Nicholas Black, and say what you will, I am determined to find him.'

The bell of Grayfriars' Kirk began to toll, calling the principal down to the college gates where he would welcome the Bishop, our chancellor, and the Earl Marischal, son of our founder and benefactor. Goblets were reluctantly set down, gowns and shoes checked one last time for cleanliness, and we filed out after Dr Dun into the light of the July sun.

The kirk was packed, and the crowd hushed only as Bishop Patrick, aged now and infirm in body, was helped to his feet. The well-beloved tones rang through chancel and nave as they had done for so many years now, and I prayed fervently with the bishop for the young men ranged before us, about to make their inaugural disputation and, God willing, take their place in the world. When the bishop regained his seat, the principal rose to give due and accustomed thanks to our patron and benefactor, and to the massed ranks of the Provost, Magistrates, and Town Council of Aberdeen arrayed before us. From my place facing them on the podium, my eyes wandered over the assembled audience, scanning, hopelessly, I knew, for the face of a man I had never seen.

Those for whom there were no seats stood, and at the very back, where the relatives of the poorest scholars jostled for space, I saw Patrick Urquhart. It gave me a jolt to see him there. In all the business of Matthew Jack, and the revelations about Richard Middleton, I had all but forgotten him, but of course he would be here, to see his brother undergo his final examination and, if found worthy, graduate. He was standing, his face like stone, as far apart from the crush as he could, almost in the shadow of the porch of the church. Not many years had passed since he had himself been laureated, *summa cum laude*, the foremost in his class, a glittering career overseas predicted for him. And now, here he stood, ready to watch his brother, so much less deserving than he, take his place amongst the ranks of the learned and walk on into a world that should have been his. He did not seem to notice me, but something further back in the far recesses of the nave took his attention. A brief, uncertain smile flickered across his face. I lifted my hand to shield my eyes from the sunlight that at that moment streamed through the window above me, blanking out the features of the people before me, and then I saw that, walking slowly and leaning on the arm of Andrew Carmichael, John Innes had entered the kirk.

So taken up was I with my search among the faces of

the crowd that the conventional ceremonies and speeches preceding the inaugural disputations were lost to me. I straightened myself in my seat and forced myself to listen. The scholars were obliged to publicly thank their bene-factors on this unique occasion, and they did so with fulsome praise in panegyrics of some exaggeration. Jaffray's eyes shone as Paul Ogston, a poor candlemaker's son from my home burgh, thanked the good doctor for all he had done for him over so many years. As the poorest and youngest of the twelve boys called to the podium by their regent, it fell to him to read the memorial to two companions of their class whom God had not spared to see this joyful day. One had succumbed to the damp and cold that clung like ivy to our college walls and the other had been drowned at the Links when a boast and an unexpected wave had carried him too far. Candles, snuffed out before the world could see their light.

Later, whether the scholars had acquitted themselves honourably, displaying the requisite learning, intellect and eloquence in defending and opposing the theses of their *praeses*, I could not have told, for my attention drifted time and again over faces in the crowd. Several could have accorded with the description of Nicholas Black that Matthew Jack had given me from the one time he had seen him, in the factor's office in Rotterdam, but none looked to be the face of a man who had done murder within these very precincts.

The theses on Logic passed me by and the propositions

on Ethics made little impression on me either until, ranging my eyes for the fifth or sixth time across the back of the church, I noticed that someone was standing alongside John Innes and Andrew Carmichael, someone who had not been there before – Richard Middleton. I could scarcely believe he had dared to come to so public a place while the threat of exposure by Matthew Jack hung over him. The principal, too, I noted, had seen him, and was struggling not to betray his unease. But Richard Middleton did not have the look of a man trying to hide himself from the sight of others. His eyes were fixed on the boy on the stage, and his every sense seemed to be locked on what he was saying. I scrambled in my head to listen, to dredge from my mind some recollection of what had already been said. The boy spoke of friendship and the longings of love and, earnestly, of the necessity of bridling our desires. It was written on Richard Middleton's face that those words were lost to him, for they had come too late.

Patrick Urquhart looked at his most alert and animated, naturally enough, when his brother was opposing the *praeses'* mathematical propositions. Malcolm clearly had his brother's gifts and his display of skill was not lost on the audience. Many watched and listened to him with increasing approval, none more so than Sir Thomas Burnett of Leys, whose pride in the erstwhile errant youth was written on his face.

The ceremony of graduation, bound by formality, proceeded without mishap, and the newly capped masters

SHONA MACLEAN

walked proudly out of Grayfriars' Kirk and into the sunshine of the street, the acclamation of friends, family, teachers and ministers in their ears.

My ceremonial duties done with for the day, I sought out my own friends in the crowd that had spilled from the kirk into the Broadgate. Jaffray was not difficult to find. I joined him in applauding the group of newly capped masters whom I had come to know well over the last four years. 'It does my heart good to see this every year, Alexander. It does the town good.'

I looked over at the labourers, servants, craftsmen and merchants who had paused in their work to acclaim the graduands. 'It is something that never ceases to astonish me,' I said, 'that they show no bitterness towards those upon whom Fate has looked more kindly than themselves. These boys have access now to a life of privilege and status, while many of those who applaud them are consigned to endless drudgery and toil.'

'Does it truly, Alexander? Does it not show you that the human heart is capable of a generosity of spirit that our unbecoming form often serves to mask? You see the washer-woman over there for instance?' He indicated a woman who might have been anything between thirty and fifty years of age, with red-chapped hands and a huge bundle of linen on her back, who had stopped a moment with her son to watch the parade.

'What of her?' I said.

'Did you not see how brightly she smiled as our proud

323

peacocks swung past? In them she sees what her child might be, if God has gifted him a mind and a spirit for study, and put charity into the hearts of those who see it. Look there at Paul Ogston, son of a Banff chandler, and he walks alongside the heir of Pitsligo — equal today, by virtue of their learning. What happened today will see Paul accepted at the table and in the company of any laird in the land. You yourself would have led quite another life had not the master's cap been placed upon your head, not so many years ago.'

I held up a hand in defeat. 'How is it that you are so often right, old friend?'

'I have had long experience in the study of my fellow man. And that experience tells me that four hours in the Grayfriars' Kirk are as many as a decent man may stomach without food and drink. Thank the good lord for the *convivium* — to mark young Paul's triumph we shall feast like gods.'

And indeed, when we entered Bella Watson's yard a quarter of an hour later, it had been transformed from being the typical dreary backland of a burgh tavern into the nearest the good widow could approximate to an Elysian grove. Garlands of ivy and honeysuckle hung from the walls, a roast of lamb turned in a corner nearest to the kitchen, and in another a well-known burgh fiddler was readying his bow. Casks of Bella's best ale stood ready by the back door and flasks of wine alternated with jars of roses, marigolds and daisies to fill the centre of the table that ran the length of the yard.

'You have outdone yourself this year,' I said to Jaffray as we surveyed the scene before us.

'Ach, it is little enough, and the boy deserves it.'

I wondered if Sir Thomas Burnett of Leys would have provided a similar *convivium* for Malcolm Urquhart, or if he would have judged that a little humility would do the boy no harm.

Alongside Paul Ogston's parents, and those of his friend and fellow poor scholar, Jaffray had, in his usual expansive way, invited a wide range of his acquaintances from the two burghs of Aberdeen. As well as myself, Dr Dun had, of course, also been invited to attend, and would do so, when protocol allowed, for he must sup first with the foremost families. From the King's College in the Old Town Andrew Carmichael was there, along with John Innes, still weak in body, but with something of the old serenity of spirit about him. Despite his boldness at appearing in the kirk, Richard Middleton, at his wife's behest I did not wonder, had judged it better not to come to the celebration. It was only for Jaffray's sake, and the boy's, that I myself had been persuaded to leave my wife in the care of Elizabeth Cargill an hour or so longer, for although I knew Matthew Jack was secure in the tolbooth, I could not feel for certain that Sarah was safe unless I was watching over her myself.

William greeted me across the table. 'I am relieved to see you here, Alexander. You will only annoy Sarah, you know, if you are hovering over her every minute. She would not wish you to be miserable – you looked so distracted throughout the disputation and graduation that I half-expected you to have wandered off somewhere else at the end of them.' He lowered his voice. 'You are still looking for him, aren't you?'

William knew me too well.

'I cannot shake from my mind the certainty that he is still amongst us, that there may still be some danger . . . and for Robert's sake.'

'For Robert's sake I think it as well that this matter is laid to rest with him. Would it not be better that it should die on the gallows with Matthew Jack?'

I could scarcely believe what he was saying to me. 'You, of all people, should advocate that?'

'You have matters to attend to at home, Alexander. And if you persist in this investigation you may find yourself with fewer friends than you began with. Many good men have things they would wish to be kept private.' He left me and went to join John Innes and Andrew Carmichael who were seating themselves at a bench at the other end of the table.

Jaffray, who had not overheard our conversation, turned to me after William passed him. 'What is the matter with our young lawyer friend?'

'I do not know,' I said quietly. 'I think perhaps he is hungry.'

'And indeed, he has my sympathy. Come,' he called to the company in general, 'let us set to this board before good Mistress Watson takes offence.'

The landlady laughed and began to shear slices of lamb off the roasting carcass to be set on platters on the table. I said the grace, and after the chorus of murmured 'amens' dishes of bread, beans and vegetables began to be passed from hand to hand and slabs of the roasted meat, its juices collected in a pan with Bella's own famed concoction of herbs, were speared on to plates. After the initial general pangs of hunger had been satisfied, the doctor banged a knife against his pewter goblet.

And then Jaffray stood up and spoke, as I had heard him do so many times before, in other years, for other boys, of his pride in the new graduate's achievements, the worthiness of the boy's family, the wonders of the grammar school of Banff, of his affection for the young man before him and of his great hopes for his future. He finished, as ever, with the admonition, 'and never forget your friends.'

When the doctor had finished, John Ogston, candlemaker of Banff, stood to give as eloquent a speech of thanks to James Jaffray as I had ever heard a man of little learning give. When it was over, Jaffray, who had been looking at his plate throughout, smiled and said a quiet 'Thank you, John,' before asking if the fiddler had fallen asleep that we were so forced to entertain ourselves.

'He is right, you know,' I said.

'Who is right?'

'John Ogston. Were it not for you, his son, however bright and gifted he might be, would be spending his days amongst the stench and grease of a tallow shed in Banff.'

'I know it,' Jaffray conceded eventually, 'and it is wrong, it is very wrong. Poverty has bound so many young men of great gifts hand and foot, and the commonwealth is the poorer because of it.'

Andrew Carmichael overheard our conversation. 'I saw an emblem once, painted on the ceiling of Sir George Bruce's house at Culross. It showed a man with one hand that was winged and reaching for the heavens, while the other was bound to a stone. The stone that bound him to the ground was poverty. It was written underneath that poverty hindered the advancement of the most able minds.' His voice dropped. 'It affected me greatly.'

I looked around the table; few amongst my companions, regardless of their gifts, would have attained to their present position in life had it not been for the goodness of others. I would myself never have progressed from the grammar school of Banff, or indeed my father's smiddy, to the King's College had it not been for the munificence of the laird of Delgatie; William Cargill and John Innes had both won bursaries to see them through studies they could otherwise never have aspired to. I thought of Richard Middleton, who owed his education to the foresight and determination of a kirk minister in Lanarkshire. In fact, only Andrew Carmichael had had the cushion of family wealth to give comfort to his years of study. His father might have been a stonemason, as he had told me, but I knew from examples all around me that gifted craftsmen could become wealthy men.

At the other end of the table, John Innes was discussing the contents of the theses they had defended with the two boys; he was happy, animated, and I thanked God that his dark days seemed to be behind him. But then their conversation turned to physics, to metaphysics and, at last, to alchemy.

'The college itself is a crucible,' said William, turning to me. 'It has changed those two boys, I daresay, as it changed us.'

'If the college is a crucible, it is but a preparation for the furnace of the world. Should we all sit down at table here together in ten years' time, I think we would find those boys much altered.'

'Perhaps, but not to each other. Friendship does not alter, does it?'

'Not to us,' I said.

And so we drank to that. And, conscious of others around the table, to new friends and, finally, to friends no longer here. Paul Ogston, rose to his feet and toasted the memory of his departed friends, those two lost boys who had set out with him on the road of scholarship but been gathered to their maker before its end.

'It was well done,' said Jaffray. 'And the dedication at the beginning of the disputation did those boys great honour. It will be a comfort to their parents that they are not forgotten.'

'But their names will live only in memory and then one day that, too, will be gone.'

Jaffray shook his head. 'You are wrong. Do you not remember what Melville the bookseller said – no doubt to distract my attention from the faulty map he was selling me?'

'What did he say?'

'That the printer was near run off his feet up the stairs, with the new fashion for printing these theses for posterity, and that the boys were never away from his door with new ideas for the dedications. The names and memory of those dead boys will live on long after those who knew them have gone, for as long as any have an interest in reading the theses of the Marischal College.'

'Which will be few enough,' said William. 'It is not a thing that I would choose to pore over in my leisure.'

'You were ever an active scholar,' said John Innes, 'but for a man of more contemplative disposition they might afford an hour or two's diversion.'

'A man like you, John,' said William, 'or like Robert, whose name we his friends should not forget either.'

And as the company toasted the memory of our murdered friend, I sat frozen, unable to take my eyes from the image in my head, the image of Robert as I had last seen him alive, the library catalogue in front of him and the box of gifted books lately arrived from Holland at his feet. Someone was trying to talk to me, saying my name, but all I could hear was Malcolm Urquhart, when I had tracked him down to Crathes, recounting to me his last interview with the librarian: 'I was angry that he wouldn't even put down the old set of theses he was reading to listen to me properly.'

'Alexander, are you all right?' It was Jaffray.

'What? Yes, yes, I am fine. But I have to go.'

'You are white as a sheet, boy. Sit back down a minute.'

'I cannot, Doctor. I must go. It is Franeker. The theses. Nicholas Black was at Franeker.'

The doctor narrowed his eyes. 'What? Alexander, you are rambling. Who *is* this Nicholas Black?'

'There is no time,' I said, throwing off the hand he had laid on my arm. 'Ask William; I must go.'

TWENTY-FIVE

Return to the Library

The library was much the same as I had left it, a dead place housing the books of dead men. It was a place of shadows and would remain so for three months, until students and masters returned to the college after the vacation, new students and new masters, some of whom would not know the name of Robert Sim. And one day, all that would be left would be a memory of a story, a tale, perhaps true, of a librarian who had been murdered here and the man who had killed him, the reason long forgotten, locked up in the pages of a book rarely opened.

Dust floated on beams of light from the windows and gathered on table tops polished smooth by thirty years of use. My every footstep in a place used to silence echoed in the sombre room, disturbing the rest of all those who had gone quietly through this place before me. A childish fear, a wish not to be left alone, made me leave the door to the outer stairway open a little. I dragged the chest of bene-facted books from its hidden corner to the space beside Robert's desk and sat down. My hand trembled slightly as

I drew the key from my belt and turned it one more time in the lock. As I pulled the lid back, I felt it jar against something beneath the desk: the box of mathematical instruments, also from Dr Gerald Duncan's benefaction, that had lain uncatalogued and unregarded since the day of Robert's death. I began to push the box further beneath the table with my foot, disturbing an astrolabe lying precariously on the top; it rolled noisily to the floor, and I made no attempt to pick it up again, transfixed as I was by something else I saw amongst the rules, set squares, compasses and sets of Napier's bones: a case such as Jaffray used – a case such as any physician might carry. I left off the books for a moment and stooped to open it up. The catch had already been broken and the inventory, old and yellowed, written in the hand of a man who had owned and gifted it, was partially torn, and yet I knew already that one item would be missing from that box. I ran my eye down the list of instruments and soon came upon the entry 'scalpels – 4'. Already I held in my hand, carefully, the scalpels from the physician's case: there were three of them. I did not know where the other was now – whether in the principal's room in another part of this college, or some safe in the chambers of the court or tolbooth, but I knew for certain that I had seen it and where it had been – cast aside in a dank corner of the library close, beneath the steps, after having been plunged in to the neck of Robert Sim. It had not been brought into the library by Robert's killer with the intention of being used as it had ultimately been used, but grabbed in haste by a man seized by some murderous madness. We had all, for some time, been misled by the nature of the weapon that had killed Robert, and amongst those unconvinced by the guilt of Matthew Jack, there were those still who believed that only a physician could have access to such an instrument. For a time, I myself had been such a one, and had harboured suspicions that would have done me no credit amongst my friends should they have become known. I knew from experience that it might not have taken too many more like me for the accusation of, and possibly retribution for, this deed to have been heaped upon an innocent man.

But there was no time for such reflection; innocent men need not fear the subversion of justice should Dr Duncan's chest hold the secret I believed it to hold. Once again I lifted out the books Robert had examined on the day of his death, conscious now of my failings, the failings of the vain scholar in the face of the diligent librarian and true lover of books and what they contained. I had seen titles, flicked through pages and made my own assumptions, and Robert had not. Today, I would do as he had done, I would do what it was that he had done that had cost him his life.

What I sought must be, I knew, somewhere near the bottom of the chest, disregarded as insignificant; at the top were the volumes I had considered to be of the greater importance. There, at the very top, was Ubbo Emmius' *History of the Frisians*. I was about to cast it aside when a thought occurred to me, a flash of curiosity, and I opened it, rifling through the pages until I found a map. I almost laughed: Jaffray had been right. I should have expected it, and yet I had dismissed the certainties of my friend as the ramblings of an old man. But Jaffray was not yet old, and he did not ramble; I had long understood that and yet I had chosen to forget it. I would apologise to him later. I laid the Emmius down and lifted out the works beneath it – works of geography, of natural history and of alchemy. I had allowed myself to be distracted for so long by the notion of the quest for Hermetic knowledge as it had been pursued in all its forms by the players in this tragedy that I had forgotten what is at the heart of all tragedy. I had sought to connect the workings and beliefs of stonemasons to the dabbling of theologians, mathematicians, physicians in their secret societies, to understand their fascination with symbols, the lessons of paintings, with myth, and I had failed to see what was ever before me, day in, day out in the streets and houses of this burgh, in the open spaces and darkened rooms, in the crowded market and lonely cell – the tragedy of fallen man. I had thought to divert myself at some later point, when all of this was over, in the company of the Greek dramatists, but I had done better to turn to them first, and see there laid bare the flaws of humanity. I came to the bottom of the chest at last, and with trembling hand lifted out the small, slight volume that I had so quickly judged to be of no significance.

I hesitated for a moment, only a moment, fearful of what I might find. *Theses Philosophicae Adolescentes Magisterii*

Candidati, in Academia Franekeria, die tres Julii, Anno 1622.
The graduation theses of Franeker University for the year
1622. I swallowed, and opened the book. On the fly leaf
was a quote from Cicero in a letter to Brutus, and underneath, the printer's date and mark. On the following page
was the dedication which I had so thoughtlessly passed over
the previous time I had held this book in my hands. I did
so again now, but only for as long as it took me to scan
the list of names of magisterial candidates at the end of it.
And there it was, as I had known it would be, a little over
halfway down the list: *Nicolus Niger* – Nicholas Black.

None of the other names meant anything to me – I should
not have expected them to – and I turned now to the dedication. It was so simple, and Robert, who had been so
precise and had taken time over everything he did, must
have seen it within moments. The dedication had not been
overly lengthy, and it had followed much the form of those
I had listened to earlier in the day in the Grayfriars' Kirk.
Honoured first had been the teachers of the class, the learned
professors who had brought them to this stage. Then had
come fulsome thanks to the States of Friesland who had
inaugurated the university, the town of Franeker, and the
benefactors who had made possible such a magnificent
education. All conventional, and telling me very little. But
then came what I had been looking for. The names of
friends, classmates, greatly loved and much mourned,
whom God had seen fit to gather to Him in the flower of
their youth. There were two boys, Frisians both, from the

island of Terschelling, who had drowned in a storm while returning to their studies after the summer vacation of their third year. I had not time to grieve their loss, for the third name was that I sought. And there it was, as it could only have been. A wealthy young Scot, matriculated at Franeker in his final year alongside his friend and fellow countryman with whom he had travelled from Germany where they had studied together at various academies and universities. While Nicholas Black, the much-pitied friend, had lived to see his graduation day, the other, higher-born and universally loved, had not. Taken by a fever in the chill and damp of the Frisian winter, he had finally succumbed in the early days of spring, his friend having nursed him three months. The loss and the sympathy were keenly felt, as genuine as I had seen in such a dedication, and I could have felt them too, would have felt them, had I not been lost in confusion, a momentary lack of comprehension, as Robert must have been, when I read the name of the man who had died. And into that confusion came a sound that almost stopped my breath, a creak on the stairs, the clicking shut of the door. I waited, unmoving, as a shadow passed over the book where it lay open on the desk before me. There could be no doubt, the confusion was gone and now I understood. I lifted my head slowly.

TWENTY-SIX

The History of Nicholas Black

Andrew Carmichael turned the key in the lock and walked towards me. 'I thought I would find you here, Alexander.' He indicated the book. 'You found it. I searched high and low, on every shelf, in every drawer. I thought he had given it to Rachel, perhaps. I had even begun to hope . . . I should not have done.'

'It was never on a shelf.' I nodded towards the corner where the library strong-box had been hidden amongst items for repair and other debris.

'Oh.' And then, 'It is such a small thing. May I look at it? I never saw it printed.'

I handed him the volume and he went with it to a window in the west wall, where the light was best. He said nothing as he turned the pages I had just turned, but a smile began to form on his lips as he read. He closed the book when he came to the end of the dedication and looked out of the window, as if he could see there the faces of the boys whose names were contained between the covers. It was almost as if he had forgotten I was there.

'Who was Andrew Carmichael?' I asked eventually.

He looked down, composing himself, his thoughts, before he answered me. 'Andrew Carmichael was my friend, the only true friend I have allowed myself to have.' I waited, while he chose where to begin. 'I grew up in the town of Lanark, where my father was a stonemason, as you know. Andrew's family was also from Lanarkshire – they held land at Skirling, near the town of Biggar. We did not know each other in those days. They were not wildly rich or influential, but they were wealthy enough and, as I understood, well-enough liked by their neighbours and tenants. Andrew's father had proved to be a disappointment to his own father; he had shown no interest in farming the family estates, and preferred the attractions of the lawyer's life in Edinburgh and then, when Edinburgh got to know his failings – for he was not a good or dependable lawyer – Glasgow.' He paused. 'I do not malign a man I never met, but I had this from Andrew himself, you understand. At any rate, Andrew's father married into a family of whom the old man in Skirling did not approve, and in time, as was inevitable, was cut off by his father. But the old man was not cruel, he was even wise, perhaps, and when Andrew was born he began to make some provision for the grandson that he knew he might never see. It was this provision, this foresight, that allowed Andrew to study for a spell at Glasgow, and then to go abroad, to Breslau, where I first met him. As fellow countrymen, we soon fell into the same company and, despite our differences in temperament and

339

station, became close friends. I was the more serious scholar of we two, he had the greater appetite to see the world. More than an appetite – an unquenchable thirst.' He smiled. 'You know the type?'

'Yes,' I said, 'I know the type. Go on.'

'Well, after travelling and studying together for three years, we decided it was time to return home. Our plan was to matriculate for our last year together at Glasgow and finally to graduate there. Andrew's father had died while we were at Frankfurt an der Oder, and so he was free to be reconciled with his grandfather. He hoped to gain the old man's blessing and help in finding a place aboard ship with the East India Company, or even in venturing to the Americas. I wanted nothing more than to find a regency in one of our own universities, to continue to study and to write, and in time to marry and have a family of my own.'

'You have not mentioned Franeker,' I said.

'No, I have not, for that was not part of our plan, and you must believe me when I say I wish with all my heart that I had never heard of or seen the place. It was in the early summer of 1621 that we were travelling by way of Utrecht to Rotterdam and the ship that would finally take us home to Scotland. Andrew, a little nervous I think at the prospect of presenting himself to his grandfather for the first time, began to think of diversions, occasions for delay in our return, but I had had enough of wandering and was so resolved to return home that I had written to the shipping office at Rotterdam weeks before we were to arrive there to book my passage home. On the road, Andrew was constantly at me to try just one more town, one more university, one more adventure, to make for ourselves one more tale to tell. And so, as we stood at the crossroads between the routes that would take us to Rotterdam or to Franeker, I finally relented; I agreed to go there with him, to visit the flat Frisian lands.' He spread out his hands the better to explain. 'And, in all, it was not an unattractive prospect for me, for there I would have the opportunity to improve my Hebrew under Sixtinus ab Amama and hear the Englishman William Ames, of whose passion and vehemence in teaching and strictness of life I had heard much. My protest that my passage home was already booked was easily overruled by Andrew, who went himself to the shipping office in Rotterdam, and sold my passage home to a fellow Scot, a physician returning home after his studies.'

In that, it seemed, as in other matters, Matthew Jack had not lied.

'And by these means,' I said, 'Andrew Carmichael, the *real* Andrew Carmichael, was architect of his own murder.'

The man who had usurped his dead friend's name looked at me with incomprehension. 'Andrew was not murdered.'

I pointed impatiently at the book of theses he still held in his hands. 'Read it,' I said. 'Read how it tells of Andrew Carmichael's fever, which he finally succumbed to after three months of nursing by his great friend Nicholas Black.'

Nicholas Black shook his head almost in disbelief. 'How could you think I murdered him? I loved him. I could not have loved him more had he been my brother. He took a fever in January, on a whaling trip he had joined on the island of Fohr. I had remained behind in Franeker to study – I had neither the means nor the interest to see the spectacle in any case. He was brought back to the town, to our lodgings, and I nursed him there until at last the fever broke, but by then the vapours from the cold and damp had descended to his chest and, finally, his lungs.' He breathed deeply, and I saw that this was truly difficult for him. 'Although he returned to lectures and to something of his old enjoyment of life, he never fully regained his strength, and when the spring fogs began to envelop the town, they carried off what strength he had left. By the time the first rays of April sun spread over the rooftops of Franeker, he was dead. And so he never did travel to the East, or see the Americas, all for the sake of his curiosity to see a small Dutch town. He was mourned, and missed, and remembered by his fellows in the pages of this book. That was Andrew Carmichael.'

He apparently believed he had told me all I would require to know, and lapsed into some memories in his own mind, almost unaware of me there with him in the now locked library.

'I see no reason to doubt what you have told me. But if that was Andrew Carmichael, then who is Nicholas Black?'

He regarded me as if beginning to wonder whether I

might be lacking in something. 'You know it already. Why would you ask it? I am Nicholas Black.'

'I grant you that. I will not dispute it, and I have racked my brains and can think of no other who might be, but tell me: who *is* Nicholas Black?'

He walked over to one of the cabinets housing the oldest books in the library's collection and gazed a long time at his reflection in its glass-fronted door. 'I do not know who Nicholas Black is, any more. But I can tell you who he was. Nicholas Black was the boy, the able scholar held down by lack of means of whom your friend Jaffray spoke only today; he was that scholar in the emblem at Culross with one hand reaching for the heavens and the other shackled to the stone of poverty.'

'I do not follow you,' I said.

And so he told me, a tale that had little in it that any might not have guessed, a familiar enough tale of a young man of gifts but few means, the third of six surviving children of a poor stonemason of the town of Lanark and his wife. The boy had been marked out at an early age for a scholar, and through the support of the kirk session had been seen through grammar school to the university at Glasgow where a year's bursary had been won. At the end of that first year, the fund depleted and no more available to a poor stonemason's son with few connections, a kindly professor, recognising the boy's abilities, had written to an old acquaintance at the university of Breslau and secured for him a place in a house for poor scholars there. Many a poor Scot had travelled the same road and returned home with a lifetime's cause for gratitude and a determination to do for others what had been done for himself. And so it might have been for Nicholas Black, had he never met Andrew Carmichael or set foot with him in the town of Franeker, had he never stood at that crossroads in Utrecht and chosen the wrong path. But Nicholas Black had fallen in with Andrew Carmichael, had gone with him to Franeker, and there had studied with him, caroused with him, nursed him and seen him die.

'What happened when Andrew died?' I asked.

'There was great sadness amongst our friends, of course. A great mourning and sense of loss.'

'What did the college authorities do?' I said, trying to keep my voice level, conscious that I should not push him too far beyond what he was prepared to tell me.

'When it was understood that Andrew's closest living kin was a grandfather he had never met, it was decided that I should be the courier who brought news of his death, and his belongings, back to his homeland. I would not graduate for three months, but there could be little harm now to Andrew or the family he had never known in keeping the news of his death from Scotland until I was able to return there and take it with me. After our graduation, my friends at Franeker pressed me to remain amongst them a little longer – indeed I told you the other evening of my eventful visit to the island of Texel, did I not?'

I nodded. I realised now that it had been that tale, along

with the man we had thought to be Andrew Carmichael's earlier assertion to us that he had never travelled as far north as Gouda, that had made Jaffray question the veracity of the bookseller's map. But there it was: the map had been accurate and the man had lied.

'Anyhow,' he continued, 'it was autumn by the time I returned to Scotland. I went first to my own family in Lanark, for I had not seen them in three years, and very seldom before that indeed, since boyhood. I thought to be welcomed, lauded, the great scholar, the first of our family to have been so, having brought honour on our name and the promise of something better for us all. But my home-coming was not as I had expected it would be. I discovered that my younger sister had been dead two winters, my father one. My brother, who had followed our father in his craft had few of his skills and all of his vices – he was more often drunk than sober, and it was I who paid another mason to carve the stone that marks my father's grave. The family had fallen deeper far into poverty even than it had been in my own childhood. And so instead of being welcomed and lauded, I was scorned, blamed by those who had been left behind. They wanted none of me or my promises for the future, for I had then no calling other than that of scholar, I had soft hands and no skill to turn a stone or work a lathe.'

He looked away from the window and back to me. 'I do not try to dissemble, Alexander: I had not seen them in many years, had not truly considered what their fortunes might have been while I indulged myself in my studies and the world they opened to me, but I had held them in my heart, held the memory of my mother's love, and that of my young sisters, in my heart. My mother had wept for her boy on the day I had left home for the college in Glasgow, and I had thought to see her weep with joy at his return. But it had not been so; she had no tears for the man who had come back in his place. And so it was that within two days of landing at Leith, I learned I had no family, no home, nowhere to go. Nowhere but Skirling, where I still had to discharge my obligations to Andrew's kin. I took myself on the road south.

'Skirling was a pretty parish, and I found the house of the Carmichaels with little difficulty; it was a sturdy, sombre-looking place, the kind of place you might imagine an old man to inhabit alone, cut off from son and grandson, surviving them both. It took a deal of banging on the door on my part before it was opened to me, and at first I took the aged manservant who answered to be old Carmichael himself. I began to tell my tale, telling him where I had come from, but on hearing the word "Franeker", the old fellow began to tremble and to babble almost, so that I had trouble understanding him. And then I knew what he was saying: "Too late, you have come home too late, Mister Andrew, for the old master is dead." I tried to tell him again who I was, but he would not hear it, repeating over and over in a mournful tone that I was come too late. I should have insisted, I should have made him hear me, and then turned and walked away, but in my mind all I could see was the emblem I had seen once as a boy, with my father at Sir George Bruce's house at Culross, and in that moment the chain binding the scholar's hand to the stone of poverty snapped.'

'You took his inheritance,' I said.

He nodded. 'I had borne the name of one dead man, my father, and seen it marked on his grave in the town of Lanark but two days before, and in that moment, there in that cold hall in the hamlet of Skirling, I took the name and the legacy of another. The house and lands had gone to a cousin of Andrew's father, not yet arrived from Berwick to take possession of them, but a substantial sum in ready money had been left to the grandson that none in the household had ever seen. I produced Andrew's testimonials and, with little ceremony and no further questioning, was handed the money. By the time it was in my hand I regretted what I had done, but it was too late, already too late . . .'

His fists were clenched, the knuckles white, and the agitation in his voice was growing. 'It was autumn – I have said that, have I not?'

'Yes, you have said it.'

He nodded. 'Yes. It was autumn, but winter was coming, I could feel it as I walked away from that house. The sun shone, bathed everything in a golden brown light, but there was a bite in the air from the north that made everything fresh, clean. The branches of the trees were almost bare already, their leaves shed in atonement for the excesses of the summer, readying themselves to become something new. When winter was past, everything would be new.'

He smiled, nearing the end of his tale. 'And so I followed the call of winter and turned from Skirling northwards, to where I was not known and where Andrew had not been known, beyond Edinburgh, beyond St Andrews, to Aberdeen, where few from Glasgow, Edinburgh or Lanarkshire would ever have cause to go, and I became the man you have known since. No longer Nicholas Black, for Nicholas Black died at my hands in the hall of Skirling House almost nine years ago, and no one mourned him.'

He had finished, and wore the look now of a man with nothing left to say. I scarcely knew what to say myself. 'Andrew, this was not a matter to kill over.'

He sat down on the window ledge, his face grey. 'I know it was not, I know that now. But do you know what I saw, what was the last thing to catch my eye as I walked out of that parish of Skirling?'

I shook my head.

'It was so brief a glimpse, that I hardly think I knew I had seen it then. But I see it now, so clear in my mind, every night since the death of Robert Sim, as I try to sleep, I cannot tear my eyes from it. I see, to the south, just as I was turning north, the gibbet on the Gallows Knowe. My end was marked from there, I think.'

'No, Andrew . . .'

But he did not seem to be listening to me any more. 'I never intended that anyone should die for the sake of my deception. And yet when you told us all that day, a few weeks ago on the Links, of having left Robert Sim poring over a benefaction from Groningen, amongst which were to be found printed theses from Franeker, I could not rest until I knew if they numbered amongst them those which would eventually tell my secret. You may think I had little to lose, but that day I believed there was much I might yet lose, some of it even that I did not yet have. I have been happy, you know, in my post at the King's College, and the companionship of John Innes and the other regents. Even between you and me it seemed there might be some possibility of friendship, if only you could forgive me Sarah, or I you.'

'You forgive me?' I was stunned.

'Yes. For despite everything that I have tried to tell myself since the day I heard you were not dead but returned from Ireland, despite the discipline I have held my feelings under for the last three years, there were days on which I knew I had not yet given up hope. You are well-liked, well-respected in these two colleges and towns, but I know that whatever manner of man you are, Alexander, you do not deserve her, that I would love and cherish her better.'

I could not believe what he was saying to me, but could say nothing as he spoke on.

'In the solitary hours of the night, where reason flees and dreams take hold, I continued to believe I might one day win her from you. All that, little enough to you, no doubt, but everything to me, would have been lost to me had my secret become known. And so, on that night after the fight on the sands between our students, I slipped down over the King's Meadows here to the New Town, and through the untended gate to your college. All I had in mind was to find the theses, to discover whether they were those that would give me away, and, if they were, to destroy them if I could, before anyone should see them. I had not expected to find Robert still at work there in the library, and as I was trying to compose my features, to think of my story, I saw from his face that he knew it all already.'

'And so you killed him.'

'No,' he shook his head, somehow desperate that I should understand. 'I pleaded with him, begged that he would not make my secret known, but he was determined that he should seek guidance from your principal. I knew it was not a thing Dr Dun would keep from the Chancellor, and that all the life I had would be over for me, but Robert would not listen. He gathered up his bag and made for the library door. I tried to hold on to him, but he shook me off and got past me. I made to go after him but stumbled on that box there' – he gestured here to the medical instruments protruding from beneath Robert's desk, and I knew what had happened next. 'By the time I had righted myself I had the knife, the scalpel, in my hand. When I caught hold of Robert a second time and he refused me again . . .'

'You plunged the knife into his throat and left him there to die.'

'I could scarcely believe what I had done. I returned by

the backways to my own college and as darkness finally fell I had almost persuaded myself that I had not done the thing at all. The first few moments of waking in the morning were the last peace I have known; for that brief time I believed I had been the victim of a nightmare while I slept. And then I saw the blood on my boots, Robert's blood, and I knew what I had done.'

I did not know what I felt as I looked upon the man who had murdered my friend and sought to take my wife from me. It was not hatred, but a sickness somewhere in my stomach, and a simmering anger.

'Did you really believe you would never be found out?'

'Sometimes. As I spoke with you and others about Robert's death it did truly seem to me as if I was talking about something I myself had no more knowledge of than you did, as if it had been another who had perpetrated that deed. And then the behaviour of Matthew Jack and the discovery of the fraternity in which John Innes and others had been involved, the dabbling in the business of the masons – it seemed that each day, each new revelation obscured the truth a little more, and set me further and further along the path of safety.'

'But then came Bernard Cummins,' I said. 'Bernard recognised you in town, did he not?'

He put the theses down on a desk in front of him. 'It was the one thing about my days at Franeker I had forgotten – the young weaver from Aberdeen. We had spent a pleasant evening together in an inn in Leiden and then I had gone my way and he his; I had never thought to see him again. And then, one day, as I was down in town on an errand, about to fetch some Greek grammars from Melville's the bookseller, I saw Bernard Cummins come out of the shop. It took me some time to place him, and by the time I had, it was too late, for he had seen me also. With him there was no hesitation: he knew me straight away. He strode up to me, his hand extended, and greeted me by my name, my own, true name. I could think of no answer but that I was not who he thought me to be, that I did not know him. He insisted upon our having met, and that he was sure I had told him my name was Nicholas Black. I insisted I had not done so, that I had never seen him before in my life, and went hastily on my way back up to the Old Town.'

He swallowed. 'It was that very day that I received a message from Sarah, urgently wishing to see me. Fool that I was, I thought she had discovered my secret somehow, and wanted to warn me. But when I met her at the Snow Kirk all her conversation was of you, and of the dangers she feared you had placed yourself in by meddling with the business of the masons.' He raised an eyebrow at me. 'You should not concern yourself in their affairs – their secrets are not yours to know.'

'I have no interest in their secrets,' I said. 'Go on.'

'I comforted her and reassured her as well as I could, and sent her home to you, although all I wanted was to beg her to leave this place with me, and go far from it and start, ourselves, again. Had it not been for your children, I would have done so, and I believe she would have come with me, but for them.'

'You are wrong, Carmichael,' I said. 'My wife loves me and will never leave me for any other man.'

He shrugged. 'It is your right to believe that. But on that day, for a moment, I felt she was mine.' He waited. 'But then she was gone. I had promised to warn you off the masons, but she had also left me knowing all about their lodge, and from my childhood memories of what my father had told me, I knew I would find Hiram's grave not far from the door. That night I went back down into town. I went into the streets where the weavers and dyers and their like live; keeping my hat down low and my collar up, I looked in the alehouses and taverns where I thought they might be found. Eventually I saw him – Bernard Cummins. I waited; when he left the alehouse I followed after him and watched him to his door. All that night I did not sleep, for I knew that he might at any time expose me. Had it not been for the death of Robert, I could have passed the name of Nicholas Black off as a youthful student prank, indulged in to while away an hour or so in a Leiden inn, but I knew it was too late for that. And so the next evening I went down into town again, as soon as my classes were over. I waited for Bernard Cummins to return to his lodgings and approached him in the street. I apologised for my strange behaviour of the previous day, excusing it by saying I had mistaken him for a passing acquaintance from the past who had more than once importuned me for money. I invited him to come and take his dinner with me, and talk over old times.'

'You walked openly with him to the King's College?' I could scarcely believe the pair had not been seen.

Carmichael shook his head. 'No, I could not do that. But there are enough narrow lanes and dark vennels, even at this time of year, between his lodging in Futty Wynd and the Middletons' house, that I could manage it without attracting undue notice.'

'You told him the Middletons' house was yours?'

'I told him I rented rooms in the lodging in their backland, but that my landlady was a harridan who would allow of no company, and so we slunk silently down by the shadow of the wall to the lodge. I take some comfort in the knowledge that he never knew he was to die; I had cut his throat from behind within a moment of us rounding the corner to the lodge, and he was in Hiram's grave not two minutes later. I was sorry for it, because I remembered our evening at the Fir-Cone in Leiden then, and it had been one of good cheer.'

And now between us there was silence; he stood before me, the murderer of two men, the usurper of the name and inheritance of another, the man who might well have taken my wife from me. A good man; a decent man, as any who could get me to listen had told me. But all that was gone. I remembered what he had done to Rachel Middleton in his search for the book he now held in his hand. I did not know if I was looking at Nicholas Black or at Andrew Carmichael, and I did not know what the man leaning against the window across the room from me would do. I glanced down at the box of medical instruments. His eyes followed mine.

'I have no weapon. And despite all, I have not the taste for blood.'

'What will you do?' I said. 'Will you come back with me, to the magistrate? Will you give yourself up?'

He shook his head. 'I have lived two men's lives. It is my choice how I should end them, how I should prepare myself to meet damnation.'

'You cannot know—' I began.

'Oh, I know. One of the elect would not do as I have done. I am destined for the flames, and it is time that I made myself ready.'

Only then did I notice that he had pulled an unlit candle from a nearby sconce on the wall. He took flint from his pouch, struck it and brought the flame to life.

'We have no need of light, Andrew,' I said carefully. 'The sun is still high in the sky.'

'And I have no mind to see it set.' He laid the flickering candle on the ledge beside him, picked up the book of theses and held it open towards the flame.

'Destroying the book will not destroy the truth, you know,' I said.

'Perhaps not, but it will be a long time before another volume such as this finds its way to the Marischal College library, and by the time it has, I and all who knew me will be long gone.'

'I will have to tell them, you know, Andrew.'

'No, you will not.'

'Andrew . . .'

'Do not be frightened, Alexander: no doubt your journey through the flames will be one of earthly torment only, and not the thing of eternity that awaits me.'

I threw back my chair and lunged at the burning book in his hands, but he was too quick for me, and had the flame at the edge of a window drape before I could reach him. The heat of the summer sun had left the thing as dry as tinder, and the whole was engulfed in a moment. I watched in horror as Carmichael swept books from their shelves and set alight as many as he could. The keys to the library door were on the window ledge where he had set them after he had first come in. I tried to reach them but a second drape caught light and barred my path.

'Andrew, for the love of God, the keys!' I shouted, as the smoke from the flames began to obscure him from my view.

'I am sorry,' he shouted, coughing, 'her life will be better without you.' His voice failed and he stumbled into the glass cabinet to his right and sent it crashing to the ground, knocking over another as it did so. I tried to clamber over the shattered fragments, but already the books that had been flung from its doors were taken up in the conflagration and formed between me and the door a barrier of fire.

I tried to shout again, above the noise of splintering glass and roaring flame, but the smoke that stung my eyes scorched my throat and filled my lungs. I could scarcely see, still less speak, and the last thing I did see before the black fumes overtook me entirely was the sight of Andrew Carmichael, or Nicholas Black as I now knew him to be, standing against the window of the Marischal College library, utterly aflame. As I passed into the nothingness he was beckoning me to, I thought the smoke had already begun to warp my mind, for I believed I heard a familiar voice call my name and an unholy cursing as William Cargill crashed through the library door.

Epilogue

The air was the cleanest I had ever breathed. I could feel it course slowly through my body, purifying as it went, reaching to where the very furthest tentacles of smoke had reached and making all clean again.

'There are those who believe fire to be the most potent of all the elements, the greatest agent of change, but I have long held it inferior to air.'

'You are better versed in these matters than I, James, and I will not argue with you.'

'That indeed will be a pleasant alteration between us.'

I allowed him his small note of triumph, for although he had made little enough of it, I knew, had I paid greater attention to him, confided more in him, I would not have been in need of the cleansing mountain air we now breathed.

'The map over your mantel-shelf will serve as a reminder to me, should I need it, of your greater wisdom, Doctor; I will take care not to dismiss your concerns again.'

'What you call my greater wisdom is nothing more than

an inclination to pay attention to people, Alexander, to listen. You paid enough attention to Andrew Carmichael – or Nicholas Black, as we must now call him – but it was all of the wrong sort. You looked at him, and try as you might, all you could see was the man whose aim was to take your wife from you. You listened to him, but you had no interest in the half of what he said. Whatever man you thought you looked upon was the creature of your own fears, and those had little to do with Nicholas Black. Had you listened to what he *said* that night at William Cargill's dinner-table, instead of worrying that he sat too close to Sarah, that burn on your leg might never have been.'

'It was not so much that, by then,' I said. 'The truth is I think I had begun to like him myself. To see him come into his own in company, revel in telling a tale, was something new to me and I believed I was seeing the man he had hidden from me because I had never given him the chance to reveal him to me until then.'

'And you were probably right. His tale of his eventful night on the island of Texel was indeed amusing, and would have given me no pause for thought other than as something I could later relate myself for the entertainment of others, had he not claimed earlier in the evening for the whole company to hear, that he had never been as far north as Gouda. Now, if there be any short-comings in that map I bought from Melville – and I am minded to invite Straloch to Banff to take a look at it – on one thing it is clear: the island of Texel is well to the north of Gouda.'

'If you had not bought that map . . .' I said.

The doctor swatted away a fly and shook his head. 'It was not just the map. It was something else he said that I thought little further on until you started rambling about Nicholas Black and Franeker before you took off for the library from Paul Ogston's graduation dinner.'

'I had not realised that I had not mentioned him to you,' I said.

'You had mentioned the name, but told me nothing else about him.' The doctor raised a wry eyebrow in my direction. 'We have of late had other topics of conversation, if you recall. But after you rushed off from the table that day, I did ask William about Nicholas Black, as you had told me to, and he explained to me about the weaver's letter to his sister and the Scots student of the name studying at Franeker. Well, a month or so ago, it was my misfortune while dining with Lindsay at Edzell to be seated at dinner next to the most boastful fellow, a physician from Angus. No doubt her ladyship thought she was doing me a good turn, in seating me next to one of my own profession with whom I might converse on acquaintances and places in common.'

'And this was not the case?'

The doctor snorted. 'It might have been, had I been able to get a word in edgeways, but the fellow commandeered the whole conversation to himself. There was hardly an open eye around the table by the time the first three courses had been dealt with, I'll tell you.' I had to suppress a smile at the image of my old friend thwarted of his own expected audience. 'Anyhow, while I was myself still awake and listening to him, he was discoursing on what he imagined to be his linguistic expertise, and shared with the company a shibboleth by which he claimed it was possible to tell a true Frisian from an impostor.' Jaffray looked at me meaningfully. 'It concerned the drinking of tea.'

'Of tea?' And then I remembered, the curious phrase Carmichael had uttered when the subject of that drink had come up at William Cargill's table. 'Butter, bread, tea, spice . . .' I began, failing badly.

But Jaffray had it exact. '"*Buyter en Brae en t'zijs goe Huwsmanne spijs.*" You see? You do not listen. Franeker is at the heart of the West Frisian lands. When I heard that the Nicholas Black whom you sought had been a student there, Andrew Carmichael came immediately to mind, and when William and I cast around the table in Bella Watson's yard and saw that he, too, had slipped away we knew we had to find you. Your mumbling to me about the Franeker theses directed us, thank God, to the library.'

And there they had found smoke billowing from the shattered windows and the door locked. William's lawyerly occupation had deprived him of little of his strength, and the doctor's determination had taken twenty years from him. Between them, they had managed to batter down the door. In the brief moments they had before the smoke threatened to overcome them, too, they had found my body, all consciousness and almost all life gone from it, and dragged me to the air. The vehemence of the inferno had forced them back, although William had tried, once, to advance into the flames towards the blazing figure he saw stumble further into the fire.

'He did not want it,' they had told me when finally I had come round and been able to make some sound issue from my scorched throat. 'Andrew Carmichael, Nicholas Black, whatever you will call him, he did not want to be saved. He chose his death, the flames rather than the hangman's rope.'

Jaffray let me indulge my thoughts a few minutes then brought a small flask from the bundle he carried with him. 'Here, swallow some of this. It will do you more good than all that sage water Sarah has been pouring down your throat.'

'She said it would heal the scorching, and indeed, I scarcely feel it now.'

'No doubt, but it is a foul enough thing for a man to stomach.' He unstoppered the flask. 'Drink down some of that instead and then I will take you to the men who make it, the true alchemists who turn water into gold.'

I did as I was bid, and followed my old friend as he led me onwards on the mountain path, through the clean air that he promised would restore my body and strengthen my soul. I promised myself with every step that I would return a different man from him who had left Aberdeen in the doctor's care; that I would prove Andrew Carmichael wrong, that there would never come a day in my wife's life when anyone could say she would have been better off without me.

Acknowledgements

I would like to thank Aberdeen University Special Libraries and Archives and Aberdeen City Archives for allowing me to consult materials in their care. I would like to thank Craig Russell and Dr Jamie Reid Baxter for their advice on matters Frisian, and most particularly to thank Professor Goffe Jensma of the Department of Frisian Language and Culture, University of Groningen, for his help with my queries on the Frisian language in the seventeenth century.

Anyone wishing to read further into the early history of Freemasonry in Scotland should consult Professor David Stevenson's *The Origins of Freemasonry: Scotland's Century, 1590-1710* (CUP, 1988). The classic account of the Rosicrucian phenomenon is Frances Yates' *The Rosicrucian Enlightenment* (Routledge, 1986). The painted ceilings of Crathes Castle can still be admired in that property, now run by the National Trust for Scotland, their symbolism explained in Michael Bath's *Renaissance Decorative Painting in Scotland* (NMS, 2003).